ENTANGLED

A Detective Sonya Reisler Novel

J. Evan Stuart

ISBN-13 978-1-943506-01-9
ISBN-10 1943506019

Cover Art by Ronnell D. Porter

jevanstuartauthor.blogspot.com

For Chris
who has supported me in my writing endeavors
and has always believed in me

For Zach
who said from the beginning
it sounded "like a real book"

CHAPTER ONE

Connor crumpled the beer can and tossed it over his shoulder into the bed of the pickup truck on whose tailgate he was sitting. The can clattered against the growing collection of twisted aluminum which included the remains of the first beer he had drunk that night. He closed his eyes to enjoy the light buzz settling over him.

"You want another one?"

Opening his eyes he saw another can of beer being held out to him by his friend, Mike. The offer was tempting. The blue and silver glinting in the moonlight and the pull to make the buzz stronger worked on him, and if it were a Saturday night he would have accepted. But it was a school night and shimmying up the old oak to the second floor of his house to sneak back in was hard enough to do sober let alone wasted. This he knew from past experience.

"Nah. I'm good for tonight." He watched as Mike withdrew the beer, popped the top and began drinking. Connor looked away. God he wished it were a Saturday night.

To take his mind off the beer he watched Brett and Josh down by the creek. They were already pretty shit faced when he arrived having contributed the most to the pile of aluminum in the back of the truck. After a few more they were completely drunk off their asses and now trying to see who could piss the farthest into the creek. Brett, trying to maximize his trajectory, was leaning too far back and fell to the ground with a thud. Josh roared with laughter and tumbled down next to Brett who also found the whole thing equally hilarious.

Connor smirked and shook his head. *Idiots,* he thought even though he knew there were many times when he easily out drank and outperformed them, and this was the place to do it. The nearest house was over a mile away and there was no danger of being caught here. The only risk was of catching hell when you got home.

The crunch and clunk let Connor know Mike finished the beer that should have been his.

"Only two beers? Your dad ain't got you scared with that military school crap has he?"

Connor turned and glared at Mike even though he knew it wouldn't register. Mike's stupid smile toward the sensitive topic indicated he was too hammered to even know when to shut up.

"I'm not scared. I just gotta climb the oak tonight to get back in and want to do it without breaking my arm again."

Mike started laughing. "You're right. You climbing a tree drunk is much scarier than your dad's talk. Good thing you were wasted enough not to feel the bone come out." He pushed himself off of the tailgate and stumbled as his feet connected with the solid ground. He started weaving his way toward the creek while unbuckling his belt. "They piss like girls."

"I'm sure you'll show them how it's done," Connor called after him.

"You know it."

Connor looked at the inside of his right forearm as the fingers of his left hand traced the length of the scar that was only about three months old. He was so drunk that night. He didn't remember falling and didn't know he broke his arm until his mom started freaking out. He didn't feel a thing as he stared at the jagged end of bone that had ruptured through his skin. But that's the great thing about alcohol. You don't feel anything.

Connor's attention broke with the static and brief chatter coming through on the Ashlin sheriff's department two-way radio laying in the bed of Mike's truck. Mike was taking the military school talk more seriously than he let on and lifted the two-way from his dad. They were trying to be careful, even laying off their usual antics that got them in trouble with the local authorities. He reached over and turned it off to save the batteries. They were just staying at the creek tonight.

This was still a risk. He had been warned. One more incident of any type and the military school talk would become more than just a scary threat. He was turning eighteen in a couple of weeks and his reprieve of being a juvenile wouldn't protect him anymore and his dad was done dealing with it. Trouble with the law seemed to run in the family. How many times did he hear he was going to turn out like his Uncle Jake? More than he could count.

But it was hard to stay out of trouble. He hated Ashlin, Nebraska. He hated ranching. He hated the boredom. Apart from leaving his friends and his little sister, he almost liked the idea of going to this military school. At least it would get him the hell out of here. Maybe even more, it would get him away from the expectations his dad held for him. Carrying on the family ranch was not what he wanted, and living with the growing disappointment his father showed toward him was pushing him to the breaking point.

Connor took a deep breath, reached behind him, and opened the cooler. He took out a beer, popped it open, and chugged it down before grabbing another. It would be quite a few beers before he was really good for the night.

CHAPTER TWO

Connor trudged through the open range of his family's ranch heading for home. He had left the creek with Mike around three-thirty and was dropped about a mile away from his house. This was the norm in an attempt to get somewhat sober before daylight hit. Sometimes it helped but more often than not it didn't, like the night with the old oak.

He looked at the horizon, saw no threatening pink tinges, and figured it still must be inside of four in the morning. Even so, he picked up his pace just to be safe. His dad was always up by five. He hiked the small rise overlooking the two story house that stood still a half mile away.

Cresting the ridge he came to a stop and instantly became sober. Red and blue lights lit up the night and reflected off the white siding of his home. It seemed all of the law enforcement of Ashlin —three patrol cars and two jeeps — were parked out front, as well as a couple of ambulances. Men with flashlights were combing the ground around the house and indistinguishable shouting could be heard.

Connor's heart began to race. He lurched a couple of steps forward, getting ready for an all out sprint, when he heard the sound of a pickup driving up behind him fast. He looked over his shoulder and saw it was Mike swerving and breaking hard just below the rise.

He jumped out and ran toward Connor, calling out, "Wait."

Connor looked back and forth between his home and Mike, his head still fogged, rendering him indecisive. Just when he decided to make the dash for home, Mike latched onto his arm. Connor could feel his friend shaking through the grip. When he looked at Mike's face, the serious look frightened him even more

"Let go," Connor said as he tried to shake loose from Mike. "Something bad's going on."

Mike tightened his hold. "Really bad, but you can't go."

Panicked, Connor gave a twisting yank and broke free. He got about three strides into his mad dash down the rise before having his legs taken out from under him by a diving Mike. Connor hit the ground hard and before he could move, Mike had crawled up and was laying on top of him.

"Get the hell off of me! Something's wrong. I got to see them."

"You can't see them." Mike's voice began to break on the last word.

Connor didn't want to hear anymore. He reached out and clawed at the ground. "I gotta go. Let me go God dammit."

"Connor ...."

"Shut up. Just shut up and let me go."

"Listen to me. They've all been shot. I don't know the details, just what I could catch on the two-way, but your whole family's been shot."

It took Connor a couple seconds before the news made its way through the haze his brain was in. Once it did, he made a wild attempt to dislodge Mike even though his friend had him by twenty pounds. He grew tired from the struggle and began begging, "Please let me go. I need to go."

"You can't go down there. They think you did it."

Connor's head rested against the cool glass of the passenger seat window of Mike's truck. The sky was awash with pink as the familiar open rolling land passed by. Chatter was still coming through on the two-way, but the boys were silent during the drive. Connor didn't ask, and really didn't care, where Mike was taking him, although the route indicated it was probably to Mike's home. If it were up to him, they would just keep driving.

They pulled onto the long dirt drive that stretched and meandered another half mile before ending at the Traynor home. Mike brought his truck to a stop right in front of the house, meaning his mom must be working a graveyard shift at the hospital. Connor already knew where Mike's dad was. He was an Ashlin deputy.

Mike jumped out of the truck. "Stay there," he told Connor before dashing up to the front door of his home. Connor watched him enter the house, then closed his eyes. His head hurt. It wasn't just the alcohol. Too much was trying to crowd into his mind. He was working so hard at shutting everything out but felt he was losing as flickers of thoughts flared up and scared him.

The sound of the banging screen door caused his eyes to open. He saw Mike carrying a grocery bag, a blanket, and some keys. "Come on," he said while giving his head a jerk indicating Connor should follow. Connor opened the truck door and woodenly followed his friend around to the side of the house.

They stopped in front of a locked storm cellar. Mike thrust the bag and blanket at Connor, then bent over to unlock the padlock securing the doors shut. Once unlocked, he pulled up on the doors whose hinges groaned and set the heavy wood panels to rest on the ground. Mike climbed down the ladder and then held his hands up to take the stuff Connor was holding. Connor climbed down the ladder after giving Mike the bag and blanket.

Mike set the stuff down on a dilapidated cot and looked around. "Nobody's been down here in awhile so it's kind of dirty."

Connor took in the small space. In the dim light he could see a heavy layer of dust and cobwebs covering every surface. It smelled musty.

"You should be safe here while I find out what the hell is going on and why the hell they think you did it." He rummaged in the bag and started showing Connor glimpses of the items he put in there. "I got you some water and stuff to eat. It's not much but it'll get you by until I get back. I also got you this." He pulled out a bottle of Jack Daniels. "I figure you might need some."

Connor took the bottle from him and stared at it.

"Anything else you can think of before I lock you in?"

Connor's eyes went wide and he grabbed Mike's arm. "Don't lock me in here."

"Dude, listen. If I don't lock it someone will notice. I'll be back after school to check on you. Trust me. This is the safest place I can think of."

Connor nodded and let go of Mike.

Mike headed for the ladder and climbed out of the small storm cellar. "I'll see you later," he called down before shutting the doors, leaving Connor in near darkness.

Connor felt a shiver run through him as he heard the padlock click shut, then Mike's retreating footsteps. He turned and sat on the cot. He glanced through the contents of the bag which included a few bottles of water, crackers, a bag of cookies, and an apple, but didn't take anything out.

Being alone in the dimly lit cellar provided no distractions and he felt it harder to keep away the frightening thoughts. Suddenly an image of his family flashed in his mind causing a sharp stabbing ache to hit him in his stomach. He began to gasp as he quickly unscrewed the cap off the bottle of Jack Daniels. He pressed the bottle to his lips and tipped his head back and filled his mouth with whiskey. He grimaced and gave a small cough as the liquid seared his throat, making the pain in his gut diminish slightly. Connor took another mouthful and swallowed, then another. Soon the pain was being overshadowed by a blanketing numbness. He let out a shaky sigh and closed his eyes. That's the great thing about alcohol. You don't feel anything.

CHAPTER THREE

Connor barely registered the heavy shove of his shoulder and his name being called. He tried to respond but his tongue was thick and seemed pasted down. Swallowing was near impossible. There was just no saliva in his parched mouth. His eyes fluttered opened and he could barely make out Mike in the darkness. Suddenly his head felt like it was splitting in two. He groaned and closed his eyes.

"Hey," Mike said as he gripped Connor's shoulder. "You need to get up. You're beginning to scare me."

As consciousness began to take a firmer hold, Connor noticed his stomach begin a slow building roil. Saliva began to flood his mouth, making him choke. He swung his legs over the side of the cot and bolted upright as the first heave began. He leaned over and aimed for the floor but Mike was quicker, shoving a bucket between his knees. Connor clutched the sides of the bucket as everything in his stomach was violently ejected. Dry heaves continued to wrack his body long after nothing was left.

Once Connor was quiet and the only movement was his trembling from the aftermath, Mike took the bucket away. Connor collapsed back onto the cot, letting a whispered, "Fuck," fall from his lips.

Mike held up the empty Jack Daniels bottle. "Damn, Dude. You were suppose to pace yourself. I came back here after school and you're out cold." He turned, setting the bottle on the floor, and began rummaging around in the grocery bag. He pulled out a bottle of water and the crackers and brought them over to Connor.

Connor struggled to sit up while Mike took a seat next to him. He uncapped the water and handed it to Connor, who took a few cautious swallows. While drinking, he took in his surroundings and the memories came back to him from earlier in the day. Without looking at Mike, he said, "Tell me."

Mike opened the package of crackers and handed one to Connor before setting the package in his friend's lap. Connor ate the cracker as Mike took a deep breath. "They're dead. Both of your parents."

He felt his throat constrict as he swallowed the dry cracker. He took a few sips of water as he steeled himself to ask his next question. "What about Skeeter?"

"She's alive. Pretty bad shape but still alive."

Connor closed his eyes and began to shake harder. His baby sister was alive.

"Dude, keep eating. You look like shit."

Connor took a sip of water and ate another cracker. "What about me?"

Mike grimaced. "They think you did it. I heard stuff on the two-way and was listening to my dad talking on the phone. There's supposedly all this shit load of evidence."

"I was with you guys."

"I thought if we told the cops that then you'd be off the hook. But they're saying the times don't match up. You know, from the time it happened to when you were with us. And they think we're covering for you. Brett and Josh weren't much help recalling even what day it was let alone times." Mike paused. "You got no alibi."

"Skeeter can tell them. She knows it wasn't me."

"She's pretty bad, Connor," Mike said quietly.

Connor felt his chest tighten and he quickly took a drink of water.

"That's not the worst of it. There's talk of trying you as an adult. They're out looking for you."

Connor heard enough. He stood and took a shaky step toward the ladder.

Mike grabbed his arm. "Where you going?"

"I gotta take a piss."

"Let me make sure it's okay out there." Mike climbed up the ladder and in a few seconds whispered, "Come on."

Connor followed him to a bush at the corner of the house. Mike turned to keep a watch on things while Connor unzipped his jeans. He took in a deep breath of the cool fall evening air to settle his nerves while he relieved himself. He zipped back up and followed Mike back to the storm cellar. He looked at the ladder leading into the dark space, then turned to face the unending expanse of rolling fields. He took a couple steps before Mike grabbed him and turned him back to the cellar.

"You need to stay here until we can figure out what to do." Mike said as he firmly took hold of Connor's shoulders to force him, if necessary, down the ladder.

Connor didn't have the strength to resist and went without complaint. Mike took out the foul bucket and stayed with him until he ate some more crackers, a few of the cookies, and finished off the bottle of water. Connor saw the empty whiskey bottle. "Hey, Mike. Do you have anything you can give me?" he asked while flicking his eyes and lifting his chin in the direction of the bottle on the floor.

Mike shook his head. "I'll probably get busted for lifting that from the cupboard." He stood and fished a hand into his pocket, pulling out two round tablets. "I brought you these instead. They should do the trick."

Connor took the offered pills and held them in his palm. "What is this?"

"It's valium. Should take the edge off." He grabbed another water bottle, opened it and handed it to Connor.

Connor looked at the pills. He'd never taken drugs before. But his splitting headache and the thought of being alone in the cellar had him opening his mouth and tossing the tablets onto the back of his tongue. He took the water bottle from Mike and washed them down without another thought.

"It'll take a little while to kick in," Mike said. "If my parents are gone in the morning, I'll check on you. Otherwise it'll be after school."

Connor nodded and watched Mike go to the ladder and climb out. The wood doors were shut and the snap of the padlock was heard, then there was silence. Connor finished off the bottle of water and waited for whatever the valium would do. Relief didn't come fast enough and the reality of what had transpired in the last twenty-four hours sucked him in faster than a rip tide.

He was helpless against the knowledge his parents were gone and his sister might be soon as well. Pain tore through him as his chest tightened, doubling him over as he curled onto the cot. He buried his face into the blanket, nearly stuffing it into his mouth, to stifle his anguished cries. When the worst of it had passed, he began to feel a numbing drowsiness start to pull him under. Connor lay there, drifting on the calming disconnect slowly taking over even though the tears continued to stream. His eye lids grew heavy and finally closed.

CHAPTER FOUR

Sonya Reisler interrupted her typing, reaching behind her to scratch her neck for the tenth time that morning. She eyed her scissors while contemplating violence against the irritating clothing tag of her new blouse. After three months she still wasn't used to the pant suits or the desk. She was beginning to regret her promotion.

Maybe it was karma or the imputative vibes coming from the glances of the other officers that made her feel undeserving of her new rank. Being only twenty-four and promoted to detective had raised a few eyebrows. She knew the behind the scenes discussions fueled by the officers passed over were of who she had slept with to seal the deal. She would be pissed if only there wasn't some truth in the rumors.

She reconciled it as a mistake made when she was a twenty year old cadet coming off a bad breakup. They had both tried to get into the academy. She made it. He didn't. Two months into the grueling training, and with her relationship in its death throes, she was ready to quit. Ray wouldn't let her.

Detective Ray Boone was thirty-five, separated, and a part-time instructor at the academy. He took note when Sonya missed her Friday roll call and classes. By late afternoon he tracked her down to a local bar. He was a good detective.

Sonya made sure she wore her cadet uniform to sway the bartender into serving her under-aged self and was nearly completely blitzed when Ray found her. After threatening the bartender that the place would be shut down if he ever caught them serving her again, he took her to his apartment to sleep it off. That weekend was the start of her becoming Ray's special project, both professionally and personally.

She never understood what it was Ray saw in her to risk his career by having an affair with a cadet. It was more than that. Ray truly believed she could be a great cop and got her to believe it herself. Under his guidance she flourished, although there were times after extra gym, firing range, and study sessions she was ready to scream. Sleeping with her instructor seemed to guarantee the furthest thing from an easy pass, but she loved him for it.

Their arrangement lasted until she graduated from the academy at the top of her class and she took a placement in Omaha. Ray went back to Lincoln and reconciled with his wife. No drama. Just life and careers setting them on different courses. Until three months ago.

When she got word of her promotion, Sonya was pleased with herself. It was all part of the plan Ray carefully laid out for her to put her on the fast track and she had followed it to the letter including completing her bachelor's degree in criminal justice. She worked hard and felt she earned her promotion. But then she received her assignment and now wasn't so sure.

Sonya glanced across the desk butted up against hers to the empty chair on the other side while trying to focus on the file in front of her. She was part of a small pool of qualified candidates when the opening came up. She also knew detectives looking for new partners had a role in the selection process. He assured her she was the best candidate, but knowing he had a big say in her being selected as his partner planted doubts she couldn't shake. Part of her hated Ray for that.

She caught a glimpse of an officer heading her way. It was Drew Snyder, one of the candidates she beat out.

"Is Ray around?" Drew asked as he reached the desk.

"He got called to Peterson's office. Do you have something for him?" Sonya lifted her hand a little indicating she could take the file.

Drew pulled it closer to him. "It's follow up information on a case we were working on a few months back."

Sonya caught a glimpse of the name on the file before he had pulled it away. "The Mickleson case. He briefed me on it. What do you got?" She reached out a little more deliberately toward the file.

"I think it'll be better if I talk to Ray about it. He knows the case backwards and forwards. Besides," he said with a smirk as he lifted his chin towards the stack of files in front of her, "it looks like you're in over your head."

Sonya bit back what she wanted to tell him to do with that file and all the other files on her desk and simply said, "He should be back soon."

"I'll catch him later." Then Drew left.

Sonya let out a deep breath. She would eventually figure out how to handle Drew and the others. What she didn't know was how she was going to handle Ray. They both needed this to be a professional relationship only and were doing a good job to keep it that way. But there was always that undercurrent present.

She hunkered down, determined to make some headway. After only a few minutes the tag dug into her skin again. Sonya gave up, grabbed the scissors, and headed to the ladies' room. Some quick steps caught up with her.

"It took me six months to get used to the suit."

Sonya continued walking as Ray kept pace. "Have you been watching me?"

"That's my job." He leaned a little closer. "And my pleasure."

She rolled her eyes while giving him a backhanded slap to his stomach.

Ray chuckled. "Here." He took the scissors from her hand causing her to stop, then moved behind her. His free hand moved aside her long blonde ponytail as the back of his fingers caressed her skin on their way to finding the offending tag.

His touch, even brief, always calmed her and she exhaled as he pulled the tag up and began snipping each stitch. She would have just hacked off the damn thing and not really solved the problem. He was thorough.

"How would you like to get out from behind that desk?" he asked as he continued to snip.

"Love to."

"Like to travel?"

"We're going on a road trip?"

"More like a solo. I think my baby needs to leave the nest and stretch her wings a bit." He moved in front of her holding up the tag and smiling.

Sonya became suspicious.

Ray shrugged. "Nothing too hard. A double homicide and attempted in Ashlin last week. Suspect identified but on the run."

She reached out slowly and took the tag. "Ashlin?" She wasn't familiar with the name.

"A little ranching town about four hours west of here in Scotts Bluff County. The Ashlin sheriff has the investigation pretty much wrapped up but the DA would like us to go over it. It would also be a good opportunity to log some field hours."

That was a load of crap. She had plenty of hours already logged even before her promotion. She gave Ray a pointed look. "Significance in the victims?"

Ray hesitated and made a small grimace. "A family. Mother and father shot to death. Six year old girl in grave condition. Good chance it'll turn into a triple. Seventeen year old son is primary suspect."

It was a good thing he was still holding the scissors. She glared at him. "Dammit, Ray."

His tone was terse. "You've got to be able to handle shit like this, Sonya. We can't pick and choose cases that'll be acceptable to our personal demons. You won't last."

She looked away, knowing he was right. He was always right.

He softened. "This one is easy. No investigating. Just check their paperwork, you know, i's and t's and all of that. Let them worry about catching the kid. You'll be there three days tops."

Sonya sighed. "When do I leave?"

"Tomorrow morning." He smiled while handing her the scissors. "And if you play your cards right, I might let you off early today to get ready."

"What do I need to do?"

"Have lunch with me."

Sonya started shaking her head and clucking her tongue. "I wish I could but my partner loaded me down with a bunch of *his* old case files and I don't think I'll have the time."

Ray grinned. "Your partner sounds like an ass."

"Don't be too hard on him. He has his good points."

"Hmmm. I think your partner could be convinced to unload some of those files on another officer, say … Drew Snyder?"

Sonya smiled. "You are so bad."

Ray laughed as he tugged the end of her ponytail. "Meet me at my car in thirty."

As Sonya watched him walk away she realized no matter by what means she came to this job, she could never view Ray as a mistake.

CHAPTER FIVE

The clock on the dash showed nine-forty. Sonya figured that should put her in Ashlin right around ten. She had gotten an early morning start, having done her packing the previous night. Even though Ray had told her to plan on at most three days, she'd over packed.

She'd like to attribute it to the better safe than sorry mindset, but she knew better. Once a suitcase was set in front of her, everything went in for fear of leaving anything behind. A habit she couldn't shake from years of packing suitcases.

Another reason for the early start was simply the sooner she got started, the sooner she could go home. Hopefully Sheriff Bennett and his deputies were good at their jobs and did indeed have the case pretty much wrapped up.

A few more minutes of driving put her within sight of a sign along the side of the road that said, Ashlin population 5,346. Because of what took place a few days ago, that figure would be reduced by two. It was awhile before Sonya reached what could be called the downtown section. Ashlin sprawled out over six square miles with numerous large farms and ranches covering the outskirts, but downtown covered about four blocks.

She checked the directions she had penciled out and, after making a couple of turns, pulled her dark grey Nebraska State Patrol sedan in front of the sheriff's station. She stepped out of the car and smoothed down her light grey slacks before opening the back door to get her matching suit jacket. She slipped it on, concealing the shoulder holster she wore over her white blouse.

Sonya took a deep breath, put on her game face, grabbed her laptop case, and headed for the door. Stepping into the station she saw a young blond haired deputy sitting at the front desk discussing things with a man she guessed to be in his fifties.

Upon her entrance, the older man broke off his conversation and looked at her. "Wow. You got here fast."

"I got an early start," Sonya said as she saw the name tag on his shirt, letting her know she was speaking to Sheriff Bennett.

The sheriff gave her a smile. "Well, we're glad you're here. With this case going on and Val's baby deciding he wanted to go ahead and make his appearance ahead of schedule, we've been a little shorthanded."

Sonya smiled back. "I'm ready to get started."

"Just to let you know, it's pretty relaxed around here. You're a little overdressed. Folks might take you for a lawyer." The blond haired deputy got up and stood back as the sheriff started pointing out things on the desk. "The job is simple enough. Take in calls and log them on the call sheet. Check against the roster to see who's working and notify them on the two-way of calls if they're not here. Filing and stuff we'll walk you through. But most important is always make sure we got coffee. Why don't you check that first before you settle in."

"Uh, I'm not here to answer phones or make coffee."

Sheriff Bennett's face began to take on a sour expression, although the deputy behind him looked amused. "Now I told that temp agency what the job would entail."

Sonya brought out her badge. "I'm Detective Reisler with the Nebraska State Patrol. I'm here to look over the Evans murder case before it's forwarded to the DA."

The sheriff definitely did not look welcoming anymore. "You're Detective Reisler? They implementing some affirmative action thing over in the State Patrol?"

Sonya's own demeanor cooled considerably. "I'm ready to get started so if you would show me where I can work and give me the case file I'll get at it."

He turned to the deputy behind him. "Kerry, get our detective here set up. I got some calls I got to make." Sheriff Bennett left without another word.

The young deputy stepped forward and held out his hand. "I'm Deputy Patrick. You can call me Kerry. What's your name?"

Sonya shook his hand but was feeling none too friendly at the moment. "You can call me Detective Reisler."

Kerry laughed. "All business, huh? Well, Detective Reisler, let me find you a desk and I'll get you what you need."

Sonya followed him into the small station that had maybe half a dozen desks placed throughout the central area. He led her to one near a wall and obviously unoccupied.

"This okay?" he asked.

Sonya nodded.

"I heard you were going to be here a couple of days. Where you staying at?"

"I was hoping I could stay somewhere in town. The nearest motel is over forty miles away."

"Let me see what I can arrange. I'll get the file for you." He went to leave but stopped. "Oh, and don't mind the sheriff too much. He knew the victims and has been putting in a lot of hours to get this thing ready."

"I'll keep that in mind."

"Help yourself to some coffee, but remember you drain it, you make it." He gave her a grin before he left.

CHAPTER SIX

Kerry brought over a large binder containing all the paperwork regarding the case along with a flash drive that contained everything as well in case she wanted to work off of her laptop. Sonya stowed the flash drive in her computer bag and set it aside. She slid the large binder in front of her and opened it. There was something about physically handling the pictures and reports that allowed her to be absorbed into the case. The first thing Sonya did was to remove all the photographs and spread them out across the top of her desk. A family photo was placed in the center and crime scene photos on either side. She always liked the constant visuals as she read through case files.

She read over the description of the victims. William Mason Evans was forty years old, owned and operated a local cattle ranch, and had lived in Ashlin most of his life. Mary Louise Parker Evans was thirty-eight years old and the wife of William. She held a part-time job at the local clinic. Madison Parker Evans is their six year old daughter.

Neither parent had been in trouble with the law and had lived a relatively quiet life since moving to Ashlin almost seventeen years ago. The ranch was originally owned by Ralph Evans, Will's father, and the couple moved in to help run the place. Ralph Evans passed away about five years ago and Will inherited the whole operation.

She picked up the family photo. They looked happy being outdoors and posing by a large tree. Picture perfect. Her eyes were drawn to a little blonde haired girl smiling widely. The image began to dredge up something in Sonya and she quickly changed her focus. She needed to keep her head clear. Best not stir up the mud.

She studied Connor Evans. Sonya heard everyone refer to him as a kid, but he really didn't look like one. He was well-built and nearly as tall as his dad, with whom he had a strong resemblance to. The hair was the main difference, with Connor's being a much lighter shade of brown. He was smiling. He didn't look like a killer, but then who usually does. Kids can snap and do horrendous things. Maybe Connor Evans just snapped.

She had spent about an hour going over autopsy and ballistic reports. Will and Mary were shot while they slept in their bed. Will had managed to at least dial 911 before he died. Madison must have heard the noise and crawled in her closet to hide before she was shot. The weapon was a Winchester M94 rifle with a custom stock that had Connor's name engraved on it. One shot was delivered to each victim. The weapon was discovered in Madison's room and ballistics confirmed it as the murder weapon. A gun safe was found open in a room used as an office. There were about six other assorted shotguns and rifles, and a couple of handguns in the safe.

Sonya sat back in her chair. A handgun would have been easier to use. Why the rifle and why the one with your name on it? She looked back at the crime scene photos as she mulled over her questions. Looking at the picture of Madison's bedroom, she noticed long streamers hanging down from the ceiling. A closer look told her they were thicker, but she couldn't make out the details. She was still studying the photo when Deputy Patrick came over to her desk.

Sonya showed him the photo. "Do you know what these are?"

"Yeah. They're a bunch of these paper animals strung together."

"Like origami?"

He nodded. "Hundreds of them. Mostly birds. By the way, I found you a place you can stay at while you're in town. If you're ready to take a break, we can head over there. It's only a couple of blocks away."

"Sounds great," Sonya said, then grabbed her jacket and left with the deputy. Kerry drove Sonya over to Ashlin Tool and Hardware.

"Miss Sara has a furnished apartment above the store here you can use," he said as he parked the car in front of the store. They walked inside and Kerry made the introductions.

Sara led them outside and around to the side of the building where a flight of stairs went up to a railed landing that ran along the side and back of the building. They climbed the stairs and Sara unlocked the door to let them in. The door opened to the living room and the open space allowed you to see to the kitchen and dining area.

Sonya followed Sara through a hallway that started between the dining and living rooms. On the left of the hall was a large bedroom and bathroom, and on the right was a smaller room and storage closets. It looked clean and well maintained and Sonya said it was fine. They discussed price and Sara handed Sonya the key.

"You had lunch yet?" Kerry asked as they got into the car to leave.

"No."

"Lori's Café has good food," he said. Only a block later he was pulling in front of a yellow store front with green trim.

They went inside the café which was covered in a bright sunflower motif. Kerry led them to a booth then pulled out his two-way to let the other deputies know where he was. A waitress came with glasses of water, rattled off the lunch specials, took Sonya's and Kerry's orders, and left.

Kerry took his straw and tore the wrapper off before sticking it in his water. "How far did you get on the report?"

"Autopsy and ballistics," she said while stirring around the ice in her glass. "Maybe you can give me some of the other highlights."

"Hmm, let's see," he said while leaning back. "No forced entry. Gun, which was later confirmed as the murder weapon, was found on premises with Connor Evans' fingerprints. Boy has experience handling firearms and it was his hunting rifle. He's been in trouble with the law since he was thirteen and has a history of not getting along with his daddy. Completed military school application was found on kitchen table which probably set the whole thing off. Kid has no alibi, is now a fugitive, and there are no other suspects."

"Sounds pretty solid."

Kerry smiled. "Like a brick."

"So why leave the gun behind?"

He shrugged. "Shock of the deed. Not thinking clearly."

"Any vehicles missing? Money?"

"No."

"Makes it kind of hard to get very far."

Kerry sat up and eyed Sonya while taking a drink from his water. "You're sounding more like devil's advocate than somebody trying to help run the paperwork through."

"I would hope I'm sounding like a detective."

"Don't know any of them to know what they sound like," he said, then grinned. "But I'd like to get to know you."

Before she could respond, the waitress brought their food and they started eating. Sonya made a personal rule against getting involved with officers after her relationship with Ray ended, but felt she might be willing to bend it for the good-looking deputy. After all, she was only going to be here a couple of nights and she wouldn't be seeing him again. Then again, two nights is one night more than what her recent relationships have lasted.

CHAPTER SEVEN

Connor stared out the passenger window. The silence wouldn't last. It never did. But they were pushing thirty minutes into their drive home and not a word had been said to him. His dad must really be pissed.

He reached behind him to adjust the strap of the sling to keep it from digging into his neck. It was going to be a long eight weeks having this cast on his arm. A long eight weeks of not being able to escape down the oak.

The action was enough to break the lack of sound barrier. The questions coming like a building storm.

"What's it going to take, Connor? Breaking your neck next time? Dying? What's it going to take before enough is enough?" His dad paused. "Answer me, boy. What's it going to take?"

"I don't know!"

"Well, you'd better figure it out damn quick. You're turning eighteen in a few months. It's time to grow up and start shouldering more responsibilities like a man. What's going to happen one day when you wake up and realize this long running party is over? What are you going to do? You think your friends will be there for you? They won't. What kind of man are you going to be? A drunken felon? A man like your uncle?" His dad paused again. "I need an answer from you. Now."

Connor turned and glared at him. "I don't know what I'm going to be, but I'm sure as hell not going to waste my life on that ranch. I'm not you. I'm nothing like you."

His dad turned and looked at him. "You don't know much, but at least you got that part right. You are nothing like me."

His dad turned and stared out the windshield, the storm over. It was silent again.

Connor blinked in response to the memory. It was more like a wince. Memories had started popping into his mind with increasing frequency. They all hurt, but that one was one of the more unpleasant ones. And there were many like that.

He stared up at the rafters. Even in the dim light he could make out the tattered and dusty draped cobwebs suspended between each board. For awhile he had lost track of the days thanks to those wonderful little pills Mike would bring him. Everything had rolled and morphed into one long vague emptiness which was fine by him.

Now he was all too aware of every passing minute of every creeping hour. Worse, he was left with his loneliness and grief which seemed to have accrued interest while he was gone on his mental check out. Payback's a bitch.

Mike had cut him off two days ago telling him his mom was going to notice the pills missing. He joked there was no way he wanted to deal with her being drug free. Connor was pissed and they almost came to blows. Mike said he needed to start dealing with *things*. Connor knew what the *things* were even if Mike didn't have the balls to say it. His parents were dead and life as he knew it was over.

The first day was easy. He spent it being angry and didn't speak to Mike at all when he came late to check on him. Mike didn't say anything either and left shortly. By the second day Connor just didn't have the energy to maintain the anger and spent the day "dealing." Mike stayed with him longer that night.

Now here he was, still hiding out in the storm cellar. Nothing in the outside world had changed. Everyone thought he was guilty and he was going to be arrested. He already felt like he was in prison. He knew he couldn't stay here forever but right now neither he nor Mike had any answers as to what to do. Until they decided the next step, this is where he would stay. At least it was safe.

Connor suddenly heard the rattle of the padlock and he immediately sat up. It seemed too early for Mike to be home from school yet and that set his heart to hammering. As the doors were pulled back, letting the sunlight stream in, he stood. When legs clad in green scrubs and white sneakers started descending the ladder, all he could think was, *Oh, shit.*

CHAPTER EIGHT

After lunch, Sonya started reading through the reports of all the times Connor was taken into custody and detained by the sheriff. It was as thick as a small phone book and dated back to when he was thirteen. The reported incidents were quite impressive and included breaking and entering into various businesses and the high school, petty theft, vandalism of private and public property, hot wiring vehicles, and public intoxication.

Some descriptions of the incidents had Sonya smiling at the sheer creativity of them. Many sounding like high school pranks. Some of the others, though, left her wondering why he wasn't arrested and officially charged. There was no juvenile record for Connor Evans. She also noticed all of the reports mentioned accomplices, but no one specifically named. One thing was for sure, he never did anything by himself.

Sonya glanced around and saw Deputy Traynor sitting at a desk, busy typing away at his computer. She got up and walked over to him, taking the thick stack of reports with her.

The deputy's eyes flicked up at her as he continued to type. "Something I can help you with?"

"I've been going through all these reports and noticed that Connor Evans was never actually arrested for anything. Some of these are serious enough to warrant jail time."

His jaw set slightly. "We like to handle things in house around here."

"I've also noticed all the reports mentioned accomplices. I'd like to get a list of all the people who were detained with Connor Evans for each of these incidents."

"The list is short. It's always the same boys — Josh Mellor, Mike Traynor, and starting two years ago, Brett Aldrich."

Sonya grabbed a pen and a sticky note and scribbled down the names. She paused. "Mike Traynor? Is he related?"

"Yeah." He paused. "He's my son."

The corner of Sonya's mouth lifted. "Good thing the sheriff likes to handle everything in house, huh?"

"Anything else you need?"

She held up the sticky. "This is good for now," she said as she returned to her desk.

A little while later Sonya's attention was broken when Deputy Traynor's cell phone went off. He looked at the screen and answered it. "Hey, Trish." There was a long pause. "Slow down. I can't make heads or tails of what you're saying." Another pause. "Yeah. What about the storm cellar?" His brows furrowed in concentration. "Who was there?" Suddenly his face blanched. "Son of a bitch." He stood. "We'll be there in a few minutes. Yeah, Trish, yeah. We're coming."

He ended the call and yelled, "Sheriff," while grabbing his hat.

Sheriff Bennett came out of his office. "What's going on, Greg?"

"The Evans kid's been spotted." Greg began to put on his jacket.

"Where?" Bennett asked while ducking into his office to get his hat and jacket.

"At my own god damned house."

"He still there?"

"No. He made a run for it about an hour ago."

"Call Cleary and Patrick and have them do a sweep of the area. It's daylight so let's hope we get lucky."

"You got it," he said and began hailing the two deputies on his two-way while heading out of the station.

Sonya got up and started putting on her suit jacket.

Sheriff Bennett looked at her. "Going somewhere?"

"I think I'll take a ride out with you, if you don't mind."

He paused briefly, then talked as he was heading for the door. "You take your own car and just stay out of the way. You're an observer only."

Sonya followed the two cars as they drove out to Deputy Traynor's home. It was about five miles from town and looked like it sat on a hefty amount of acreage, though none of it seemed to be in use. As they drove up the long dirt drive, Sonya could see a woman in green scrubs pacing in front of the house, then stopping as she saw the cars heading her way.

Deputy Traynor got out of his vehicle and went to the woman. He put an arm around her and was leading her over to the sheriff as Sonya parked her vehicle. She assumed the woman to be Deputy Traynor's wife and walked up to listen to the sheriff asking the woman questions.

"Where did you see him, Trish?"

"He was in our storm cellar. It was locked. Mike must have put him in there."

"Did you see which way he went?"

"No. He closed the doors on me and it took me awhile to push them open."

The sheriff spoke to the deputy. "The boy could have covered a lot of ground by now. Have Cleary and Patrick continue the sweep, focusing three miles in every direction from here."

Sonya was pretty sure they were wasting their time looking anywhere but on a path heading northwest. She figured Connor wouldn't let his friend walk into a shit-load of trouble without a heads up. He was making his way to Ashlin High. She looked at the sheriff, still giving out instructions, and decided she'd let him waste his time.

Trish finally took notice of Sonya and her eyes grew large. She turned and gripped her husband's arms. "Who is that, Greg? Is that the detective from Lincoln? What's going to happen to Mike? Is she going to charge him with something?" She was growing more hysterical by the second.

Sonya closed the distance between her and Trish. "The sheriff will handle this, Mrs. Traynor," Sonya said. "I'm just here to look over the paperwork of the case."

Trish calmed down and let go of Greg, who went back to the sheriff.

"Mike and Connor been friends a long time?" Sonya asked.

Trish nodded. "Since grade school."

"Could I take a look at where Connor was hiding?"

"Sure. It's around the side. I'll show you."

Sonya followed Trish to the side of the house and went down into the cellar. Other than food wrappers and empty water bottles, nothing seemed too remarkable. As she climbed out, she asked Trish, "What made you decide to open the cellar?"

"I got off early today and thought maybe I'd start cleaning."

"I bet you were surprised."

She let out a shaky laugh. "I'll say."

"Were you afraid of him?"

"No. Startled, yes. Afraid, no."

"He didn't try to harm you?"

"No. He bolted around me and shut the doors. That's all."

"Thank you, Mrs. Traynor," Sonya said and turned to leave.

Trish took hold of Sonya's arm. "You meant what you said, right? About letting the sheriff handle this?"

Sonya gave her a reassuring smile. "I meant it." Trish nodded and let go of Sonya, who went back to her car. She looked at the clock on the dash. The high school would be letting out soon if it hadn't already. Sonya decided to take a drive by the school before heading back to the station.

CHAPTER NINE

Connor reached the edge of the corn field he'd been cutting through. The tall stalks had become tan and brittle from the hard frost they'd had about two weeks ago. Luckily they hadn't been plowed under yet and provided him cover to get him fairly close to the school.

He peered out across the street toward the school parking lot. He easily spotted Mike's navy blue Ford truck smack in the middle of the lot. School hadn't let out yet so only a few people were milling around. Enough to where he ran the risk of getting spotted. He had on a sweatshirt but since the day was warm, it would look odd if he was walking around with the hood up. He decided he would just have to go for it and leave the hood off.

Stepping out of the field, he quickly crossed the street and then slowed his walk down to look casual. He wove between the parked cars until he got to Mike's truck. A quick glance told him it was locked. Connor went to the passenger side. Somebody passed close by so Connor bent down and pretended to be examining the front tire. When the person was gone, he stood and went to the bed of the truck. He pushed the bed liner away from the side of the bed and reached his hand down. As soon as he felt the metal wire he relaxed a bit.

He withdrew the stiff wire and looked around. No one was too close to get a good view of him. Connor took the hooked end of the wire and pushed it between the rubber seal and the window, feeding it into the interior of the door. He moved the wire around until he felt the locking armature, hooked it, and gave a tug. The lock popped and Connor opened the passenger door. He put the wire back in its hiding spot, before shutting himself in the cab of the truck. He crawled into the backseat and scrunched down while peeking out the side windows. Nobody was coming.

While he was looking he noticed a dark grey sedan with some official looking emblem on the side, drive by on the street he'd crossed earlier. He had an uneasy feeling when the car turned around and parked on the street next to the lot and across from the corn field. Connor kept watch but no one got out of the vehicle. He would be willing to bet they were watching for someone. Probably him.

Connor lay on the back seat and waited. He didn't have to wait long, all of maybe fifteen or twenty minutes, before the dismissal bell sounded. It was another ten minutes before Mike showed up. He unlocked his door, tossed his backpack in the passenger seat, and climbed in.

As soon as the door shut, Connor said a quiet, "Hey, Mike."

"Jesus," erupted from Mike's mouth as he jumped and whipped his body around to look at Connor. Shock turned to confusion. "What are ... Oh, shit." He closed his eyes and his shoulders slumped.

"It was your mom. Sorry."

"Not your fault." He gave Connor a halfhearted grin.

"I need you to do me a favor before you go home and your parents wind up locking you in that cellar."

Mike let out a laugh. "Sure. Doesn't sound like going home will be any fun right now."

"I need you to take me to Scottsbluff."

Mike raised an eyebrow.

"I gotta see Skeeter."

"How the hell you going to do that?"

"It's a forty-five minute drive. We'll think of something."

"It's a bad idea."

Connor continued to look at him.

Mike finally threw up his hands. "What the fuck. Let's go."

CHAPTER TEN

Connor was laying across the back seat enjoying the fresh air blowing through the cab of the truck. Mike had the music turned up and all the windows down, taking full advantage of the warmth the Indian summer was providing. They had just crossed the bridge over the Hennessey Reservoir which lay on the extreme outskirts of Ashlin, and after being shut in that cellar for nearly a week, nothing felt better to Connor than the breeze and the feel of the highway passing under the tires.

He saw a light purple sheet of paper sticking out of the myriad of crap Mike left in his truck and had now wound up on the floor. Connor fished it out of the pile and turned it over. There wasn't much writing on the other side so it would work. He folded over the end and tore it off to make the paper square, then started to fold it.

"That wasn't anything important, was it?" Mike asked as he glanced at Connor.

"Flier for the homecoming dance next week."

"Not important anymore," Mike grumbled.

Mike's parents had been blowing up his phone with calls and texts since he and Connor left the high school until he finally just shut it off. Connor knew his friend was already going to be in trouble for some time for the cellar incident. Going to Scottsbluff? Just more icing.

"What are you going to do now? You know, now that the cellar is blown."

Connor shrugged and kept folding. "I don't know. I'm thinking of seeing my Uncle Jake. Maybe he'd be willing to drive me to Colorado or Wyoming."

"So, you're thinking of leaving?"

"Just thinking. That's why I got to see Skeeter. Just in case."

Mike was silent for awhile. "I heard they brought in a Detective Reisler from Lincoln. He's staying here in town a couple of days to go over the case. Maybe he'll find something and they'll realize it wasn't you."

"Maybe," Connor said. He wasn't going to hope but was still curious. "Where's he staying at?"

"Above the tool and hardware store." Mike glanced at him. "So, maybe you should stick around till he leaves."

"I might." His answer was enough to satisfy Mike for now, but Connor knew staying in Ashlin wasn't safe. There were just too many people who could recognize him.

Connor continued folding the paper until a purple paper crane was sitting in the palm of his hand.

About twenty minutes later they entered Scottsbluff and the hospital was only another five away.

"What's the plan?" Mike asked.

"Go around to the back and try to park."

"You got it. Then what?"

Connor looked down at his clothes. They were smudged with dirt and grime from his days spent in the filthy storm cellar. He began looking through the pile of stuff on the floor and found a sweatshirt and sweatpants that needed washing from P.E. but they were cleaner than what he had on. He began to take off his shoes and unbutton his jeans. "I'm going to try and go in the back and find a staff changing room. They probably have some lockers I could get into. I need to find some scrubs. Do you happen to know what floor they're on?"

"I think my mom said the ladies' one is on the fifth. Men's is probably there too. You going to try and pass yourself off as a doctor?"

"No. I couldn't pull that off. But I might be able to do an orderly."

"They all wear badges, you know. My mom says they're really strict about it."

"I'll figure that out if I get that far." He finished shucking off his jeans and slipped on the sweats. His brows furrowed a bit. "Is your mom on tonight?"

"No. She's not on until tomorrow afternoon. Is there anything you want me to do?"

Connor pulled off his own sweatshirt and t-shirt before pulling on Mike's, then shook his head. "I'm going to do this by myself. If I get caught I don't want you to be around."

Mike nodded his head but didn't seem too happy. "You sure this is worth it?"

Connor put his wallet in one of the sweatpants' pocket and the purple paper crane in the other. "Not if I'm caught before I get to see her."

Mike parked his truck near the back. It was quiet. No other vehicles and no people. "Now what?" he asked.

Connor crawled up front next to him. "What time is it?"

"Three forty-five."

"Let's wait until four and see if someone comes with a delivery. If not, I'll chance going through the front doors."

Ten minutes later they heard the rumblings of a truck backing in the loading area. Connor and Mike watched as the driver got out and rang a bell by a set of double doors. In a few minutes they swung outwards and the door stops were lowered to hold them open. The delivery man gave the hospital staff person papers to sign and the staffer soon left with a copy. The delivery guy opened the back of his truck, loaded up a dolly, wheeled it off his truck, and through the open double doors.

"I'm going to check it out," Connor said while getting out of the truck.

"Once you're in, I'm going to go and get something to eat and come back."

"That's fine. This is probably going to take me awhile. I'll plan on meeting you here if everything goes well." Connor got a nod from Mike, then headed toward the delivery truck at a slow jog.

He reached the front of the truck and peered around it to look through the open doors. The short hall was empty. Connor took a step around the truck but suddenly saw the dolly round the corner. He quickly went back and crouched behind the front of the truck as the delivery man went into the back of it. After a few minutes, the guy must have reloaded the dolly and was leaving the truck, heading through the doors again. As soon as he rounded the corner, Connor followed.

He peeked around the corner and saw the man and dolly disappear into a room. Connor started walking down the hall swiftly and peeked into the room the man had entered. The man and the hospital staff person were talking and counting boxes. When both had their backs to the doorway, Connor quickly passed by, headed up the hall, and turned another corner until he reached a set of elevators. He punched the up button and the door immediately opened to an empty elevator. Connor pressed for floor five and the doors closed.

It seemed like the elevator stopped at every floor on the way to five, picking up more and more people. Connor stayed in the back and kept his head turned away from the other occupants. Once reaching the fifth floor, one other person got off with him. She looked to be a nurse. Connor followed her at a distance to see if by chance she was going to the staff changing rooms. He watched as she entered a door and then walked by it. The sign said "Authorized Female Personnel Only" and there was the female symbol on the door. Several feet away there was another one for males.

Connor pushed open the door and entered what looked like a lounge area with many chairs and a coffee table with magazines strewn across the top. There was nobody there. Off to the left were a few doors leading to private bathrooms. Farther back and to the right were numerous lockers. Connor walked over to them and looked over the locks of those that were in use. Many were combination type, but there were a few that required keys. Connor selected one of those lockers and took out his wallet. He opened it and selected a small bent wire from an assortment he carried with him. He gave a quick glance of the room and then stuck the wire in the lock and went to work on it. In a few seconds there was a click and the lock opened.

At the same time somebody came in and Connor prayed this was not the guy's locker. The guy went up to one several feet away and became busy spinning the dial on his combination lock. Connor let out a breath and opened the locker. There were a couple sets of scrubs and a toiletry bag, but more importantly, no street clothes. He took the shaving kit and a set of scrubs, then headed for one of the bathrooms.

Connor stripped off his clothes and washed up best he could at the sink. Looking at himself in the mirror, he thought he looked a bit too scruffy. He went through the shaving kit and brought out a razor and shaving cream and set to work. When he was done he wet down his hair and combed it back, making it look different from how he would normally wear it.

He put on the scrubs and found them to be on the large side, but they would do. After putting his wallet in one of the pockets and the purple crane in the other, he gathered everything up and stepped out into the main room. It was empty once again. He went to the locker, stowed all his clothes inside, and shut it. He decided not to lock it but positioned the little padlock so it would appear locked when given a cursory glance.

Connor saw it was ten to five on the wall clock. He took a seat in one of the chairs and picked up a magazine. He figured the administrative offices would close at five, giving him about twenty minutes to kill before he headed over there.

The time passed slowly and his nerves didn't allow him to fully focus on the content of the various magazines he casually flipped through. One guy entered and grabbed something out of his locker while Connor was waiting. They glanced at each other and nodded a quick greeting before the guy left. When the clock said ten after five, Connor put his magazine down and left the room. He walked to the floor directory posted directly across from the elevators. Out of all the choices, the personnel office was probably the best place to start. He set off to find room 521.

He found the office easily with "Personnel" being clearly marked on the door. There were no windows so from the outside it was hard to tell if it was, in fact, closed for the day. He put his hand on the knob and slowly tested to see if it was locked. It wouldn't turn.

"May I help you?"

Connor started at the unexpected voice coming from behind him. He turned and saw a lady wearing a skirt and a blouse and carrying her purse like she was leaving for the day exiting the office behind him. "Uh, I lost my ID badge. I need to get a replacement."

"The personnel office closes at five. You just missed them. You'll have to come back tomorrow."

"I'll do that. Thanks."

Connor walked down the hall in the opposite direction from where she was heading and went around the corner. He stopped, turned, and peeked back down the hall he just came from. He watched as the lady disappeared from view, then hurried back to the office door. After looking at the lock for a few seconds, he took out his wallet and selected two wires from an assortment that comprised his homemade lock pick set, then put his wallet back in his pocket.

He took a quick glance down the hall before taking the L-shaped wire and shoving the short end into the lower part of the key opening. The other wire was straight except for a carefully formed wavy w-shape at the end. Connor gripped the L-shaped wire and applied tension on the key hole as he inserted the wavy wire.

He glanced down the hall again before working the wavy wire against the locking pins. He kept applying tension on the key hole and began to feel it move. He continued to work at it until the L-shape wire swung upwards, unlocking the door. Connor grabbed the handle and turned it, opening the door. He removed the wires from the lock, entered the office, shut the door behind him, and returned the wires to his wallet.

He flipped on the lights and saw a long desk with a computer near the back wall. He walked over to the desk and around it, then took a seat in front of the computer. There was a golf ball sized camera attached to the top of the monitor that pointed to a plain white screen set up about three feet from the desk. Next to the monitor was a small boxy card printer.

Connor jiggled the mouse and the screen came to life. He looked through the icons and clicked on a few until one of them produced an ID badge template with the hospital name and logo. There were a couple of blank fields for name and employee number. There was also a larger square into which you would import a picture. In the blank fields he typed in Mason Parker and a fake employee number.

A quick glance told him he could not take the picture where the screen was positioned. He unfastened the camera and flipped it around to face him, then got up and carried the portable screen behind the desk and moved the chair out of the way. With a couple clicks of the mouse he had the camera activated. Standing in front of the screen, he looked at the image on the monitor. He went back and made a couple adjustments to the camera until the image looked good, then took the mouse off the desk and placed it in the palm of his hand while his other hand maneuvered it. He watched the screen until the cursor hovered over the button to take the picture. Positioning himself in front of the screen, he clicked the mouse, then went back to the computer and imported the picture into the ID template, and clicked print. In a few seconds the little box by the monitor spit out his plastic ID badge.

Connor searched through nearby drawers and found the blue lanyards with the hospital name printed in white running along the length, clipped his new badge to one, and put it around his neck. He turned the camera back around and returned everything to its proper spot. Walking to the door, he opened it a crack to look down the hall. He heard whistling and saw a janitor coming out of a room about a dozen feet away.

Softly closing the door, Connor stood with his back to the wall hoping the janitor would pass by this room. When he heard a key going in the knob he knew there was going to be no such luck. Connor cringed farther into the wall as the door swung open, almost making contact with his feet. The janitor continued to whistle as he pushed his cart in. Once the man was clear of the door, Connor quickly grabbed the edge of it before it started swinging shut and quietly scooted around it. He turned his body so he was facing the office and had his hand on the door handle to slow the closing. Suddenly the whistling stopped.

"You looking for someone?" the man asked.

Connor forced a smile and tried to appear relaxed despite not knowing at what point the man had spotted him. "I saw you go in and thought they were still here."

The man gave him a smile back. "Sorry. They're closed already."

"That's okay," Connor said while raising his hand in a parting wave, then turned and started walking down the hall. Before the door closed, he heard the whistling resume and he took a deep breath to calm his rattled nerves.

CHAPTER ELEVEN

Connor was casually wandering the halls of the hospital trying to figure out his next move, all the while keeping his eyes sharp. He needed to find Skeeter's room and he knew he would be more convincing if he had some sort of prop. After turning a corner, he spotted a tall canvas bag suspended in a metal frame with wheels sitting outside of a room and walked over to it. Looking inside he saw what looked like rumpled bed sheets in the bottom. A laundry cart could be the ticket to making him look like he was working and give him a good reason to go into Skeeter's room. He took it and began pushing it ahead of him as he walked.

He went to the elevator and studied the directory. His best guess would be floors two and three. He punched the down button and decided to start with two. It housed the pediatric unit. The doors opened and he pushed the cart on in, joining three others in the roomy elevator. Nobody gave him a second look. When the doors opened at the second floor, Connor exited and began his search. After quite a few minutes he had walked the entire floor but didn't find her name by any of the doors. He went back to the elevator and headed for the third floor.

When the door opened, it seemed this floor was much busier. It contained the ICU. With the activity going on, he pushed the cart with much more purpose to make himself seem as busy as the other personnel. Name after name he passed but none of them were hers. Nearing the end of one hall he saw a uniformed guard standing outside one of the doors. Connor paused. He had a sinking feeling that was Skeeter's room.

He studied the uniform carefully and felt a small sense of relief. It was only hospital security, not police. The guard would only be looking for the obvious and Connor doubted hospital personnel would garner close scrutiny. At least that was what he was counting on.

Taking a deep breath, he pushed the cart at a good clip toward the guard. When he got to the door he lifted his ID badge for the officer to see. The guard glanced at it and then to his face and gave him a nod as he opened the door for Connor. Connor pushed the cart ahead of him and entered the room. The guard closed the door behind him.

He looked at the lone bed in the room and saw a small blond haired girl lying very still. Swallowing hard, he made his way around the cart and went to the side of her bed where she looked so small lying against the white sheets. She was on oxygen and there were a couple other machines keeping tabs on her vitals, as well as an IV running into her arm.

Connor leaned over to place a soft kiss on her head. "Hey, Skeeter girl," he whispered. "You need to get better for me." He reached in his pocket and pulled out the purple crane. "I made you this so when you wake up you'd know I was here." He placed the crane in front of a bunch of cards that were on a rolling tray. He turned back to her and kissed her on the head again as her eyelids gave a brief flutter. He had to fight back the tears that were forming. "I'm sorry. I wish I could stay here until you wake up. I love you, girl, and I'll try to come see you again."

He took a step back. He didn't want to leave but if he took too long the guard would become suspicious. Reluctantly, he went back to the cart and pulled it toward the door. Before turning the knob, he took one more look at her, then opened the door. He pulled the cart clear and gave a parting nod to the guard before heading down the hall.

Connor was lost in thought and didn't register right away someone was talking to him until a nurse touched his back. His heart was hammering as he turned and looked at her.

"I need your help changing a bed in room 317," a middle-aged nurse with short brown hair said to him.

"Uh, yeah, sure," Connor said as he had no choice but to follow her to room 317.

Upon entering the room, he saw a large elderly man sleeping. "Help me roll him and I'll keep him there while you change the bed."

Connor's eyes grew big as he left the cart and followed her over to the bed. She pulled off the top sheet and handed it to Connor, who wadded it up and tossed it into the cart.

"Come on this side," she instructed and Connor went and stood by her. "Okay. Ready?"

Connor quickly positioned his hands on the unconscious man similarly to the way the nurse's were.

"One, two, three," she said and they rolled him onto his side. "I got him," she said.

Connor went around the bed to the other side and started removing the bottom sheet from the corners and pushed it to the center. Then he paused.

"Behind you," she said with a lift of her chin.

He looked and on the other bed was a clean set of sheets. He separated out one of them, his shaking hands making the task take longer. Unfolding it he tried to make sure he got it lengthwise all the while being aware the nurse was watching him.

"I haven't seen you on this floor. Are you new?" she asked as he struggled to tuck the sheet under the mattress and fold it around the corners.

Connor cleared his dry throat. "Ah, yeah. Started a few days ago." He got both corners done and smoothed the sheet to the halfway point.

"Okay. Help me lower him."

He went back around and helped her ease the man down, then they went to the other side to repeat the process. Connor removed the dirty sheet, putting it into the cart with the other one, then finished smoothing out and tucking in the clean sheet.

"If you can finish up here I'd appreciate it, uh... What's your name?"

"Mason," Connor said.

"Thanks, Mason," she said and then exited the room.

Connor quickly placed a sheet over the man and tucked it in and then laid a blanket over him. He quickly pushed the cart out of the room and headed for the elevators. He ditched the cart once on the fifth floor and hurried to the changing room. Only one other guy was present, sitting in a chair and reading a magazine. He gave Connor a glance and said, "Hi," before going back to the magazine.

Connor was glad he didn't lock the locker. Picking a lock with an audience was sure to raise questions. He opened the locker and changed back into his clothes, folded the scrubs and put them back before locking the locker. The ID tag he kept around his neck just in case.

He exited and made his way to the back doors. Once outside, he looked around but saw no Mike. Connor paused for a moment, knowing Mike wouldn't have ditched him and that something must have happened to make him leave. He decided to walk on the sidewalk by the street and head toward the front of the hospital thinking Mike might have parked in the main lot. He didn't get too far when the familiar truck pulled up.

Connor hopped in and asked, "What happened?"

"A security vehicle came by and said I had to move. I wasn't 'authorized,'" he said while giving the word air quotes, "to park in the loading area. So I parked down the street and have been looking out for you." He reached over, picked up Connor's ID badge, and looked it over. He smirked. "Nice."

"Thanks," Connor said as he crawled into the backseat to change.

"So, did you see her?" Mike asked as he began to drive.

"Yeah," Connor said as he pulled Mike's sweatshirt off and pulled his own on.

"Was it worth going through all this?"

"Definitely." Connor finished changing and made sure his wallet and ID badge were safely stowed in his jean pockets before he climbed back up next to Mike.

"Here," Mike said as he reached down, grabbed a bag, and handed it to Connor.

Connor could already smell the burger and fries before he even opened the bag and his stomach growled in response. "Thanks," he said while reaching into the bag.

"No problem."

As Connor ate, he noticed they were driving back to Ashlin. Mike wasn't going to entertain other options right now which was okay. Connor really didn't have any idea where he wanted to go nor what he would do once there. At least Ashlin was familiar. He also had the feeling Mike was placing a lot of hope in that detective.

On the drive back they listened to music and talked about completely trivial and random topics, avoiding anything remotely related to Connor's predicament. It almost seemed normal except when they lapsed into silence as they studied any oncoming vehicles. They were infrequent on this road and after being identified as just a regular car their talking would resume.

They were about ten minutes outside of Ashlin when they saw headlights heading toward them. Mike and Connor stopped talking as the oncoming vehicle passed. It was a sheriff's car. Mike's eyes kept flicking to the rearview mirror and Connor turned in his seat and peered out the back window. They let out a collective, "Shit," as they saw the red and blue lights come on and the vehicle start to make a u-turn.

CHAPTER TWELVE

Sonya took a sip of her lukewarm coffee as she turned a page in the binder. It was pushing eight o'clock and she could've ended the day earlier but was finding herself interested in what was going on in the station since this afternoon. The sighting of Connor Evans had everyone scrambling to find him. Sonya was secretly pleased her hunch about Connor going to the high school was in all likelihood correct.

Mike Traynor had not been seen since school let out. And by the curses spewing from Deputy Traynor every time a text or voice mail went unanswered, it was clear Mike wasn't interested in coming home or speaking to his dad just yet. The sheriff had issued an APB with the license plate and make of Mike's truck to the surrounding counties, so he and the deputy were still in the station waiting to see if somebody spotted the vehicle.

Sonya was curious about what the boys were doing. She doubted they were going on the run. Connor probably had little if any cash on him and from the conversations she was overhearing between the sheriff and Deputy Traynor, Mike didn't have much money either. Between that and little time for planning, she was convinced Mike would make his way home eventually.

To pass the time, Sonya began looking at possible suspects or persons of interest the sheriff had identified. It was pretty much a list of one — Jacob Evans. He was the younger brother of William Evans. Sonya looked at his photos, which happened to be mug shots. Sonya could see a strong resemblance to his older brother, though he seemed to have a slightly smaller build.

She flipped through his prison record. First conviction was for statutory rape at age twenty for which he served two years. Second conviction was for first degree burglary at age twenty-four landing him in prison for three years. Third conviction at age twenty-eight was for fraud which he served five years. He moved back to Ashlin five years ago after being released. Now at age thirty-eight, he currently lived in an apartment above Harris's Feed and Farm Supply where he was also employed. Even with the close proximity, it was noted he was estranged from his brother and his family.

Despite having a shady past, Jacob Evans had not so much as a parking violation since moving to Ashlin. He also had an alibi for the night his brother was murdered. A signed statement was given by a veterinarian named Dr. Randall Veckle who resided in Morrill County, a good ninety minutes away from Ashlin. Jacob Evans was at the doctor's home at eleven-thirty that same evening. Since the murders took place close to twelve-thirty, he was ruled out as a suspect.

She found statements given by three of Connor's friends saying he was with them that night out at a creek drinking. The same three friends he gets into trouble with. The three accounts didn't match up according to times and one of the stories even got the day wrong. They were dismissed as not credible and in no way could be used as even a reasonable alibi.

Sonya thought back to the time of death. It was strongly established by a 911 call Will supposedly placed at twelve-twenty-six while he was dying. She flipped to the autopsy report and read over it. The damage to his chest from the rifle blast was extensive. In Sonya's opinion he would have been dead in short seconds. Being able to place a 911 call seemed doubtful, but she had seen dying people do some pretty incredible things to where it was possible.

Curious about the call, Sonya took out her laptop, fired it up, and inserted the flash drive that held the recording. She started playing it and heard the standard operator greeting followed by silence and then the operator again inquiring about the nature of the emergency. More silence followed.

With the injuries Will sustained, especially the punctured lung, there should have been some noise. Unless he died while the call went through. Again, that was possible. Sonya went back and looked at the crime scene photos. Will and Mary were in their bed, obviously shot within seconds of each other. Madison was shot in her room meaning she was shot before or after her parents. If she was shot before, Sonya doubted her parents would have remained in bed. If she was shot after, which Sonya believed was the case based on finding Madison in her closet, why wasn't anything heard on the 911 recording? The recording went on for long minutes after it was placed but not a sound was heard. Unless the call was placed after all the shooting was done and that would mean the murderer placed the call.

So how did the 911 call factor in all of this? It helped solidify Jacob Evans' alibi with regards to the timeline and ultimately saved Madison's life by getting the authorities to come and check out the house. It also served to raise more questions in Sonya's mind.

She was still pondering the call when the phone suddenly rang in Sheriff Bennett's office. After a few seconds of conversation, he came flying out of the office. "Greg! A patrol spotted your boy's truck on Route 47 near Hennessey Reservoir heading back to Ashlin. He's in pursuit. We can head him off at the bridge."

CHAPTER THIRTEEN

Mike punched the accelerator as Connor watched the sheriff's vehicle complete its u-turn and the siren began to blare. He let out a slew of curses as the truck sped down the road. "I can't believe my dad put out an APB on me."

"Gee, Mike. Who wouldn't want their son out and about with a suspected murderer."

"Ha, ha, so funny," he said, then grew quiet. "You know I can't out run them."

Connor looked over at his friend and saw worry shadow his face. "I know."

"What do we do?"

Connor thought for a few seconds. "Can you get us to the reservoir bridge?"

Mike's brows drew together. "Yeah. Probably. Why?"

"I need you to drive to the middle of the bridge."

Confusion transformed to understanding as Mike's eyes went wide. "Are you out of your fucking mind?"

"It's the only chance I got."

"Jumping off the fucking bridge? No way."

"Mike. Listen to me. It's only like a twenty maybe thirty foot drop to the water. It'll be a cake walk and they won't follow me in."

Mike continued to scowl but didn't say anything.

"If you drop me off anywhere else, they'll catch me. This is my best shot."

"Alright," Mike said with a frustrated groan. "Just make sure tomorrow you contact me somehow, okay? So I know you didn't break your god damned neck."

"Deal," Connor said as he took off his seat belt.

The bridge was within sight and the sheriff's car was gaining. Just before the tires hit the beginning of the expanse, Connor could see more flashing lights on the other side of the reservoir. As Mike neared the halfway point, Connor placed his hands on the dash and gave his friend a nod. Mike jammed on the brakes, sending the truck screeching and sliding to a halt.

Connor flung open the door, hurdled the barrier, grabbed a quick breath before launching himself towards the black water waiting far below.

Even though he entered feet first, Connor hit the water hard. The impact and cold temperature left him dazed as his muscles constricted. A few seconds passed before he was able to move and fight against the weight of his soaked clothes. He was disoriented and out of air. Making strong pulls with his arms he headed to the surface. As he neared, he slowed his ascent and quietly surfaced, taking deep breaths. He looked around and saw the sheriff cars that were on the other side of the reservoir were now coming to a stop on the bridge.

A quick glance told him the bank to his right had more vegetation starting about a couple hundred yards past the bridge. He pulled in a deep breath, sank down and began to swim, keeping himself well below the surface. Connor swam until his lungs began to burn, then surfaced again. Looking back at the bridge, he saw a couple deputies training hand-held searchlights onto the water's surface.

One beam of light began to sweep his way and he quickly went under the water and watched until the brightness faded. Resurfacing, he sucked in a deep breath before going back under and began swimming toward the bank again. A few lungfuls of air later his feet started striking mud. He turned to look back toward the bridge and saw the lights trained elsewhere, then began to scramble out of the water and crawl through the vegetation. He collapsed in the midst of some larger bushes and lay there breathing hard. After awhile he began to shiver.

Connor knew he had to keep moving and find somewhere safe to spend the night and get out of these wet clothes. He kept following along the line of thick vegetation, putting more distance between himself and the bridge until the lights could no longer reach. He hiked up the bank and took a look around. In the distance he saw a large empty field with a mountain of recently baled hay covered in large tarps. *That could work,* he thought and set out at a brisk pace for the bales.

CHAPTER FOURTEEN

Sonya stared unseeing at the paper in front of her as her mind wandered to the events from last night. She had followed the sheriff and Deputy Traynor to the reservoir after the call came in. When the bridge came into sight, Sonya watched as a truck raced onto the bridge, slammed on its breaks, and slid to a halt. In the glare of the headlights coming up behind it she could see the passenger door open, a person get out, run and leap over the side of the bridge.

Sonya had gotten out of her car, walked to the spot, and looked over the edge. She estimated it to be a good thirty foot drop into the water. Not something for the faint of heart. The limited search for Connor Evans turned up nothing and Sheriff Bennett was fit to be tied. Questions came to Sonya's mind but Deputy Traynor hustled his son away before she could get near him to ask.

Her eyes drifted to the family photo and she picked it up. She stared at the smiling image of Connor Evans. For the first time, looking at his image caused her discomfort. There were things bothering her about the case. It was the small things. Things that could easily be explained away or discounted by the solid evidence. Maybe that's what bothered her more. Everything that needed to be there was there. No need to look any further than what was staring you in the face.

Sonya's phone rang and she set down the photo. She saw the name and answered. "Hey, Ray."

"Hey, Partner. You finished early. You planning on coming home today?"

"No, I'm not done yet. I still got a few hours to go on the case before I send it off."

There was a pause. "You didn't send it off yet?"

"No. Why?"

"I got word that the DA filed charges on the kid."

"What? When did you hear this?"

"This morning. Somebody forwarded the file to him."

Sonya's jaw clenched. "I gotta go, Ray."

"Sonya, don't go off half cocked. This isn't your case. We're doing this on behalf of the DA. If he already has it and it's good, then we're done with it unless you find something."

"I gotta go, Ray."

"Sonya ..."

"I'll call you later. Bye," she said and promptly hung up.

Ray immediately called back but she sent it directly to voice mail as she got up and headed for Sheriff Bennett's office. She walked in and interrupted a discussion he was having with Traynor and Cleary. "Nothing was suppose to be sent off until I finished looking at it."

Sheriff Bennett and the two deputies turned and looked at Sonya. "It was just a preliminary report that was sent in," he said.

"So why'd the DA already have charges made?"

Sheriff Bennett shrugged. "Guess he liked what he saw."

"Why the rush?"

"I'll tell you why," he said while leaning forward in his chair. "The faster we bring charges against that son of a bitch the better chances we have of catching him. Rewards and press have a way of enticing the public to become heroes."

"It also increases the chances of him getting hurt or killed in the process."

"That's just another form of justice."

"He's just a kid."

Sheriff Bennett slowly smiled. "Not according to the DA."

Sonya's stomach dropped. "He's going to be tried as an adult."

The sheriff nodded. "If we catch him. And I do plan on catching him, one way or the other."

Sonya turned on her heels and went back to her desk and resumed her work on the file.

Sheriff Bennett left his office with the two deputies following him. "You're job here is done, Detective Reisler. You're wasting your time."

"It's mine to waste."

An exasperated looking Sheriff Bennett turned from Sonya and faced his deputies present in the station. "I don't believe we got the full introduction yesterday, boys. Detective Sonya Reisler, twenty-four years old, has been a detective a whole three months and change. Before that she spent the last two and a half years working undercover as a high school student. And that was after nine months as a field officer. This is what the great state of Nebraska sent us to look over our work."

Sheriff Bennett walked back to his office as Sonya fought back the burn she began to feel in her cheeks. She was going to finish this file more for herself than anything and then get the hell out of Ashlin. With that thought, she took the family photo with Connor's face and placed it under a large stack of papers.

CHAPTER FIFTEEN

Connor planned on staying in bed all day. Third grade sucked and being in the warm, semi-darkness seemed to make things better.

The covers came off his head. "Time to get up for school."

He knew it wasn't a good thing because it was his dad this time. His mother obviously wasn't as convinced as he thought. "I'm sick," he said as he kept his eyes closed and did his best to sound miserable which, in reality, he didn't have to try too hard.

He felt a hand lay on his forehead. "You're fine. Get up."

"I got a stomachache." That wasn't a lie.

He felt the hand go to his stomach. "You're fine. Get up."

Connor scowled at his dad. "You can't tell if my stomach hurts."

"But I can tell if you're trying to get out of going to school." His dad sat on the edge of the bed. "Avoiding school isn't going to make you feel better."

Connor knew his dad was wrong. If he stayed home he wouldn't have to face them and that would make him feel a whole heck of a lot better.

"Your mother told me a couple of boys are giving you a bad time."

"Nobody is giving me a bad time."

"So you're saying Mrs. Graham and your mother are lying?"

"No, sir."

"You need to stand up to those boys, Connor."

"I tell them to stop but they won't listen to me."

"I'll tell you a little secret. Just between you and me. Sometimes boys need to talk with their fists."

"They're bigger than me," he said quietly.

"Bigger doesn't matter. Just means you need to talk harder. Now get dressed. Bus is coming."

Connor reluctantly got ready, was handed a piece of toast while heading out the front door, and got on the bus to go to school. He sat near the front because in the back were those two boys. When the bus reached school, he quickly got off and went to the playground.

He was wandering around, wishing for the ache in his stomach to go away, when a swift shove sent him skittering to the ground. Connor turned over and looked up at the dark haired boy and his sandy haired friend.

"That's for telling on us, asswipe," the dark haired boy said, then turned around and left.

Connor got up and looked at his hands. They curled into fists. Yeah. It was time for this kid to hear him. He ran up behind the boy and yelled, "Hey!"

The kid turned around and Connor slugged him in the face, sending him staggering back. Connor threw himself at the bigger kid and they fell in a heap as fists and feet started flying. The sandy haired kid joined the fray, falling on top of Connor. Putting every ounce of strength into each kick and punch, Connor repeatedly struck any part within his reach. Every blow that landed on him hurt like hell, but he was convinced these two were finally hearing him.

Sitting outside of the principal's office, Connor was too busy talking and laughing to even notice his father's arrival. When he finally looked up, he smiled. He threw his arms around the shoulders of the two boys flanking him, who looked every bit as bruised, scraped, dirty, and torn as he did. "These are my two new best friends — Mike and Josh."

Connor shifted under the heavy canvas tarp as he stirred from his sleep. He yawned, taking in a deep breath of the sweet green alfalfa hay stacked around him. Reaching over, he felt his various pieces of clothing to see how dry they'd gotten and found them still a little damp in places. His sneakers were a lost cause. They wouldn't be dry for days. The afternoon sun would help but he wasn't going to take the risk of setting his clothes out.

He pulled the section of tarp closer around him and thought about the dream still vivid in his mind. God that scene took place so long ago. He remembered the fight, and he, Mike, and Josh still joked about it from time to time.

But now it was the memory of his dad talking with him he didn't want to forget. Connor felt tears start to build knowing there were going to be no more conversations like that. Hell, he'd even settle for one of their fights. Anything so he just wouldn't feel alone in all of this.

Connor felt he was back in third grade, hiding under covers and running from bullies. A big difference now was he couldn't face his bullies without getting his ass arrested and they weren't going to listen to him no matter how hard he fought. He couldn't run and hide forever. Time and luck were going to run out on him. He knew Mike was doing his best to help him but this was something too big for either of them. He needed someone who could actually help him.

He suddenly thought of the detective Mike mentioned who was going over the case. He also remembered this Detective Reisler from the city was leaving tomorrow, along with any chance of his being cleared. At this point he had nothing to lose. He'd have to try and get that detective to hear him.

CHAPTER SIXTEEN

By four o'clock Sonya had finished going over the case file. She placed the binder neatly in the center of the desk and left the station. She grabbed a quick meal at Lori's Café and drove the two blocks to the apartment. Only one more night to spend in Ashlin. Earlier in the day she thought she would just leave for home when she was done, but she was tired, still angry, and didn't feel like making the four plus hour drive to Lincoln.

Sonya climbed the stairs to the apartment and let herself in. She took off her jacket and tossed it on the couch, shrugged off her shoulder holster and draped it across the back of the nearest kitchen chair before heading to the bedroom. She unbuttoned her blouse as she went to the dresser to pull out a t-shirt and a pair of sweatpants. She laid them on the bed, kicked off her shoes, finished undressing, and headed for the shower.

The hot water did help to leach the anger from her body, but left an unsettling melancholy behind. She knew it was the case. The report checked out. Motive, means, timelines, evidence ... everything was there. But the whole thing felt wrong.

After many long minutes, Sonya got out, dried off, and went into the bedroom to dress. Once in comfier clothes, she sat heavily on the edge of the bed and closed her eyes while taking a deep breath. A cool breeze from the window next to the bed touched her cheek. She blinked and looked at the curtain gently fluttering as a tremor ran up her spine. The window was closed this morning.

Sonya sprinted out of the room and to the kitchen. Her socked feet slid across the linoleum to the kitchen chair. Her holster was empty.

She slowly raised her hands to make them visible. "Are you going to shoot me or not?" she asked, more irritated by someone having the drop on her than fear.

"Maybe."

Sonya slowly turned around to face Connor Evans. Her hours spent staring at his photos made him easy enough to recognize, but the live version looked tired and a bit worn. She found herself feeling oddly relieved to see him okay even though this situation should elicit anything but. A quick evaluation told her he had her by about four inches and a good forty pounds. He also had her Glock 26 pointed at her. It was rock steady in his hand indicating someone who knew how to use a gun and who was in control of his emotions and intent.

He dropped a pair of handcuffs on the floor by his feet and kicked them to her. "Wrist and chair," he instructed.

Sonya reached down for the cuffs while glancing at Connor. The gun followed her every move. She decided it best to go along with whatever he had planned. She stood and placed her wrist in the one cuff and closed it with a click. Her feeble attempt at keeping the cuff loose was instantly thwarted.

"Let's hear a couple more clicks."

Sonya's lips lifted in a slight smirk as she gave the two more requested clicks. It was worth a shot even if she was trying to outsmart a guy who has had regular run-ins with handcuffs. She then secured the other cuff around one of the dowels of the chair back. She looked Connor in the eyes. "Okay, now what?"

"We talk." He paused and took a breath. "I didn't kill my parents and I didn't shoot my sister."

Sonya saw the brief play of emotions cross his face and how the gun moved to emphasize his points, but he was doing a good job at keeping himself under control. Engaging him in conversation could be dicey if she pushed him the wrong way, but curiosity of why he would risk coming here had her slowly pulling out the chair she was cuffed to. She turned herself and took a seat. She kept her tone soft and non-accusatory. "There's a lot of evidence that says otherwise."

Connor paused while giving the place a quick glance and then went back to focusing on Sonya. With his free hand he grabbed the back of the nearest kitchen chair, spun it around backwards, and sat down straddling it. The gun was still very much trained on her. "How much evidence?"

"Enough where the sheriff thinks you're guilty and wants the case closed."

Connor scowled. "I bet he does."

"He's not your biggest fan." She paused. "The case was forwarded to the District Attorney. They've charged you with two counts of murder and one of attempted. They want to try you as an adult."

She watched his face to gauge his reaction. He didn't seem surprised. They slipped into silence, each studying the other.

"Do you think I did it?" Connor asked.

It was the first time she broke eye contact with him. The finger of her free hand began tracing the patterns on the printed tablecloth. "Evidence says you could've done it."

"But …"

Sonya gave a small shrug. "Maybe I'm not totally convinced."

Connor abruptly stood and Sonya's eyes were back on him. "Listen. You're a detective, right? I need you to stay and find out who did this."

He backed away, gun still pointed as he reached into the front pocket of his jeans and pulled out a set of keys. Her keys. He set them on the table before his hand went back to rummaging in his pocket. "I know this was a real shit way of doing it, but I came here to ask for your help, Detective Reisler."

"Sonya."

Connor withdrew a fistful of something from his pocket and paused. "What?"

"My name is Sonya." She thought she saw the corner of his mouth lift slightly before he brought his hand to the table and deposited a dozen bullets near her keys.

He took another step back and laid the gun on the edge of the table. "See you around, Sonya," he said before disappearing down the hall.

She reached out and grabbed her key ring, separating out the smaller handcuff key from the others. After unlocking the cuff on her wrist, she collected her bullets and gun before heading to the bedroom. She didn't hurry, knowing full well Connor was long gone. Sonya sat down on her bed, checked and saw the chamber of her gun was empty, ejected the empty magazine and reloaded it while she thought about the unexpected meeting. When loaded, she snapped the magazine in place, put the safety on, then grabbed her cell phone. Quite a few minutes later, she dialed.

It rang only once. "Please tell me you're back home."

Sonya grinned at the desperation in Ray's voice. "Sounds like someone is missing me."

"What can I say. I'm lost without you."

"Temporary partner not working out?"

"Drew's driving me nuts. I miss my work wife."

"You should've thought of that before you sent me here. Besides, isn't one wife enough for you?"

"More than enough. I take it you're still in Ashlin. You still planning on leaving tomorrow?"

"Actually, I would like to stay on a few more days to work the case."

"Got leads on the kid's whereabouts?"

"No. More like working on the details of the case itself."

There was a pause. "It seemed pretty well tied up for the DA."

"A little too neatly packaged. Some things aren't adding up."

"Concrete or gut?"

"More gut right now."

"You don't have to go above and beyond to prove yourself. You earned your position, Sonya."

"My self-esteem is fine according to my shrink. I just want to make sure the right person is caught, not the convenient person."

"Are the locals on board with your thinking?"

"No. They want the kid to hang."

He paused. "You have my blessing for another week. After that, we'll have to have it be more than gut for the investigation to continue."

"Thanks, Ray."

"Are you sure it's the case and not some hunky local that has your guts a fluttering?"

"Would you be jealous?"

"Of course."

"You have a wife, Ray."

"I can still have my fantasies."

"Goodbye, Ray."

"Love you, Sonya."

"Love you, too."

After hanging up, she leaned over to shut her window, but ended up staring out into the darkness. She wasn't that surprised she'd agreed to stay. His visit was an all or nothing gamble that took a lot of guts and conviction. It also could have gone very wrong and she was sure he knew that. But the gamble did have a pay off. It solidified in her mind Connor Evans was innocent.

CHAPTER SEVENTEEN

Sonya tossed and turned most of the night. She didn't even know where to begin on this case and worse was the thought of delivering the news to Sheriff Bennett that she was staying in town. When she finally crawled out of bed and went to the closet, the sight of one of her pant suits made her groan. "Screw this," she muttered, and grabbed a pair of jeans, a t-shirt, and her black leather motorcycle jacket. "They don't take me seriously anyway so I might as well be comfortable." Once dressed, she slipped on her shoulder holster, grabbed her jacket and headed out the door. It was still fairly early and looking like it was going to be another warm day so Sonya decided to walk the two blocks to the sheriff station.

Sonya's pace slowed as she crossed in front of Lydia's Bakery. Strengthening her resolve with a hefty dose of caffeine and sugar before facing the sheriff seemed like a good idea. She opened the door, causing the bells at the top to jingle, and was met with the warm smells of baked doughnuts and freshly brewed coffee. Sonya paused, closed her eyes and pulled in a deep breath.

"It's okay to come in, honey."

Sonya opened her eyes and saw a middle-aged woman with short dyed red hair wearing a yellow baker's apron smiling and looking bright as any Nebraska sunrise. The lady gave her a wink. "We don't bite."

"Speak for yourself, Lydia," said an older heavy set man in a faded John Deer cap and even more faded coveralls seated at a small table. His smile was warm in his teasing. "She's so cute she deserves at least a nibble."

"Behave yourself, Hank. I don't need you scaring off customers." She waved Sonya to come in. "I promise he'll keep his teeth to himself."

Sonya smiled and entered the shop. She stepped up to the case next to the counter and began looking over the various baked goods.

"What can I start you off with?" Lydia asked.

"Definitely a large coffee."

Lydia gave a small laugh as she turned to get the coffee. "Too long of night or too early of a morning?"

"Both," Sonya said as she looked at the bran muffins but glanced longingly at the chocolate covered custard doughnuts.

Lydia set a large cup of steaming coffee on the counter and watched Sonya. "I make the custard myself. They've won blue ribbons at the state fair."

Sonya grinned at Lydia. "You sold me. I'll take one."

"Now, Lydia, you go filling her with those sweets of yours and it'll be too tempting not to take a little bite," Hank called from his table.

Lydia placed the doughnut on a plate and rang up the sale. "You be careful. She's packin' enough heat to keep you at bay."

Sonya took her coffee and plate and turned toward Hank so he could see what Lydia was talking about. His eyebrows raised as he took in Sonya's gun, then gave her a wink. "I like my women on the feisty side."

Lydia rolled her eyes. "Oh Lord, Hank. Did Marcy mix up your blood pressure meds with your Viagra this morning?"

Hank looked thoughtful. "Huh. I was wondering why there seemed to be extra spring in my steps." He laughed as he stood and went up to the counter. "Here I thought it was all in my feet."

Lydia shook her head while smiling and handed him a small bag before he headed out the door. "See you tomorrow, Hank. Say hi to Marcy."

"Will do," he said before touching the brim of his cap in Sonya's direction, then stepped out the door.

Sonya sat down at one of the small tables in front of the store window and took a grateful sip of her steaming coffee. The door dinged and she looked up to see Deputy Patrick enter the shop.

"I'll have that order ready for you in a few minutes, Kerry," Lydia said.

"No problem, Lydia." He glanced over and smiled at seeing Sonya. Without waiting for an invite, he walked over and took a seat at her table. "I thought you'd be heading back to the big city already, Detective."

Sonya carefully picked up her doughnut with one hand and turned it over in the air. With her free hand she pulled off a piece of the bottom and popped it into her mouth, chewed, and swallowed. "Actually, I'm going to be staying here for a few more days."

Kerry gave her a smirk. "Does Sheriff Bennett know about this?"

Sonya took a long drink of her coffee before pulling off another piece from the bottom of her doughnut, exposing more of the golden custard. "Not yet," she said before putting the piece in her mouth.

"He's not going to be thrilled with the idea of you hanging around and second guessing his work."

Sonya shrugged. "He's got no choice. I already got the okay from my boss to check some things out."

Kerry frowned. "That doesn't sound like you're going to be staying in the station going over the file."

"Nope." She took a long swallow of coffee while watching the deputy across from her.

"Jesus," he said while leaning back in his chair. "They gave you permission to conduct your own investigation."

Sonya nodded as she pulled the last piece of the bottom off of her doughnut and ate it.

"I don't get it," Kerry said. "All the evidence points to the kid. What do you think you'll find that we didn't?"

"I don't know." Then she gave him a grin while bringing up what was left of the upside down doughnut to her mouth. "But that's what makes the job fun. That and pissing off small town sheriffs."

Kerry watched her as she took a bite and proceeded to get a dot of custard on the tip of her nose. He began to chuckle. "Who the hell eats a doughnut like that?"

"I've always eaten them this way."

Kerry leaned forward, reached out, and gently wiped the custard off Sonya's nose with his fingertip. "You must have missed the doughnut procedural training at the academy. It would be remiss on my part if I didn't offer my services in instructing you on proper doughnut handling techniques." He grinned at her before licking the custard off his finger.

"That's very generous of you but I don't think Sheriff Bennett would approve," Sonya said while grinning back.

"I don't need his approval if it's conducted after hours. I figure with as ingrained as that habit of yours is, it's going to take many evenings and many hours to get it worked out of your system."

Before Sonya could respond, Lydia came up to the table with a box that she handed to Kerry. "You leave her alone. I think the way she eats her doughnut is cute."

"It's definitely unique," he said while standing. He winked at Sonya. "Let me know when you're ready to take me up on my offer."

"I'll be sure to do that, Deputy Patrick," Sonya said before taking another bite while looking at him.

He smiled, took the box from Lydia, and headed out the door.

Lydia took a seat in Kerry's vacated one. "So what do you think?"

Sonya swallowed her last bite of the doughnut and smiled. "That is the best chocolate covered custard doughnut I've ever had."

"I'm glad to hear it," Lydia said while beaming.

"I know the way I eat them looks crazy, but it started when I was a kid." Sonya shrugged. "Don't know why."

"Just so you know, you're not the only one who eats them that way."

"Really?"

Lydia nodded. "Connor Evans. The boy accused of killing his parents. He eats them that way too."

CHAPTER EIGHTEEN

Lydia's face took on a troubled look once her words were out.

"Do you know Connor Evans well?" Sonya asked.

"A bit better than most of the kids around here. He spent two months working off damages he and his friends caused about a year back. Got to know him pretty well."

"What's he like?"

"At the heart of it, he's a good kid. Small town life isn't for everyone. Not a lot of entertainment around here. Some kids get bored when all there is to do is school and working on the family farms. Connor and his friends are those kind of kids. They end up creating their own fun."

Sonya nodded. "Oh, I've seen the list."

Lydia chuckled in response. "I'm sure it's a long one."

"Was he a good worker?"

"Apart from the fact he had to be here, yeah, he worked out real good. I swear that boy can fix anything. I had a mixer making an awful racket and he had the thing apart, identified the problem, figured out how to fix it, and had it all put back together in no time. Saved me a lot of time and money."

"Do you think he could've killed his parents?"

"I know he was a handful and his dad and him didn't see eye to eye on things, but I can't see him doing something like that. And shooting his sister? He loves that little girl. Would always bring her home something from here." Lydia stood, then looked at Sonya. "Are you going to help him?"

"I'm going to try," Sonya said while pushing her chair away from the table. "Do you know of anyone who would want Will and Mary Evans dead?"

"No. They were good hard working people. Never had a problem with anyone."

Sonya stood. "Thanks, Lydia. I'll be sure to stop by again," she said before heading out the door.

She walked the remaining block to the sheriff station and took a deep breath before entering. Sonya walked straight to Sheriff Bennett's office. The door was open so she went in.

Sheriff Bennett looked up from something he was reading. "I thought you'd be long gone by now, Detective. Did you forget something?"

"Yeah. I kinda forgot to give my gut a little more credit as far as the Evans case goes."

"Not quite following you."

"I believe Connor Evans is not the one who killed Will and Mary Evans."

The sheriff sat there a moment, then smiled. "Is this some kind of parting joke?"

"No joke. I have permission to stay here in Ashlin for a week in order to conduct my own investigation into the murder."

"You listen here," Sheriff Bennett said as he stood and pointed a finger at Sonya, "that boy killed his parents. The case has gone to the DA and it's solid. I'm not going to have you poking around and raising questions defense attorneys will be frothing at the bit to latch onto to tear it apart."

Sonya gripped the front edge of the desk and leaned in, drawing closer to the sheriff's extended finger. Her voice was steeled. "You don't have a choice."

The sheriff withdrew his finger and slowly sat down. He looked Sonya in the eye. "You know what they say about fighting the current? You just get tired and drown. Go ahead and conduct your investigation. You won't find anything. You'll run out of time and you'll be called back." He went back to focusing on the sheet of paper in front of him. "Best be off, Detective. Clock is ticking."

CHAPTER NINETEEN

The sheriff was right about one thing when he said the clock was ticking. Sonya needed to make progress and she needed to make it fast. There were certain people she needed to key in on and this morning would be the start.

Sonya drove to Ashlin High School. She went to the office and formally introduced herself and said she was there to interview students who knew Connor Evans. She asked if there was a private office she could use and was shown to the guidance counselor's office. Sonya requested Mike Traynor be told simply to report to the office.

In about five minutes the door opened and Mike stepped in. He was a big kid, about six two with dark wavy hair. Sonya indicated he should take the seat across from her. He closed the door behind him and sat looking completely relaxed with a slight smirk on his face. He maintained eye contact with Sonya without so much as a flinch. He was well practiced.

"Mike Traynor?" Sonya asked.

"Maybe."

"I hope I'm not taking you away from anything important."

Mike's smirk grew. "You can get me out of fucking American Government anytime."

"More exciting to watch shit dry in the sun, huh?"

Mike's smirk was gone and his eyes narrowed a bit. "Are you a guidance counselor?"

"Of sorts," Sonya said as she couldn't help her own smirk from touching her lips. "I'm Detective Reisler."

Surprise colored Mike's face. "You're Detective Reisler?"

"You've heard of me?"

Mike regained his composure. "I keep my ears open."

"Easier when your dad's a deputy."

"I thought you were leaving today."

"So did I, until somebody paid me a visit last night."

Mike grinned. "He has more balls than I thought."

"Even more when you ask him how he changed my mind." Sonya paused. "I'm trying to help him. I've got an okay to be here a week but that's as long as Connor doesn't get caught. He needs to lay low and not take chances. I need you to tell him that."

Mike shook his head. "Haven't seen him." Then he smiled.

Sonya stood. "I'll be back if I have any questions I think you could answer... or information that needs forwarding." Then she smiled.

Mike stood and headed for the door. "Alright, but only if you come at ten."

"American Government?"

Mike grinned as he touched his finger to the tip of his nose, then turned and left.

Sonya followed, thanked the secretary as she made her way out of the office, and headed toward her car. She actually had questions she wanted to ask Mike but knew she wouldn't get anywhere with him until he verified things with Connor.

Sonya sat in her car and flipped through her notes. Maybe she could get somewhere with Jacob Evans. He works at Harris's Feed and Farm Supply. She took note of the address and started her car. After driving a half dozen blocks she spotted a building covered in dark wood with a large painted white sign with blue letters. She pulled up in front of Harris's Feed and Farm Supply.

Sonya entered the store and headed for the checkout counter. An elderly man looked up from the ledger books he was working on. "May I help you?"

"I was told Jacob Evans works here."

"Yeah, Jake works here. He's out back loading a delivery." He pointed to a set of doors at the back of the store. "You can go through those and that should put you in sight of him."

"Thanks," Sonya said and headed for the doors that led out to the bagged feed storage and loading area. She spotted two men loading a flatbed truck that was parked a couple hundred feet away next to a mountain of stacked alfalfa hay.

Sonya jumped down from the dock and headed towards the men wielding hay hooks. The one guy who was navigating the mountain of hay looked young, not too long out of high school. He would hook a bale and toss it down to the bed of the truck to where the other guy would impale the sides with the black metal hooks and position it next to other carefully stacked bales.

Sonya walked up to the truck. "Jake Evans?"

The man gave Sonya a sidelong glance while hoisting a bale up onto another one. "Who wants to know?" he grunted.

"Detective Reisler, Nebraska State Patrol. I'd like to talk to you for a few minutes."

He removed the hooks out of the bale and turned to face her. Despite showing the mileage of a hard life, making him look older than his thirty-eight years, there was no mistaking the family resemblance. "What about?"

"I'm investigating the murder of your brother and his wife."

Jake studied Sonya for a few seconds before jumping down from the flatbed. He set down the hooks and removed his work gloves. He turned towards the guy waiting on the tower of alfalfa. "Take ten, Jess." The young man nodded and scrambled down.

Jake gave a nod of his head to indicate he was going to walk and Sonya could follow. "Not much to investigate, I imagine. My dear sweet nephew let his daddy issues get the better of him and he took it upon himself to solve them. Permanently."

"So you think Connor's the guy?"

"Listen," he said as they reached a red Chevy diesel quad cab truck and he opened the door, pulling out a water jug. "The kid had his reasons. My brother was not an easy man to live under. I'm not saying what Connor did was right, but I know all too well what the kid dealt with." He took a long drink from the jug.

"I take it you didn't get along with your brother."

Jake smirked while wiping his mouth with the back of his hand. "Oh, I got along. Our daddy gave us no choice until I could get the hell out. As soon as I could, I did."

"So why'd you come back?"

"Jail has a way of limiting one's options."

"When did you come back here?"

"About five years back."

"Isn't that around the time your father died?"

"More coincidence than planning."

"Seems kind of unfair that your brother got the ranch and you're working here."

"Our daddy had no tolerance for stepping out of line. My brother toed that line until he would bleed. I didn't. My daddy rewarded obedience. Simple as that." Jake shrugged. "Didn't want the ranch anyways. Ranching was the old man's dream, not mine. He lived and died that dream. Guess him and my brother were even more alike than I thought."

"So you got nothing?"

Jake smirked. "Now I didn't say that. I got what was owed to me. So I guess it's all kind of fair after all."

Sonya began to study the shiny red truck with a little more interest. "Nice truck. Had it long?"

"Almost a year now."

"Work must be pretty good here. This a full time gig?"

"Nah. You know how it goes in small business. Keep everyone under forty and you don't have to pay the bennies." He took one last drink from the jug before placing it back in the truck and closing the door. "And as seeing how I would like to keep my job, I think our pleasant chat will need to end so I can get back to work."

"Thanks for your time. I'll be in touch if I have any more questions."

"I'm sure you will," Jake said as he started walking back to the flatbed. He brought his fingers to his mouth and let out a shrill whistle. "Breaks over, Jess," he yelled and the young man was soon seen scrambling back up the hay mountain.

Before leaving, Sonya walked to the back of the truck and took a picture of the license plate with her phone, noting it still had the dealer's license plate frame. The truck sure was nice. Nicer than what an ex-con working a part-time minimum wage job could afford on his own. This might be worth checking into.

CHAPTER TWENTY

Ray ran the plate and it came back Jake was the owner of the truck. Sonya asked Ray to get a warrant for Jake's bank records and run his credit report, then, after a quick lunch, decided to take a drive to the dealership that was advertised on the license plate frame.

Sonya pulled into Westcott's Chevrolet dealership in Scottsbluff. Before heading into the office she went over to where the trucks were lined up. She slowly walked down the row trying to spot a similar model to the one Jake owned.

"Got something particular in mind you're looking for?"

Sonya turned to see a middle-aged man with an eager smile heading towards her. She showed him her badge. "I'm looking for information."

The smile dimmed a little, but he still extended his hand to her. "Ned. Ned Simon. I'll help you if I can."

Sonya shook his hand. "I'm Detective Reisler with the Nebraska State Patrol. I want to get some information on a truck that was sold about a year ago to this man." Sonya showed the man a photograph of Jake Evans. "It was a red diesel quad cab."

The salesman studied the photo for only a few seconds. "Oh yeah. I remember the guy and the truck. He specifically wanted red. He even waited two weeks for one to come up from our other dealership in Lincoln."

"Why red?"

"He said he wanted it bright enough to make sure his brother would see it every time he came into town."

Sonya raised an eyebrow. "Sounds like he wanted to rub him."

Ned chuckled. "No kidding. There must be some bad blood there."

"So, did he finance it?"

"No way. He paid cash."

"Cash?"

"Yep. That's why he sticks in my mind. Brought in wads of hundreds."

"How much was the truck?"

"I don't know exactly, but it was around thirty-five thousand. He didn't get all the bells and whistles, but got enough of them. I can probably dig up the paperwork. Might take awhile though."

"I'd appreciate that." Sonya handed him a card. "If you find it, you can either fax it or email it to me."

"I'll see what I can do. Here's my card. We offer a discount to law enforcement so I can fix you up with a really sweet deal."

Sonya gave him a smile. "I'll keep that in mind."

Ned's attention was caught by a couple coming onto the lot. "It was nice meeting you, Detective," he said while hurrying away to meet a potential commission.

Sonya left the dealership and headed back to Ashlin. Ray sent her a text saying the warrants were ready and he was faxing them to the sheriff's office. She swung by the office and was flagged down by Kerry, who was sitting at his desk.

"These came in for you," he said as he handed her the faxed warrant. "Jake Evans?"

"Just doing some checking," she said as she glanced over the papers.

"He has an alibi," came out of Kerry in a rather sing-song way.

Sonya threw him a dirty look. "I know. Like I said, just checking."

Kerry chuckled. "You have at it, Miss Bloodhound."

Sonya raised her eyebrows and gave him a, "Woof," before turning away. She heard him laughing as she headed for the door and found herself grinning too.

***

Sonya absently took a bite of the chicken pot pie, the dinner special of the night at Lori's, while looking over the five years worth of statements she had gotten from the bank. Jake only had a checking account and seemed to be living paycheck to paycheck. The deposit and withdrawals were very consistent and nothing of interest popped out at her.

The credit report Ray had faxed later in the day was unremarkable as well. Apart from the low score that was earned before his coming to Ashlin, nothing jumped out except for the fact he did not finance that red truck of his. The question was, how did he buy the truck? She mulled that over until her pot pie was done, then gathered all the statements and put them back in the manila envelope the bank provided her.

As she was going to the counter to pay her bill, she saw Kerry, still in uniform, getting a large thermos handed to him. "You still on duty?" Sonya asked him.

"I got the six to midnight shift at the Evans house tonight and I'm running late."

"Sheriff still having you watch the place?" Sonya asked while paying her bill.

"Yeah. Probably until the kid is caught. You find anything in the bank records?"

"No." Sonya said as she started walking out with Kerry. Suddenly a thought came to her. "Did personal records of the Evans family get taken in as evidence?"

They reached his car and he put the thermos on the roof while unlocking his door. "Personal records? You mean like financial stuff?"

Sonya nodded.

"I think all that stuff is still at the house," he said while taking the thermos and getting in his car. "Why? You interested in it?"

"Yeah."

"I'll see if Cleary will help me box it up and bring it to you on his way home."

Sonya smiled. "That would be great."

Kerry smiled back at her. "He won't be helping me if I don't get my ass out there soon. See you, Detective."

Sonya waved a goodbye as he took off, then she headed back to her apartment. An hour and a half later, Deputy Cleary showed up with four file boxes full of papers and documents. He told her they'd emptied the contents of a large file cabinet in a room used as an office. Sonya helped him lug the boxes up the stairs and into the living room.

After he left, Sonya opened the boxes, glancing through the contents of each until she saw something that looked like bank statements. Pushing the coffee table back towards the couch, Sonya began removing the papers and placed them in stacks on the floor. She sat down cross-legged in the middle of them and began looking for what she wanted.

Sometime later, she found and put into chronological order bank statements for the last five years. Sonya looked for patterns. There were large infrequent deposits based on cattle sales and small regularly timed payroll deposits. Basic utility payments, varying credit card payments, and miscellaneous expenditures involving the ranch showed up. One thing that also showed up regularly was a cash withdrawal of seven hundred fifty dollars taking place on the first of every month, unless the first fell on a Sunday, then it would be on the second.

Sonya traced the withdrawal history of this amount to almost five years back. Beyond that, it didn't exist. Five years ago is also the time Jake Evans came back to Ashlin. Sonya did some quick figuring. Seven hundred fifty dollars over four years would add up to thirty-six thousand dollars. Roughly the amount Jake's truck cost when he bought it about a year ago.

She was sure they were connected, but to be positive more time would need to be spent looking through the contents of the other boxes to eliminate possible places the cash went. Right now it was pushing past midnight and her eyes were tired.

Sonya gathered all the bank statements and put them back in the file box. Looking back at the floor, she saw the birth certificates of the Evans family mixed in with the various documents. She picked up Connor's. County of birth was listed as Scotts Bluff and the date of birth was recorded as October sixteenth. That was going to be in three days. She shook her head. What a crappy way to spend your eighteenth birthday.

She started to set it in the box when she stopped. Another date listed caught her eye. The filing date. She frowned. The date was March twenty-fourth, a good five months after he was born.

Sonya set the certificate back down, then found his sister's. It was recorded within two weeks of her birth. The difference in dates puzzled her and that's all it took for her to be making plans to visit the hospital in Scottsbluff. It may not be related in any way to the case but at least it will satisfy her curiosity.

CHAPTER TWENTY-ONE

Sonya stopped by Lori's Café to grab breakfast and an order to go before heading over to the high school. She arrived right at ten, got set up in the counselor's office, and had the secretary call up Mike.

A few minutes later the door opened and immediately an, "Oh, hell yeah. This is what I'm talking about," came out of Mike's mouth as he spied the plate of food on the table across from Sonya.

"Figure you wouldn't mind brunch. School lunches are probably still pretty crappy."

"The worst," he said while looking at the omelet, hash browns, and bacon piled high on the plate.

Sonya pointed to the two cups next to the plate. "Orange juice and coffee. Didn't know which you liked."

"Both," he said while digging in.

Sonya took a sip of her own coffee and snagged a piece of bacon off of Mike's plate.

After quite a few bites, he grinned at her. "Heard you like handcuffs."

She grinned back and took another strip of bacon off his plate. "Only with the right company."

Mike let out a laugh before taking a long drink of orange juice and went back to eating. After a time he asked, "How are things going for our boy?"

"Not as well as I would like. I got some leads I'm checking into today, but I might be chasing rabbits." Sonya took a sip of coffee while watching Mike finish the last bite of food left on the plate. "What do you know about Connor's Uncle Jake?"

Mike shrugged as he dumped a couple creamers in his coffee. "Not much. Connor wasn't allowed to hang around him. His parents thought he was a bad influence with his being in jail and all."

"From the files I've read it sounds like Connor didn't need his uncle's influence. He was getting into plenty of trouble with the help of a certain group of friends."

Mike smiled before taking a sip of coffee.

"So what gives?" Sonya asked.

"Have you seen this place? It's boring as hell here. The only entertainment is fucking girls or causing trouble."

"Seems you guys cause trouble a lot."

Mike grinned. "We do both a lot. It's just fucking doesn't get you arrested."

"Sounds equally dangerous, though."

"Girls more so. Nothing will lock you down tighter in this town than if you knock a girl up. *Always* gotta be careful. Causing trouble? You just have to *try* to be careful."

"So how do you fit into all those pages and pages of misadventures, besides having the get out of jail free card?"

"I guess you would say I'm the creative force," Mike said while smiling. "I come up with the ideas and Connor makes them happen."

"So the technical stuff like hot wiring and lock picking, that's all Connor?"

"Way more than that, but yeah, that's Connor. He can figure things out really quick and make them work."

"What about Brett and Josh?"

"They're eager participants."

"The night Connor's parents died, you were all together drinking?"

"Yeah. Out at this creek we usually go to."

"Tell me about it."

"Not much to tell. Me, Brett, and Josh had already been there awhile before Connor showed up. We drank beer and headed home around three-thirty. I dropped Connor off about a mile from his house. I was heading home and heard what was going down on the two-way I have, then turned around to stop Connor. I took him to my house and had him hide in the storm cellar."

"What time did Connor show up that night?"

"None of us knows for sure."

"Did anybody see you that might be able to provide Connor with an alibi?"

"No."

"Is there anything you can think of that might help me?"

"Other than knowing he didn't do it, I got nothing."

They slipped into silence while each sipped their coffee.

After awhile, Sonya asked, "Why does the sheriff have it in for him so bad?"

The question caused a slight wince to pass across Mike's face. "Probably because of me. As Connor's, uh, skills were developing I got more creative with what we did."

"So closer to felony territory than misdemeanors."

Mike nodded. "It was getting harder for the sheriff to smooth things over. My dad figured it was Connor who had the talent in the group and him and the sheriff have been trying to pin actual charges on him. They thought if they could then the trouble would stop."

"So why didn't they?"

"We don't work that way. Either we all get away or we all get busted. And we all keep our mouths shut about Connor doing anything. This thing is like a dream come true for them." Mike toyed with his coffee cup for a moment. "He's really counting on you, you know?"

Sonya nodded. "I know."

Mike shrugged. "I'm sorta counting on you, too."

Sonya watched him as he took another sip of coffee, then took out her phone. "You got a phone?"

"Yeah," he said and pulled his phone out of his pocket.

"What's your number?"

Mike told her and soon his phone was buzzing in his hand.

"Give me a call if anything comes up."

"You got it."

Sonya stood. "I'd better get going. It's looking like I have a lot of work to do."

Mike stood as well, tossed his trash, and grabbed his cup of coffee. "Thanks for brunch. We should do it again."

"Let me guess," she said as they headed toward the door. "As long as it's at ten and I'm buying?"

He shrugged and smiled. "Sounds good to me."

Sonya gave him a quick poke to the stomach, causing him to laugh. She smiled at him before heading through the door. "See you later, Mike."

"See ya," he called after her.

CHAPTER TWENTY-TWO

Sonya made the forty-five minute drive to Scottsbluff and easily found the hospital. She parked her car, grabbed her notebook, and headed in. Sonya knew Madison Evans was hospitalized here but she wasn't going to see the little girl. Her demons were going to win this round.

Sonya looked at the directory by the elevators and found she needed to go to the fifth floor. Up the elevator and down a hall led her to the administrator's office. She greeted the receptionist and introduced herself, saying she needed to speak with the administrator. The receptionist left and came back to usher Sonya in.

A nicely dressed, balding man with round glasses stood from behind his desk and extended his hand. "I'm Ron Albright. How may I help you, Detective Reisler?"

Sonya shook his hand, then sat in a chair in front of the desk. "I need access to the medical records of Mary Louise Evans."

"May I inquire the nature of the request?" he asked while taking his seat again.

"I'm conducting an investigation into her murder."

Ron grimaced. "I can pull up the records here. Do you need them printed?"

"I'm mainly interested in the two times she was admitted to give birth." Sonya handed him the birth certificates she pulled from her notebook.

After a few clicks his face became puzzled. "According to our records, she was only admitted once to give birth to a baby girl."

Sonya's brows drew together. "Is there another hospital nearby?"

"We're the only hospital in Scotts Bluff County." Ron tapped Connor's birth certificate. "He was born here."

"Could she have given birth at home and brought him here after?"

"Rather unlikely. Nothing shows up around that October date. And there's this." He swiveled his monitor around for Sonya to see. "Admitting paperwork shows her reporting no previous pregnancies. The little girl was her first and only pregnancy."

Sonya was silent for a few seconds. "Can you tell me how many live male births occurred on the same date as Connor Evans?"

He looked apprehensive. "Still part of the investigation?"

Sonya nodded.

Still looking unsure, Ron turned the monitor back towards him and started clicking. "Looks like seven."

"Any by the name of Evans?"

"No."

Sonya became quiet as Ron patiently waited. After awhile, she asked, "How many were by unmarried mothers?"

He went back to work, this request taking a little longer to process. "There were two."

"I need their names."

He hesitated.

"I'm not asking to look at their medical records. I just need the names."

He shifted in his chair and let out a breath. "Karen Unger and Rain Meadows."

Sonya quickly jotted down the names and thanked him. She left the office and rode the elevator down to the entrance. From the hospital, it was a short walk to the vital statistics office for the county of Scotts Bluff.

Sonya went to the office and made her request to the worker and waited. After a fair amount of time had passed, the worker returned with only one piece of paper. "I can give you the birth certificate for the baby of Rain Meadows, but the one for the baby of Karen Unger is sealed. I can give you the paperwork needed for the judge to review your request to have it unsealed."

"That won't be necessary," Sonya said as she took the copy of the one birth certificate and said her thanks. As she made her way out of the building, she knew of only one reason why a birth certificate was sealed. The baby was adopted in a closed adoption. With all she learned, she couldn't help but think Connor Evans was adopted.

It took awhile but Ray was able to get an address for Karen Unger, now Karen Harper. She was located a couple counties away in Kimball. Sonya finally pulled up in front of a small older mobile home with a dirt yard strewn with toys and weeds. A couple dogs were running around as well as three kids.

Sonya didn't get out of her car right away. The setting was eerily familiar to her even though she'd never been here before. She took a deep breath to settle her growing discomfort and got out of her car.

Sonya carefully picked her way through the clutter and reached the torn screen door of the light blue and white mobile. She could hear the blaring of a reality television show coming from inside. Sonya rapped loudly and was met with a loud, "Hold on."

The door opened revealing a small ratty-looking woman with a baby on her hip and a toddler clinging to her leg. She looked at Sonya with suspicion which increased when she saw the clearly marked state patrol vehicle sitting in the drive. "What can I do for you?"

"I'm Detective Reisler, Nebraska State Patrol. Are you Karen Harper?"

"Yes."

"Is your maiden name Unger?"

The woman shifted nervously. "Yes."

"I wanted to talk to you about a baby boy you gave birth to eighteen years ago."

Karen's eyes grew big. She swallowed and then called out, "Andy and Sara, come here and take the baby and Ellie with you for a few minutes." Soon the older of the three children out in the yard came to collect the baby and the toddler. After handing them off, Karen held open the screen door for Sonya. "Come in."

Sonya entered the cluttered mobile and felt her tension mount. Memories began to rise to the surface as she was led to a couch that was covered with half folded laundry and empty juice cups. Karen quickly shoved the piles to the side so Sonya could sit and then took a seat on a nearby chair after turning off the television. Her hands fidgeted nervously in her lap. "I don't need you stirring up trouble around here. My Johnny don't know about the baby."

The woman's words drew Sonya back to the task at hand. "I don't want to cause you trouble."

Karen looked nervous again. "Is this about the murder?"

Sonya was certain she'd found the right woman. "It might be related. I just have a few questions."

Karen shifted in her seat and tried to smooth down her disheveled hair. She nodded at Sonya.

"Do you know who adopted your baby?"

"Sure. It was Will and Mary Evans."

"It wasn't a closed adoption?"

"Pretty much. Closed to the kid mainly."

"How was it set up?"

"Through an attorney Will got. He knew I couldn't afford to raise the kid, especially after my parents kicked me out when they found out I was pregnant. I was only fifteen. He and Mary offered to adopt Connor as long as it was closed. No contact in exchange for some money. I was actually glad. Clean slate and all. I think he felt responsible in a way for what happened to me. Wanted to make it right if he could."

Sonya's brows drew together. "Was Will the father?"

Karen let out a wry laugh. "If only I was that lucky. Jake Evans is the father."

CHAPTER TWENTY-THREE

The sun was starting to set, casting the sky with shades of orange and pink. Sonya drove one handed while her head rested against the fingertips of her other hand. Her head was feeling a mess right now. Karen's revelation was not expected. She told Sonya she knew Jake briefly and her parents caught them having sex. Her parents pressed charges against him which brought about the statutory rape conviction. Karen had become pregnant and didn't tell anyone. After the trial, her parents discovered the pregnancy and threw her out. She had nowhere else to go so she went to Will and Mary. After having the baby, Karen decided it would be best for her to give it up. Will and Mary ended up adopting Connor.

Sonya wanted to focus on how all this factored into the case, but she couldn't. Instead she found herself reliving past events she'd buried and had no interest in exhuming. The visit to that mobile home set things in motion inside of Sonya, dredging everything to the surface.

Driving back through Scottsbluff on her way to Ashlin, Sonya found herself heading back to the hospital. She parked her car and walked to the entrance. This was probably a bad idea but she couldn't think of anything else to do to get her head back in the case.

Sonya's feet felt like lead as she walked toward Madison Evans' hospital room. She showed her badge to the guard standing by the door. After a glance and a nod from him, she pushed open the door. Lying on the bed was the little six year old girl surrounded by a few machines standing watch. The room was filled with balloons, stuffed animals, flowers, and cards. Sonya knew most of them would be from strangers who heard of the tragic story.

She walked closer even though she felt like turning and bolting for the door. Each step forced until she was right next to the bed, looking down into the face of the unconscious child. Sonya reached out and took hold of the blanket, carefully lifting it back. While staring at the outline of the large bandages under the thin hospital gown, the memories began to flood in. Sonya's breathing came in gasps and she began to shake. She managed to place the blanket back over the child before her knees started to give way. She collapsed into the nearest chair, buried her hands in her face, and began to cry.

Tears flowed until nothing was left, but a numbing emptiness. Sonya sat in the emptiness for the longest time until flickers of the present started to bring her back. She absently swiped her hand across her cheeks, but the tears had long dried. She stood and headed for the bathroom, accidentally bumping into the rolling tray holding the numerous get well cards and sending half of them tumbling to the floor. After washing her face with cold water, she came out to pick up the mess she made. She gathered up the scattered cards and began setting them back up on the tray.

Something purple on the tray caught her eye. She picked it up to get a closer look. It was a folded paper bird. Something about it was familiar, but she couldn't place it. She set it down on the tray and took a picture of it with her phone. Sonya took one more look at Madison and left the room. She got to her car and began the drive back to her place. She drove in the darkness with the radio off, the emptiness of the highway magnifying the emptiness Sonya continued to feel. The need to fill it began to dangerously grow.

Sonya drove past a bar she saw, fighting the temptation to pull in, and went straight to the apartment. She let herself in, headed to the bathroom, and turned on the lights. Mirrors weren't scary as long as she was fully clothed, but events today had pushed many of her emotional buttons and she was feeling reckless. What was pushing one more? She swallowed hard as she gripped the bottom edge of her t-shirt, and removed it. Tears began to form again and a few spilled over as she watched her fingers trace around the large round pink scar on her chest and the matching one on her abdomen.

After a couple of passes, she flipped the lights off and went over to her bed. She slipped off her jeans, pulled her phone out of the pocket, then crawled under the covers while wiping away tears.

She dialed a number and it only rang once.

"Hey, Sonya."

"Hey." It came out soft and weak.

"You okay?"

Sonya took in a ragged breath. "I went and saw the little girl today."

Ray cursed softly on the other end. "Oh, Baby. Where are you?"

"I'm at my place."

"No alcohol?"

"No alcohol."

"That's my girl. Do you need me to come?"

She hesitated. "No."

"Tell me what you need."

"Talk to me, Ray. Just talk to me."

"For as long as you need. I'm here for as long as you need."

Sonya rolled over and blinked a couple of times while focusing on the clock on her nightstand. Ray had talked to her for well over an hour before she dozed off. Now it was ten-thirty and she found herself wide awake with the case on her mind.

She slipped out of bed and went to the kitchen to get a drink of water. While filling the glass, she thought about the purple paper crane she found in Madison's hospital room. Sonya took the glass with her back to her bedroom. Taking a long drink, she looked at her phone setting on the nightstand. She set down the glass and picked up the phone and scrolled to the photo of the purple paper bird. As she stared at it her eyes suddenly grew large. She got up and began pulling her jeans on while trying for the life of her to figure out how he did it.

CHAPTER TWENTY-FOUR

Connor crept over the ridge and scanned the terrain leading to his home. Mike had tried discouraging him from going, thinking it was stupid to take the risk just to get a change of clothes. And it probably was if that was all he wanted to do. It was in no way logical, but part of him was hoping if he returned home somehow all of this would go away. Things would be right again and this nightmare would be over. It was a need that had been growing, so here he was.

Everything seemed unchanged, except for the presence of an Ashlin sheriff's car parked on the dirt drive in front of the house. He could see the old oak and his bedroom window on the side of the house that faced him. All he had to do was make it to the tree and sneak in as he had done countless times over the years.

Seeing no movement, Connor kept low and made his way down the gentle slope. After covering several hundred feet, he finally made it to the grassy area that became the yard. He was skirting the swing set when he heard a car coming down the long drive.

Connor took a split second to decide between going back or continuing on. He went ahead and scrambled behind Skeeter's play house. He spied the dark car pulling next to the lighter sheriff's vehicle. The view didn't allow him to make out the deputies and he was too far away to make out voices. Soon, though, he heard a couple car doors slam and saw the lighter car start up, turn around, and head down the dirt drive. Must be a shift change. He stayed put and silence resumed.

He glanced toward the oak. There was only about fifty feet of open ground to reach it. From this angle he could only see the back end of the patrol car and nothing else. Deciding to go for it, he stepped swiftly and lightly to the base of the large tree. He reached up, made a little jump, and took hold of the stout branch about eight feet off the ground. He lifted and twisted himself so he was laying along the length of the limb, then got his feet under him and stood.

Connor took hold of a branch higher up. The shorter distance allowed him to hike his leg up and step onto the second limb. He once again stood and stretched forward to snag the third branch that led to his bedroom window. He hoisted himself up and shimmied his way along the rough bark until he reached the window.

Connor looked it over and saw it was just the way he left it. His fingers felt along the edge of the wood window frame and found the flat piece of metal with the end bent into an L-shape wedged in tight. He removed it and fit the bent end into the groove he had filed into the bottom of the wood encased window. He pulled up on the metal and the window slid silently open. He returned his window pry to its hiding spot before gripping the sill to pull himself into his room. Once his waist was resting on the sill, he dropped his hands to the floor and pulled himself forward until he could bring his feet clear of the window and silently drop them to the floor.

He stood and glanced over everything in the darkness. Things looked relatively the same as the last time he had been here, but he could tell things had been gone through. A few more papers scattered about and a couple things set in the wrong places. He wanted to take a walk around the rest of the house but looking at his dresser made him decide a change of clothes would be the first priority.

He slid open the drawers and tossed a pair of socks, underwear, t-shirt, and jeans onto his bed. He slipped off his sweat shirt and sneakers, then quickly started undressing. After putting on the clean clothes, he shoved all the dirty ones under his bed. He went to the closet and pulled out a hooded sweatshirt, slipped it over his head and jammed his arms through the sleeves before finding another pair of sneakers he quickly put on.

Something on his nightstand caught Connor's eye. He turned and found a photo frame lying face down. He tentatively reached forward and touched the back of the frame. He swallowed past a growing lump in his throat before picking it up. He turned it over.

The frame was easy enough to identify. It was a kindergarten project Skeeter had made for him and given to him a year ago. A cheap wood craft frame painted blue with glued on sequins, macaroni, and other assorted trinkets that would catch a five year old's eye. "My Family" was scrawled in messy yellow script at the top. And in the center was a picture of Connor and his family.

He wanted to stop looking but couldn't take his eyes off the smiling faces captured around the time the frame was made. His chest tightened, making it hard to breathe, causing his breath to come out in gasps. His vision was blurring through the tears that began to form.

"Don't do this now," he whispered as he closed his eyes, causing a couple heavy tears to fall onto the frame. Coming here was a bad idea. He needed to leave before he started really losing it. He carefully set the frame back down on the nightstand and was ready to turn when he heard an ominous racking of a pistol, coming from right behind him.

CHAPTER TWENTY-FIVE

Connor's heart was racing as he slowly lifted his hands. Otherwise he stayed stock still, waiting for the cop to say something. After a few seconds of silence, his nerves were strung so taut he was ready to scream. He gritted his teeth to control his voice. "Are you going to shoot me or arrest me?"

"Neither. At least for right now."

Connor recognized the female voice and the breath he'd bottled up inside him came out in a heavy whoosh. With his hands still up he cautiously turned around to face Sonya. Her gun was not aimed at him, but the sight of it kept him from lowering his hands. He didn't move a muscle as she studied him.

"You do like taking chances, Connor Evans," she said while holstering her weapon.

Connor was wary, wondering what kind of game she was playing. His brows furrowed in his confusion. "Aren't you going to arrest me?"

"Do you want me to?" she asked while taking a seat near the foot of Connor's bed.

He slowly let his hands drop. "Not really."

He watched as she drew her legs up to sit cross legged, facing the headboard. A movement of her hand indicated he should take a seat.

Hesitating briefly, Connor went ahead and took a seat on the edge of his bed, not feeling he had much of a choice. He turned himself a little so he could look at her. "You scared the crap out of me."

"Good. A healthy dose of fear will keep you safe." A light smirk touched her lips. "At least now I feel we're even."

Before Connor could help himself, a small grin pulled at the corners of his mouth at remembering their last encounter. "Uh, not quite."

Her one hand took hold of the cuffs on her belt and he watched her fight a smile. "You want to argue?"

He started shaking his head as his grin grew. "No. No. We're definitely even." Connor felt himself start to relax despite wondering what the hell was going on between him and this cop. He decided he had nothing to lose by getting comfortable. He brought his legs up onto the bed to stretch out and let his back rest against the headboard.

He watched her watching him. She looked young for a cop, let alone a detective. It was the same impression he got from the first time he saw her. Before he could stop himself, he asked, "How old are you?"

"I'm twenty-four."

"You must be good if you're a detective already." He watched as his words caused a flicker of some emotion to pass over her face, but she recovered quickly and tossed a question at him.

"Why'd you come here?"

Connor shrugged. "I just needed to come. Get some clothes and see the place." His head turned slightly toward the picture on the nightstand. "This still doesn't seem real."

"I know what you mean."

His face contorted into a scowl. She didn't know shit. He turned and was ready to tell her so, but stopped when he caught a glimpse of something in her face before she diverted her eyes. He continued to watch her and became curious. "So why'd you come here?"

"Got thinking about the case and couldn't sleep," she said as she pulled her phone out of her pocket and began touching the screen before showing it to him. "I also found this today and it had me curious."

He looked at the photo of the origami crane he made for Skeeter before handing her phone back.

"How'd you do it?" she asked.

Connor kept his face serious. "First you fold an end over and tear it off so your paper is square and…" She smacked his sneaker and he chuckled as he watched her fight a smile. It actually felt good to joke and laugh. It seemed like it'd been forever.

"You know what I mean," she said while trying unsuccessfully to suppress her smile.

"Yeah, but I think for right now I'll invoke my right to remain silent if that's okay." Connor couldn't help but think he may want to see Skeeter again and didn't want to give all his secrets away. That was assuming Sonya wasn't going to arrest him.

"It's not, but I'll take a rain check. There are hundreds of those origami birds strung in your sister's bedroom. What's the story?"

Connor shrugged. "It started when she got her big bed. She didn't like sleeping in it so we made a deal. Every night she slept in her bed I would make her a paper crane. I told her once she got a thousand of them she could make a wish and it would come true." Connor grinned a little. "Skeeter sure wants that wish." His grin faded when remembering how she looked in the hospital. "If she woke up I just wanted her to know I was thinking about her."

Sonya looked confused. "Skeeter?"

Connor felt the corners of his mouth kick up again. "It's a nickname I gave her. When she was learning to talk she wouldn't shut up. All the time, yak, yak, yak, and half of it wouldn't make sense. Like the buzzing of a mosquito. Soon we all called her that."

Sonya was smiling at him and he liked that she was.

"You saw her today?" he asked,

She nodded.

"How is she doing?"

"She's proving to be a tough kid. Been upgraded to critical." She paused. "How are you doing?"

Connor just looked at her for a few seconds. "I don't know." He paused again. "Sometimes I think I'll just wake up from this, you know?"

She nodded. Something told him she really did know.

He continued without really knowing what was going to come out. "I mean, I know I'm innocent, but everybody thinks I did it, then there is someone out there who really did do it and I wonder who it is and why, and then I'm hiding all the time, just waiting till they catch me and scared of what will happen when they do, and…" After a few seconds he added, "I'm really screwed, aren't I?"

Sonya's tone was soft. "Your sister maybe can clear you. But if I can find who actually killed your parents, that would be best."

"You think I'm innocent?"

She nodded her head. "I just need more time to work on this."

Suddenly Connor heard the crunch of tires coming toward the house. His eyes flashed to Sonya.

She bolted off the bed. "That'll be a deputy. I'll distract him so you can leave."

Connor raised an eyebrow. "You're going to let me go?"

"Yes."

"Can't you get in trouble for that?"

"Yeah. A shit load. So don't get caught. Now go."

Connor headed for the window, then turned. "Thanks, Sonya."

She gave him a nod and left the room, then Connor slipped out the window.

CHAPTER TWENTY-SIX

Sonya headed down the stairs and came out the front door as Deputy Moore took a step onto the front porch. She engaged him in some chit chat for a good ten minutes so Connor had time to get away from the house. Then she went to her car and got ready to leave. She paused, then popped open her trunk.

Walking to the back of the car, she told Moore there were some things of interest that might prove useful in the investigation. She pulled out a collapsed unused evidence box and returned to Connor's room. In reality, she was going to put a few changes of clean clothes in the box in case she ran into Connor again.

Sonya assembled the box and placed it on his bed. As she went through the drawers and closet selecting various items, she chided herself. She should have arrested him. For his own good as well as hers. If he was caught and anybody got wind of what happened tonight, she ran the risk of losing her job. But she knew why she was taking the risk. She really wanted the chance to solve this case. A chance to prove to herself she was worthy of the job she was putting in jeopardy. She also knew that was only part of the reason.

Once the box was full, she put the lid on it and carried it out into the hallway. She paused at Madison's room and looked through the doorway. Even in the nighttime darkness she could make out the bright colors of the carefully folded birds. Hundreds of them strung together and hanging from the ceiling. All made by an adoring big brother. She imagined what it would be like to lay on the bed and look up to see them hovering above you, making you feel safe and loved.

Sonya quickly turned away and hurried down the hall. There was something even more riskier at stake here. Feelings for the victims, criminals, and the like are a detriment in this line of work. It clouds your thinking and causes you to make mistakes. She didn't even know when it happened but Connor Evans had gotten under her skin.

Sonya stirred from her sleep. She was lying on her stomach and turned her head toward the noise that had disturbed her. It was her phone. Reaching out, she grabbed it, and dragged it across the sheets to her face. "Hello?" she mumbled.

Ray chuckled on the other end. "Tough night?"

Sonya rolled over. "Didn't get much sleep."

His voice was suddenly serious. "You doing okay?"

"Yeah. Better. Been thinking about the case."

"Gotten any farther with that Jacob Evans you were checking out?"

"Not a lot, but there is something funny going on money-wise. I'm planning on finding the lawyer that handled his father's will and see what I can find."

"I take it that he's going to be your focus?"

"Yeah. Going after the evidence is a waste of time. I need to find a stronger motive than what they have on Connor and I'm convinced this Jake guy has one."

"So, are you thinking the kid is innocent?"

"He's innocent."

"You sound sure."

"I am."

"Do you need me to come down and help?"

Sonya smiled. "Are you just looking for an excuse to get away from Drew or your wife?"

Ray chuckled. "It would be a good one for both, wouldn't it?"

"Yes, but I think I'm okay for now."

"Darn. I was hoping you were missing me."

"I do miss you." She paused. "Do you believe I'm right about this?"

"Listen. I don't know how this will turn out, but you're my partner and I will support you in this investigation. At some point, though, I may have to pull the plug. That'll have nothing to do with me believing you or not, or whether you're a good cop or not. I need you to understand that, Sonya."

"I understand."

"Good. Keep me updated and, if you need anything, call me."

"I'll call you when I find out more."

"Sounds good. Love ya, girl."

"Love you, too."

After hanging up she looked at the time on her phone. She groaned. It was already ten-thirty. She got out of bed and got ready in short order.

Sonya stopped into Lori's and got an early lunch. While eating her chicken salad, she got a text from Mike. It said, *No brunch. Highly disappointed.* She responded, *Not seeing me or the food?* Her phone dinged with his reply. *If I say you, will that better my chances?* She smiled as she tapped back, *Most definitely.* He responded, *LOL. Later.* She sent back a final, *Later.*

When she was almost done eating, she asked the waitress if there was a law office in town and was told there was. The waitress supplied directions. Sonya thought she would stop in there on a gamble they handled Ralph Evans' will. If not, she would have to stop in at the sheriff station and she was hoping to not have to do that.

After lunch, she headed over to the law office of Dandridge and Dandridge. It was situated on the outer edge of the main downtown area and, unlike the surrounding businesses, this one used to be a home until it was converted into an office. She stepped through the front door and was greeted by the receptionist who was a well-dressed middle-aged woman.

"My name is Detective Reisler and I'm investigating the murder of Will and Mary Evans. I was wondering if I could speak to one of the lawyers here."

"I'll see if Mr. Dandridge is available," she said while picking up the phone. She pushed a button and was waiting. "The whole thing is shocking. Nothing ever like that has happened here before." Her attention broke from Sonya to the person on the other end of the phone. "There is a Detective Reisler here to see you." A pause. "Alright," she said and hung up. "He'll be right out to see you."

"Thank you," Sonya said as a door opened.

A tall man with a slender build and slightly graying hair entered. He smiled warmly and extended his hand. "Hello. I'm Thomas Dandridge."

"I'm Detective Sonya Reisler," she said while shaking his hand. "I wanted to know if you were the attorney for Ralph Evans."

"My father was Ralph's attorney."

"Did he draw up the will for Ralph Evans."

"Yes, he did."

"I would like to look at the will if I could."

"My father has pretty much retired, but his files are still in his office. You can follow me."

Sonya followed Thomas to a large well appointed office. He indicated Sonya should sit on the couch. He then proceeded to look through a large file cabinet and pulled out a folder. He took a seat on the couch next to Sonya and laid the folder on the coffee table. "Here it is. Pretty straight forward. Everything was left to William Evans."

Sonya began glancing through the papers. "Nothing was left to Jacob Evans?"

"Not a dime. My father advised against cutting Jake out completely. No good ever comes out of wills drawn up that way. But Ralph was a stubborn man. Forgiveness wasn't in his vocabulary."

"Did your father do a will for William Evans?"

"I actually handled that one."

"How is the property division going to be handled?"

"Everything is to be split between Connor and Madison. Will was like his dad in so many ways but not when it came to Connor."

"How so?"

He shrugged. "Just when you consider everything."

"Did you or your father handle drawing up the adoption papers?"

Thomas paused for a moment and looked at Sonya. "I did not draw up adoption papers."

Sonya figured he gave her the answer she wanted in a backwards way and went on to her next question. "So what happens to the estate of William Evans?"

"Well, if Connor is convicted of his parents' murder he will not be allowed to inherit anything. It will all go to Madison."

"What if Madison doesn't make it?"

"The estate will go to probate and the nearest blood relative will inherit the estate."

"Jake Evans."

Thomas nodded. "Almost more of a headache to inherit the place at this point, I imagine."

"What do you mean?"

"A decade ago they had to take out a second mortgage close to the value of the place to pay for nursing home expenses after Ralph had his stroke. I doubt they have unburied themselves much from that debt." He shrugged. "Sure you'd get the place, if that's what you want. But cold hard cash? Not a lot to inherit."

CHAPTER TWENTY-SEVEN

After speaking with Thomas Dandridge, Sonya went back to her place, set up her laptop, and began looking through more of the financial records of Will and Mary Evans. She wanted to piece together the financial history of the family to see if Dandridge was accurate. Hours were spent pouring over the documents and bank statements and everything was tracked and plotted on a spreadsheet. Sonya made calls to real estate agents specializing in farms and ranches to get a current value on the Evans property. After all her number crunching was done, she realized Dandridge was right. There was maybe twenty thousand dollars in property equity. A good portion of the livestock was already sold off for the winter, so not a lot of cash there either.

What she did know was the Evans family was just getting by and the seven hundred and fifty dollar withdrawal could not be accounted for in any of her searches. She was sure the money was going to Jake and she had a bad feeling it was not being given to him as a loving gesture. So what was the reason? She couldn't help thinking it maybe had something to do with Connor.

Her stomach growled and she looked at her phone. It was just about eight. She boxed everything up and decided to get something to eat. She drove around the town to see if there was some place other than Lori's to eat at. Her drive took her closer to the outskirts of the downtown area. A bright red truck sitting in a nearly full parking lot caught her eye so she pulled in.

Sonya wandered into The Stockade Bar and Grill. It was a small, dimly lit place with loud music and even louder patrons. A few booths were set against the left side wall and small tables were scattered through the center. A couple waitresses were darting around taking orders. The right side had a juke box in the back corner, a pool table, and a small open area where a few people were dancing.

The bar stretched out along the back with large mirrors placed on the wall behind. Sonya studied the faces of the patrons reflected in the mirror. She made out the face of Jake Evans sitting alone on the far right. He was already eyeing her reflection in the mirror. Sonya made her way around the crowded tables and took a seat on the stool next to Jake. He didn't look at her.

"I bet you get carded every time you set foot in a bar," he said before taking a drink from his bottle of beer.

"Most times," she responded before the bar tender asked what she would have. Sonya ordered a Coke.

Jake smirked and finally turned his head toward her. "How old are you?"

"I thought country boys were raised with better manners than to ask a woman her age."

"Manners went out the window after the one time I didn't ask."

"Karen Unger?"

Jake turned back to his beer. "And I thought this was a social call." He took another drink. "If you came here to ask me questions, it's going to cost you a dance."

"I could just take you in."

"You could." He turned back to her. "But it'd be a whole lot easier to just dance with me." Jake stood and held his hand out to her.

Sonya downed a long drink from her Coke the bar tender had set down before standing and giving her hand to Jake. He led her into the open area, weaving between some of the other couples. Upon reaching the spot, he turned to her, raised her hand, twirled Sonya once before pulling her tight against him. It didn't matter what was playing, this was going to be a slow dance.

Jake settled a hand in the middle of her back, keeping her close to him. "I had no idea Karen was fifteen, but it didn't matter. I was twenty and screwed. I'm a lot more careful now, hence the rudeness."

"Understandable," Sonya said as she swayed with Jake. "What I don't understand is how you afforded that big pretty truck of yours."

Jake grinned at her. "Now look who's lacking in the manners department. You're not suppose to ask money questions of people."

"My job encourages rudeness."

Jake let out a chuckle. "Don't I know it. Well, let's see, I suppose I got it the way most folks might go about getting things."

"Hmm. You're credit score isn't all that stellar so financing is out. Your bank balance has never been over eight hundred in the last five years. No savings account. Oh, and the copy of your father's will showed you got nothing. Last time I checked, you need money or credit to purchase things." Sonya watched as the muscles in his jaw tensed.

"I didn't steal the truck. I own it."

"I know you do. Paid cash for it."

Jake loosened his hold on her. "What are you driving at, Detective?"

"Where did the money come from?"

"You tell me."

"I've been going over your brother's bank statements and for almost five years now he has been withdrawing seven hundred fifty dollars every month on the same date like clockwork. Doing a little math tells me that comes pretty darn close to what that truck of yours cost."

"Is that so?"

"What did you have hanging over him to get him to pay you that sum every month?"

"Why you taking all this interest in me?"

"Trying to establish a possible motive you might have for killing your brother."

Jake stopped moving. "According to Sheriff Bennett, the motive, the means, and the evidence all point to my nephew."

"I think we both know he's a bit more than your nephew."

His eyes narrowed sharply. "My, my, you are creative. Well let's think about this. If, and I say if, my brother was paying me every month that kind of money you're talking about, then why would I want to cut off the head of my golden goose? Think on that one, Detective." Jake let go of her hand and took a step back, his pleasant demeanor gone. "Thanks for the dance. Oh, and I'm sure you won't mind picking up my tab seein' as how I must be hard up for cash now." With that, he turned and headed out of the bar.

Sonya walked back to the bar and took a drink of her Coke. She heard a light chuckling as someone slid onto the stool next to her. It was Kerry. He was out of uniform and looking quite relaxed in faded jeans and a tight light blue t-shirt that nearly matched his eyes. Sonya had to admit after giving him an appraising glance, he was looking really good.

"You sure do have a way with people, Detective Reisler. Just what were you getting ol' Jake all riled up about?"

"He didn't like some of my questions."

Kerry groaned. "He just lost his brother and sister-in-law. You should cut him some slack."

"Not when he's a suspect."

"Do you mind sharing why you think he's a suspect?"

"Not yet."

"Well, good. That means we're officially off-duty. Can I get you something a little stronger than that Coke?"

Sonya shook her head. "I don't drink anymore."

"You're a little young to be calling it quits already."

"I've done enough drinking in the past to cover this lifetime and half of the next one."

"So, you were quite the partier."

"Something like that."

"Can I at least get you something to eat?"

"Sure."

Kerry flagged down a waitress and they placed their orders of burgers and fries. They chatted while they ate, Kerry revealing much more about himself than Sonya did about herself. When they were done, Sonya found she was being pulled onto the dance floor again. Kerry was a much better dancer than Jake and she found herself having a good time. By eleven-thirty Sonya was ready to call it a night. They finished paying their tab, grabbed the leftover containers, and headed outside to the parking lot.

Kerry's car was parked next to Sonya's. He opened his passenger side door to set the left over containers on the seat next to his two-way. Sonya leaned against her driver's side door, enjoying the view of the young deputy bending to reach into his car. He turned to face her, then reached out, letting his fingers lift a few strands of her long blond hair that had fallen onto her cheek. "I've decided I'm going to start calling you Sonya whether I have your permission or not."

"Why's that?" she asked as she looked into the deputy's blue eyes.

Kerry moved in closer. "Because I only kiss people I'm on a first name basis with," he said as he placed his lips on hers. Sonya draped her arms around Kerry's neck and began kissing him back. He pulled her closer against him and Sonya let him deepen the kiss. It went on with neither one wanting to stop until the crackle of the two-way and the words coming through made Sonya tear away from Kerry with a gasp.

"Need available deputies to respond to a citizen's arrest at Harris's Feed and Farm Supply. A Jake Evans called in reporting he has captured Connor Evans."

CHAPTER TWENTY-EIGHT

Uncle Jake's place was dark and the bright red pickup he tooled around in was nowhere to be seen. Connor had scaled the chain link fence surrounding the back lot of Harris's Feed and Farm Supply and was lurking in the shadows cast by the yard lights. He made himself comfortable between the bales of straw and hay and waited.

After many long minutes, a pair of headlights swept around and were facing the chained gate by the side of the building. A figure got out, unlocked the gate, and swung it inwards before returning to the vehicle. The red truck drove through and parked. Connor watched his uncle get out and slam his truck door a bit harder than necessary. He walked to the bed of the truck, gripped the edge, hung his head, and stayed like that for awhile. Something must have pissed him off and Connor was tempted to rethink his plan. Soon, his uncle raised his head, tilting it toward the night sky, then pushed himself away from the truck. He walked towards the gate and began to shut it.

Connor scrambled across the distance and let out a low, "Uncle Jake."

Jake's eyes snapped up. "Connor? Holy shit, boy. What are you doing here?"

"I need your help."

Jake stared at him a few seconds then glanced around before opening the gate again. "Let's get you inside before you're seen."

Connor hesitated. "You know I didn't do it, right?"

"I know. Now come on."

Connor slipped through the gate and his uncle finished closing and locking it. He followed Jake up the stairs leading to a small landing in front of the apartment door. The older man opened it and let Connor enter. Glancing around the place, it wasn't much to look at except for an extremely large flat screen TV on the wall, stereo and DVD equipment, and a gaming console. All of it looked newer and expensive.

"Can I get you something to drink?"

The words broke Connor from his study of the place. "Um, I could really use a beer."

His uncle let out a chuckle. "I bet you could. I think I can do that," he said and headed for the kitchen.

Connor followed and watched Jake take a beer out of the fridge and twist the cap off. He handed Connor the beer. "So what kind of help are you looking for?"

He only meant to take a quick pull from the bottle before answering, but found himself draining it dry.

His uncle grinned while eyeing him. "Looks like you need another," he said while taking the empty bottle and setting it on the counter, then opened the fridge to fish out another.

"Yeah," Connor said while taking the newly offered bottle and put it to his lips. This time he took a controlled sip. "It's been awhile."

"So?" his uncle prodded.

"I need to get out of town for a little while."

Jake's brows drew together. "Why now? Seems like you would've done that already."

"There's this detective working on the case. I need to buy her some time so she can figure out who really killed my parents."

He paused. "Are you sure that's what she's doing?"

"Well, yeah. She thinks I'm innocent."

Jake let out a small chuckle as his lips quirked up and he looked Connor in the eyes. "Almost sounds like you've been talking with this detective, in person like."

Connor shrugged and glanced away. "Nah. I just hear stuff." He drained the second beer and set it down on the counter before looking back at his uncle. "So can you get me out of town?"

"I can maybe do that if you think it will help."

"That'd be great," he said with an exhale of relief.

"I should probably call my boss and let him know I won't be in tomorrow. Why don't you hand me my cell phone. It's on the table behind you."

Connor turned, but saw no cell phone. He started to turn back when something hard slammed against the side his head sending him to the floor. His ears were ringing and his vision blurred. He couldn't get his body to cooperate as he struggled to get up.

An empty beer bottle dropped to the floor next to him, then strong hands grabbed his wrists and started dragging him across the floor. Connor closed his eyes. His head was already spinning and the extra movement made it worse. Soon his arms were dropped and he felt someone walk past him and then heard the shutting of a door.

Connor lay there in the dark room as his head began to pound. He could make out Jake talking in the background but couldn't tell what was being said. He rolled over and struggled to get his knees under him. He felt nauseous and his stomach heaved, sending the watery contents splattering over the floor.

His breathing was ragged and strained as he pulled himself to a standing position and immediately staggered dizzily into the nearest wall. He felt something wet running down his cheek and wiped it with his fingers. Pulling them back he saw they were covered with blood.

Resting against the wall he took in the room. It was a bedroom with a bed in the center and a nightstand with a lamp by a window. Next to him was the door. He reached out to turn the knob but it was locked. Automatically his hand went for his wallet, but he stopped. Even if he could manage to pick the lock in his state, he was in no condition to take on his uncle.

He looked back to the window, then stumbled over to it. He tried to open it but it was painted shut. Even if he got it open, there was no landing. It was a straight two story drop to the ground. Despite this, the window was still his best bet.

Connor did a quick assessment of the room and settled on the lamp. The base was metal and rather long and could probably do a number on the window. With shaky hands he began to strip the bed. He tied the ends of the two sheets together, then tied one end to the leg of the bed and pulled that corner of the bed close to the window. He grabbed the lamp off the nightstand yanking the cord out of the wall and knocked off the shade. He made sure he had a good grip on the top of the base and took a couple deep breaths to muster all the strength he could. The noise would bring his uncle and he had to clear a big enough opening to crawl through.

One more breath and he swung. Glass shattered in the lower half. Another swing took care of the upper half and a final swing was brought down on the center wood cross section, splintering it in two. He tossed the sheets out the opening and backed himself out of the window. Taking a hold of the sheet he began sliding down the length of it, the friction burning his hands. He halted at the knot, repositioned his hands and started to slide again. The end of the sheet slipped past his hands and the last five feet was a free fall to the ground. Connor's feet hit the ground and he fell hard on his back, the impact bringing on fresh waves of pain and dizziness. He glanced up and saw a head poke out the window and look down at him. Connor scrambled to his feet and took off running.

CHAPTER TWENTY-NINE

Sonya brought her car to a screeching halt in front of Harris's and Kerry was right behind her. She threw open her door and started running to the side of the building. Kerry caught up with her and she saw he had a gun.

"You'd better let me handle this," he said as he beat her to the steps and started climbing up.

Sonya fell in behind him. No way was she going to wait down below.

Kerry knocked on the door and Jake opened it. His eyes briefly flicked past Kerry to Sonya before letting them both in.

"Where's Connor?" Kerry asked.

"He's locked in a back room. Won't be much of a problem."

Sonya pushed past Kerry and went right up to Jake. "What do you mean?"

"Simple. He started threatening me, demanding my truck keys, so I clocked him."

Sonya gritted her teeth. "Where is he?"

Jake motioned them to follow him, but no sooner had they taken a step before they heard a loud crash followed by a couple more.

"Shit. You stay there," Kerry ordered Jake as he ran down the hall. He got to a door and tried the handle. It was locked. He banged into it with his shoulder a couple of times before stepping back and kicking it open. He ran in with Sonya right behind him.

Light from the hall flooded the room. The window was broken and she saw no sign of Connor. Kerry ran over, shoved the bed out of the way and peered down. He stuck his gun out the window. "Halt or I'll shoot!" Kerry took aim at Connor.

Sonya grabbed Kerry's arm and shoved it far left of his target. The suddenness caused Kerry to fire off a round. Pushing Sonya away, he tried to regain sight of Connor, but he had disappeared.

Kerry slammed his hands on the window sill. "God damn it!" He rounded on Sonya. "What the hell was that? I had a clear shot to take him down. Don't tell me you're squeamish about shooting people for Christ's sake."

Sonya was still shaking as her eyes glanced to the window, then back to Kerry.

Disbelief momentarily displaced the anger on his face. "Oh my God. You wanted him to get away."

Sonya remained silent as the sound of a siren began to be heard in the distance and was growing louder by the second.

The anger returned as Kerry glared at Sonya. "What the hell kind of cop are you? If you've forgotten, we're suppose to arrest Connor Evans. That's our job. At least it's my job." He pushed past her and went to the door.

Sonya followed him out of the room

Kerry pointed a finger at Jake. "You stay put. We're going to need a statement," he said before heading down the stairs.

Sonya continued to follow but lingered quite a few feet back

Sheriff Bennett had pulled up and was already out of his car. "What happened?" the sheriff asked as Kerry walked up.

"Connor Evans got away. Escaped through a window."

Sheriff Bennett pointed to Kerry's still drawn weapon. "Did you get a shot off?"

"Yeah, but I missed."

Sheriff Bennett slammed his hand on the hood of his car. "God damn it. Do you need more time on the firing range to learn how to use that thing, Deputy?" He got back into his car and started hailing Deputy Moore to sweep the area. When he was done he turned back to Kerry. "I need you to stay and take a statement from Jake and do a report on what happened. I'm going to help Danny with the sweep."

"Yes, sir," Kerry said, then Sheriff Bennett drove off. He turned and stalked back to Sonya.

"You didn't tell him," she said.

"No I didn't tell him. But you're going to tell me what the hell is going on in that head of yours, Detective. Right now, though, it's looking like I'm back to work and I'm on duty all day tomorrow. That should give you plenty of time to figure your shit out and decide which side of the law you're really working for. So if you'd excuse me," he said and headed for the stairs to Jake's apartment.

CHAPTER THIRTY

The sound of the gunshot put Connor's adrenaline rush into overdrive as he tore over the dirt lot and darted between feed sheds to the back fence. He scaled over it and dropped to the ground into the storage lot of an auto repair shop that butted up against the feed store property.

Connor only made it a few yards before he was coming off his adrenaline high and stumbling between the parked cars. He tripped and fell, then crawled between two closely parked vehicles to catch his breath.

He didn't feel well. The dizziness came back with a vengeance after his drop from the window and he felt queasy and drenched with sweat. There was no way he could make it out of town and was growing doubtful of even making it a few feet with the way he was feeling. Staying here was in no way an option.

Ashlin Tool and Hardware was one block over. He needed to get to Sonya's. If anyone was going to arrest him, it might as well be her.

Connor grabbed the car's bumper and pushed himself to standing. He leaned over as his stomach gave a heave, but there was nothing left to come up. He drew in a shaky breath and started moving one foot in front of the other until he reached the front fence. Slowly hand over hand he gripped the chain link and got himself over. His knees began to buckle as his feet touched the ground and he quickly gripped the fence to support himself. A few more breaths and he felt steady enough to let go and begin walking.

The street was dark and all the businesses long closed. He fought the urge to run and kept his pace steady. He was halfway down the block when he saw headlights shining from a side street up ahead. Flashing blue and red lights reflected off the facing storefront windows. The car began to turn the corner to head his way. Connor saw a break in the buildings about ten feet ahead and ran for it, his head pounding with every step. He slipped in between the buildings and continued running until he was able to duck behind the back of the smaller one. Just as he did, a bright light lit up the narrow space he'd just passed through.

The car drove slowly by and continued down the road. Darkness returned and Connor crept between the buildings. When he reached the front, he looked down the street and saw the sheriff's car make another turn. He began his walk again at a brisker pace and finally made it to Ashlin Tool and Hardware. He looked up but saw no lights on in the overhead apartment.

Connor stumbled up the steps to Sonya's door and knocked. After a few seconds, he pulled out his wallet and fumbled through it till he found two metal wires and removed them. Jamming his wallet into his back pocket, he swayed and struggled to remain upright. Shoving the L-shaped wire into the bottom of the lock opening, he applied tension as he inserted the wavy ended wire into the lock and began working it against the locking pins.

Coldness began to seep through him and his sweat felt clammy against his skin as he continued to work the lock. "Just a few more seconds," he whispered to himself. As the tension wire began to turn, his vision started to cloud. He gritted his teeth. "Don't fucking pass out yet," he hissed. The handle finally turned free and he removed the wires as the door opened. Once inside, he leaned against the door to shut it and fumbled with the knob to lock it as everything clouded black. His fingers slipped as his knees gave way, sending him to the floor in a heap.

CHAPTER THIRTY-ONE

Sonya pulled up to Ashlin Tool and Hardware, still shaking as she got out of her car. She was thankful Kerry didn't throw her under the bus even though part of her knew she deserved it. He was spot on in his accusation. She wanted Connor to get away and the price she'd pay for Kerry's silence was delivering an explanation to him. He made it very clear she owed him that.

She would think of what to tell him later. Right now her thoughts were consumed with Connor. She drove around, circling every block, hoping to spot him but had no luck. A large part of her felt responsible for what happened to him tonight. She purposely put some pressure on Jake to see what he would do and he didn't disappoint. She just hadn't planned on Connor crossing paths with him. Right now she was worried about Connor and wanted more than anything to know he was safe.

Sonya climbed the steps to the apartment, reached into her pocket to pull out her keys, then froze. There were some dark smudges around the handle of the door. She withdrew her gun and unlocked the door. Slowly she opened the door but it stopped, blocked by something heavy on the other side. Sonya shoved harder, getting the door to open a few more inches so she could squeeze by.

Once through, she drew in a quick breath and holstered her gun as she dropped to the floor next to Connor. She rolled him over and saw the half dried trail of blood running from his scalp down his cheek. Sonya quickly checked his pulse and breathing and felt relief after determining they were okay. Stroking his face with the back of her fingers, she began calling his name.

After quite a few seconds, she began to get a response. His eyelids fluttered open but he seemed to have trouble focusing. "Sonya," he said as they closed again. His voice was rough as he tried to talk. "Had nowhere else to go."

"It's all right. You're safe."

"My uncle…"

"I know. I was there."

He gave a small movement of his head to indicate he understood and then grew still.

Sonya gave him a shake and said, "Connor."

He stirred again and opened his eyes.

"We got to get you off the floor. I need you to help me." After much pushing, pulling, and prodding, Sonya was able to get Connor to his feet. Wrapping an arm around his waist and pulling his one arm around her shoulders, she supported him as he began taking tentative steps. He stumbled after a dozen feet into their journey, almost sending both of them to the floor. Sonya found herself buckling under his weight but managed to half-walk half-drag him into her bedroom before letting him collapse onto the bed.

He was out cold as she began removing his shoes, socks, and the rest of his clothing, leaving him only in his underwear. She looked him over for any injuries before getting him settled under the covers. The sight of a long scar running along the inside of his forearm did pique her interest, but other than various scrapes and bruises and the nasty looking lump on his head, he seemed okay.

She went back out to her car, retrieved a first aid kit, came back and set it on the bed. Sonya went to the bathroom to get a wet wash cloth. She sat on the edge of the bed and began to wash the blood off his face. When she finished, she went back to the bathroom, rinsed the cloth out, returned to the bedroom and opened the first aid kit. She took out an instant cold pack, gave it a few squeezes until it grew cold, then gently laid it over the lump on his head.

She went to the kitchen and wet a paper towel to clean the smudges of blood off her door. After she finished, she filled a glass with water, brought it back to the room, and set it on the nightstand. She rummaged through the first-aid kit and found a few packets of pain reliever, setting them next to the glass. He was definitely going to need those when he woke up.

Sitting on the edge of the bed, she took out her phone and set the alarm to go off in an hour. Removing her shoes, she pulled her feet up onto the bed and settled next to Connor. She was pretty sure he had a concussion and that meant it was going to be a long night in making sure he was okay. As she reached over and touched his hair, stroking it off his forehead, she wondered what the hell she'd gotten herself into.

CHAPTER THIRTY-TWO

Connor was out in his yard tossing a baseball up in the air and catching it in his glove. Mom and Dad sent him out of the house. Grandpa wasn't doing good and they were discussing things they thought he was too young to hear. He was almost thirteen. That's old enough to understand about dying.

He couldn't help but think there was something more going on than just Grandpa. These private talks started a couple weeks ago. He tried to get close to listen but they were careful. Connor began to feel they were talking about him.

He stopped tossing the ball as he saw a man walking up the drive. Connor continued to watch him as he drew closer. The man looked familiar even though he was sure he'd never seen him before.

The man smiled at him. "Hi there. You must be Connor."

Connor eyed the man suspiciously. "Who are you?"

"I'm Jake. Jake Evans. I guess we can call me your... uncle. Maybe your folks told you about me. I moved to town not too long ago."

Connor shook his head. "They haven't mentioned you."

The man chuckled. "No I suppose they wouldn't. Will's my brother and we never got along too well."

"How come?"

"We just see things differently. I was hoping we'd have a chance to patch things up a bit but it's looking more like he's not interested."

Connor found this hard to believe. His dad seemed to get along with everybody and always seemed fair. "Have you talked to him?"

"I talked to him a couple weeks back. Got no response so I decided to come here and get the answer in person like. Your folks home?"

"Yeah. They're inside."

"You mind showin' me to the door? I'd like for them to see how eager I am to get to know you."

Connor led Jake to the front door and opened it. He called, "Mom. Dad. Someone here to see you."

When his parents came into view they froze. His mother's face paled while his dad's contorted with anger. "I told you not to come around here," his dad said as he advanced on his brother.

"Thought maybe you weren't taking my offer seriously."

Connor was confused by the reaction his parent's had toward this man. "Uncle Jake came…"

"Uncle Jake? That's who you introduced yourself as?"

"At least for now. Depends on how our talk goes."

"Connor, go out into the yard."

Connor's eyes were darting back and forth between the two.

"Now," his dad thundered.

Connor hurried outside, letting the screen door slam behind him.

Connor was sitting on the ground near the corner of his house, waiting. It wasn't too long before he heard the front door open. Connor stood and came around to see up onto the front porch. Uncle Jake had an envelope in his hand and seemed rather pleased. Connor was beginning to think maybe he and his dad had worked things out until he saw his dad come out onto the porch. He still looked angry.

"You got what you wanted, Jake. Don't come around here again."

Jake caught a glimpse of Connor. "Nice meeting you, kid." He turned and started walking off the porch. "And I'll be seeing you, Big Brother, on the first. Don't be late."

123

As Jake walked down the gravel drive, Connor went up on the porch and stood by his dad. His dad's face was still hard. "I want you to listen to me good, Connor. I don't want you going near that man. If he ever tries talking to you, you tell me straight away."

Connor began to scowl. "Uncle Jake seems nice. He said he wanted to patch things up with you. Aren't you going to give him a chance?"

"First off, you can't believe a word that man says. He has no interest in family unless it benefits him."

"But people can change. It wouldn't be fair not to give him a chance."

"That man has spent the last thirteen years going in and out of prison. He hasn't changed. And as far as fair goes, he's getting what he really wants out of me. And it ain't patching things up."

"But..."

"There are no buts. He is not part of our family and you are to stay away from him. End of discussion." He abruptly turned and went into the house, leaving Connor alone on the porch trying to understand a side of his dad he hadn't seen before.

Even though he was fairly awake, Connor kept his eyes closed. His head ached worse than any hangover he'd experienced. His first thought was he should have listened to his dad's advice all those years ago. He was right. Family had no meaning to Uncle Jake. Connor thought back on the scene. After that visit by Uncle Jake, it changed how he thought about his dad. The visit also changed his dad. Things were never the same between them anymore and nothing seemed to make it better.

It was a short time later after he began getting in trouble the comparisons between him and Uncle Jake began to come out during his dad's lectures. Knowing how his dad felt about his brother made the remarks cut all the more deeply, increasing their distance and leaving Connor feeling empty.

He felt movement to the side of him and opened his eyes. Connor saw Sonya, curled on her side sleeping next to him, cell phone laying in her hand. He could only remember the evening in bits and pieces after he got to her place, but recalled her often waking him up, asking him his name and her name and even how many of her fingers he could see.

Suddenly a sharp beeping sounded and her eyes instantly opened to his. She stared at him a few seconds before tapping her phone to silence the alarm. "How are you feeling?" she asked.

"Like I have a hangover from hell."

She smiled and sat up, reaching over to the nightstand to get the glass of water and one of the small packets. "I figured as much," she said while handing him the packet. "Your uncle gave you one nasty bump."

Connor looked at the packet. It was some sort of pain reliever. He turned and propped himself up on an elbow while biting back a groan. He ripped open the packet, popped the tablets in his mouth, took the offered glass of water, and quickly downed them. After giving Sonya back the glass, he collapsed onto his pillow letting out his suppressed groan, knowing it would be awhile before any relief would come. After a few seconds of silence he looked over to see Sonya watching him, concern shadowing her face.

"Any blurred vision? Dizziness? Nauseous? she asked.

"No. Just a headache."

Sonya nodded her head, then asked, "Why did you go to your uncle?"

"I asked him if he would drive me out of state. I wanted to buy you more time to work on this thing. Guess it was a pretty stupid idea. Didn't think he would try to turn me in." He brought his right arm up and draped it across his forehead. He closed his eyes and focused on his breathing. He felt a light touch running down the length of his scar.

"How'd you get this?" she asked.

Connor smirked. "Another stupid idea I had." He opened his eyes to look at her as her fingers continued to trace the length of it. "You know that tree outside my bedroom window?"

She nodded.

"I tried climbing it drunk so I could get back in my house. I didn't make it and wound up with a compound fracture."

"You're lucky it was only your arm."

"I know."

She paused. "How do you guys get the alcohol?"

"We all chip in for it and Brett's the one who brings it."

"How does he get it?"

"Don't really know. He never says."

They lapsed into silence until his stomach made a loud grumble.

She let out a laugh. "Sounds like I better get you some food since you're going to be stuck here recuperating. Speaking of which, you're to stay put in this bed till I get back."

His brows furrowed. "Does that mean you're not planning on arresting me?"

"Not today," she said as she made to get off the bed.

His furrow deepened. "Why are you helping me?"

Sonya paused. "You asked me to."

Connor knew there was more to it. She must have sensed he was gearing up to ask a follow-up question because she quickly got off the bed and crossed the room before he could ask.

Connor watched as she went through the drawers of the dresser and picked out some clothes before heading into the bathroom. He pulled the covers farther up and settled into the bed as he heard the shower start to run. He drew in a deep breath and closed his eyes. With the shape he was in he had no choice but to go along with whatever she had planned.

CHAPTER THIRTY-THREE

Sonya looked up at the sky. All traces of the Indian summer were gone with the gathering dark clouds and the wind hinting at the chill to come. It wouldn't be long before a cold rain would start pelting everything in sight. Deciding an extra layer of clothing wouldn't hurt, she threw on a zippered sweatshirt over her long sleeved t-shirt and shoulder holster, then donned her leather jacket. She opted to drive but still hoped to make it back from Lori's before the sky let loose.

As she drove the couple of blocks to the café, she thought about her guest holed up in her apartment. Now that he was there, she knew she was playing with fire. Turning a blind eye in letting him escape was one thing. Nobody would know unless Connor told. Interfering with his arrest was a bigger problem. Now she had to count on Kerry not telling. Hiding him in her apartment? That was going to get her burned.

Once at the café, she looked over the menu. She decided on ordering a variety of meals that would cover lunch and dinner today, and breakfast tomorrow. After glancing at the dessert menu, a thought came to her. Sonya added two slices of chocolate cake to the order and asked if they could give her a candle and a book of matches. The waitress said she would put those in the bag for her.

About twenty minutes later, three large take out bags were placed in front of her. Sonya paid the bill, gathered the bags, and headed for the door, then drew up short when she saw Kerry enter. His face was serious as he walked up and took her by the elbow, then started herding her back into the restaurant.

Sonya tried to get free of his grip without jostling the food bags too much. Her brows were driven together and her jaw set. "I was leaving."

He tightened his grip as he steered her to an empty booth in the back. "Change of plans. You owe me an explanation," he said as he deposited Sonya onto the seat and took the one across from her.

A waitress came over but left rather swiftly, saying, "I'll give you folks a few minutes."

Kerry looked Sonya in the eyes, his face showing hints of the anger from yesterday. "Okay. Start talking."

Sonya glared at him. "Connor Evans is innocent."

Kerry rolled his eyes and clenched his fists. He took in a deep breath before responding. "Okay. Let's say he's innocent. Who murdered Will and Mary Evans?"

"Jake Evans."

"He's got an alibi."

"Let's say he doesn't," she snapped.

"Okay, let's. What's his motive?"

"Money. Revenge."

"Why do you say that?"

Sonya calmed a bit and let out a breath. "Didn't get along with his father and brother. Father cut him out of the will and his brother inherited everything. He also started blackmailing his brother shortly after he moved here to Ashlin."

Kerry's eyebrows raised. "Why?"

"I think it has something to do with Connor. He's actually Jake's son. He was adopted by Will and Mary." She saw the surprise on Kerry's face turn to interest before she continued. "Jake was getting cash every month to the tune of seven hundred and fifty dollars from Will. But something happened to make him want more. I think he wants the ranch. If he killed the family and framed Connor, he could get the ranch through probate."

"But the girl is alive."

"Yeah. She isn't suppose to be. I think he screwed up on that one. But I got some problems of my own. I ran numbers for the value of the ranch. It was mortgaged to the hilt to pay for nursing home expenses for the elder Evans. Selling wouldn't bring about enough money to justify murder."

"Could for revenge."

Sonya shook her head. "Jake is all about the money. There has to be money somewhere in all of this."

Kerry paused. "You know your theory has so many holes it makes Swiss cheese look respectable."

"I prefer to think of it as a puzzle with some pieces missing."

"And the longer the kid is on the lam the more you can justify being here to find those missing pieces."

Sonya nodded and gave a quiet, "Yeah."

Kerry sat there studying her. His eyes narrowed. "Do you know where he is?"

Sonya didn't say anything.

"What if you're wrong about him?"

"I'm not."

"What if you can't find the missing pieces? Is this worth risking your career over?"

Sonya paused. "Yes."

Kerry ran his hand through his hair and leaned back in his seat. He was silent as he looked at her. Finally he groaned and leaned forward. "You should probably go after the alibi to see if it actually holds up. We just took it as is. You find something wrong with it, give me a call. Then, and only then, will I try to help."

She gave him a small smile. "Thanks, Kerry."

"Yeah, yeah. If Bennett finds out I might be looking for a new career myself." He pulled out his phone. "What's your number?" She told him and soon her phone was buzzing. "Okay, you got mine," he said as he pocketed his phone. Kerry reached across the table and touched her arm. "Just be careful, Sonya. If you're right about Jake, you're probably starting to get him a little nervous. Murderers who are nervous can get you hurt."

"I know."

Kerry's eyes flicked over to the food bags. "You'd better get going. Don't want his food getting cold."

CHAPTER THIRTY-FOUR

The hot water felt so good running over his body. Connor couldn't recall how many days it'd been since he'd taken a shower. His dip in the Hennessey Reservoir didn't count at all. He knew Sonya had left explicit instructions to stay in bed, but after many minutes of debating with himself and a few minutes of walking around and testing his balance he figured he'd risk it. There was also the fact that he was going to be around Sonya all day which was a different motivation altogether.

Avoiding the bump, he carefully washed his hair using Sonya's shampoo. It smelled about as girly as a hair product could get but his hair was so bad he really didn't care. He found her body wash was even worse, but used it anyway. It was after he ran his hand over his days old stubble and saw her very feminine pink razor that he drew the line. The stubble would stay.

When the hot water finally began to run out, he turned the shower off, slid open the glass doors, and stepped out. He toweled himself off then raised his arms to dry his hair. The action in the tight quarters caused his elbow to strike the glass door, causing a loud bang but little else. He was in the midst of vigorously rubbing his hair when the bathroom door flew open.

"Jesus," erupted from his mouth as he swiftly brought the towel down to cover himself. He glared at a panicked-looking Sonya. "Ever heard of knocking?"

"Yes. Ever heard of doing what you're told?"

Connor rolled his eyes.

Sonya began to grin. "So I guess this serves you right."

"Wonderful. Now, do you mind?" He lifted his chin indicating she should leave.

"No, I don't mind." Instead of leaving, she turned, leaned against the bathroom counter, and continued to grin at him, blatantly letting her eyes roam up and down.

Leaving one hand firmly on his towel, the other one grabbed the wet washcloth draped on top of the shower door. Sonya bolted from the bathroom as Connor flung it at her, hitting her in the back with a loud thwack against her sweatshirt, and causing her to laugh. Before he closed the door, he stuck his head out and shouted, "Perv," but failed to keep the laughter out of his voice.

A few minutes later he exited the bathroom with his towel firmly in place and looked around. The bedroom door was closed and the curtain was drawn. He saw clothes set out on the bed and was surprised to find they were his. As he dressed in jeans and a long-sleeved t-shirt, he wondered where his old jeans were, particularly his wallet. When finished, he went to the window and pulled back the curtain a bit to take a look. The rain was coming down hard outside. He left the room and noticed the curtain was drawn in the living room as well. Sonya was in the kitchen putting take out containers in the fridge. Her sweatshirt, now with a large wet spot on the back, was hanging on a kitchen chair and caused him to grin.

She looked up, giving him a small smile as she closed the fridge door. "How's the head?"

"Still got a headache, but the shower helped." He paused. "The jeans I had on last night…"

"Your stuff is on the coffee table."

Connor turned and saw his wallet, the hospital ID badge, and the two wires he used to pick her door lock all laying on the table. He opened his wallet to return the two wires and took inventory of the others and found they were all there. He stuffed the wallet and the ID card in his back pocket. He turned and looked back at her, waiting for her questions.

Sonya only nodded toward the kitchen table and said, "You got your choice of a burger or a grilled chicken sandwich. Both came with fries."

Connor took a seat at the table and read what was written on the nearest container and pulled it towards him. "I'll have the burger."

"Ah, a true rancher." Sonya said as she took the seat across from him and slid the chicken sandwich in front of her.

Connor groaned. "No way. I hate cows."

"What'd they ever do to you?"

He smiled. "Scarred me for life, that's what. When I was ten, my dad thought I was old enough to start helping on the ranch. He took me out on the range and I was walking by this steer. Right when I got near its head it turned, clocking me a good one so I fell right on my ass. My dad thought it was funny as hell. Teased me forever about it." He grew quiet with the memory and took a bite of his burger. He swallowed and continued. "It's just, with a ranch, you're always tied to it." Connor deepened his voice. "Cattle don't take care of themselves, son." He shrugged. "We never could get away from it."

"Your family didn't go on vacations?"

"Not really," he said before taking another bite. He started waving his finger in self-correction before swallowing. "We actually went to Colorado over this last Labor Day weekend. Just four days, but it was good. Well, good until we got back."

"Why? What happened?"

"Cattle busted through a section of barbed wire fence. A few of them got cut up pretty bad. Ended up spending a lot of time fixing the fence and patching up the injured cows."

"Why would they go through barbed wire like that?"

"If they're spooked, they don't care what's in their way. Something must have set them off." He watched Sonya eat her sandwich for a few seconds. "What about you? You go on vacations with your family?"

Sonya shook her head. "No." The empty distant look he was growing familiar with was quickly replaced with a question she tossed back to him. "If you could go anywhere, where would you go?"

He chuckled. "I know this will sound totally like a little kid, but I would like to go to Disneyland with Skeeter. The place just sounds amazing. I know she would love it."

Sonya gave him a small grin. "I always wanted to go to Disneyland, too." She grabbed a few fries. "So, if you don't like ranching, what do you want to do?" she asked before popping them in her mouth.

He shrugged as he grabbed a couple of fries of his own. "The counselor at school thought I should look into becoming a mechanical engineer."

Sonya nodded. "I can see that. Did your dad know about what the counselor said?"

"I brought home college information she gave me. He said why waste money on going to college when chances were I might not even get a job and I had a guaranteed livelihood with the ranch. Heard on and on about how my grandfather worked so hard to build it up from nothing. Ended up feeling guilty for wanting something different."

"What did you do?"

Connor shrugged. "Threw all the college info in the trash and went out with Mike and my friends. Got drunk, raised hell, and my dad had to pick me up at the sheriff station at three in the morning."

"I'm curious. Where'd you learn to pick locks, hot wire cars and stuff?"

Connor laughed. "YouTube. You can learn anything from YouTube and then it's just a lot of practice." They ate for a bit before Connor asked her a question. "Why'd you want to become a cop?"

"I didn't."

He raised an eyebrow.

Sonya smiled. "Well, not at first. An old boyfriend thought it would be cool if we became cops. I think he watched too many police shows on television. I thought, what the hell, and took all the entrance exams. I got in and he didn't."

"Ouch."

"Yeah. His ego couldn't handle being beaten by a girl. Needless to say our relationship ended shortly after that."

Connor focused on the food in front of him. "Got a boyfriend now?"

"No."

He glanced up and saw her grinning at him. He quickly averted his eyes before his embarrassment could take hold and asked, "Have you been a detective long?"

She shook her head. "Just the last three months. I actually worked undercover the last two and a half years with a narcotics unit."

"Doing what?"

"Posing as a high school student."

He chuckled. "Seriously?"

Sonya nodded. "We were targeting suppliers. I liked it, but they had plans to pull me after last school year ended."

"Why?"

"They thought I was looking too old to pull off high school, so I took the detective exam and applied for an opening that came up. Now I'm surrounded by people who think I'm too young to do this job. Kind of stuck between two worlds."

Connor nodded, understanding what that feels like. Although he wanted to keep talking to her his head began to throb and distracted his thoughts. They ate for awhile in silence until their food was gone. When he got up to toss his trash, he swayed a little.

Sonya must have noticed because she was instantly next to him, her hand on his back. "Are you okay?"

"Headache's worse."

"I think you should lay down."

"No argument on that one," he said as he made his way back to the bedroom. Sonya followed him and gave him more pain reliever to take. He took the tablets and laid down on the pillow, listening to the rain fall outside.

Sonya watched him for a few seconds, then turned to leave.

"Hey," he said, causing her to turn back to him. "Could...could you stay for a little while? I mean, I've just spent so many days..." His voice trailed off.

She sat on the edge of the bed. "I'll stay till you fall asleep."

Connor nodded but found, even though he wanted her there, he couldn't relax. His eyes would shift from looking at the ceiling to glancing at Sonya, the constant movement not helping his headache.

"Hey," she softly said as his eyes flitted to hers for the umpteenth time. "Close your eyes."

Connor settled his head back on the pillow and drew in a deep breath as his eyes closed. He let out his breath slowly and kept his eyes shut. The feel of her hand slipping under his caused him to start slightly, but the slow circular movements of her thumb on the sensitive skin of the top of his hand soothed him. His mind focused on the warmth of the contact and with each pass of her thumb he felt himself drifting away.

CHAPTER THIRTY-FIVE

When Connor's breathing slowed and his body went slack, Sonya slowly withdrew her hand from under his and left the room. She went to the living room, plopped down on the couch, and dragged out her laptop that was stashed between the couch and end table. As she started up her laptop, a large yawn escaped her and she fought the temptation to lay down on the couch to catch a nap herself. Her short night of sleep was catching up to her but she was behind in compiling her notes for her investigation. With Connor asleep she could work without worry of him seeing things.

Sonya took out her yellow notepad and began going over what she had. After lengthy minutes she let out a long frustrated breath. Kerry was right. Holes. And lots of them. Every time she uncovered something it raised more questions instead of answering the ones she needed to.

Her phone buzzed, interrupting her from her thoughts, and she looked at the screen. She answered, "Hey, Ray."

"Hey, Sonya. You haven't sent anything in and Peterson asked me about it. Got time to give me an update?"

"Yeah. I'm working on updating the report now."

"No investigating today?"

"It's raining cats and dogs here, so I'm sticking close to home."

"Weather hasn't stopped you before."

"I'm sticking close to home today."

"I guess that's my cue to leave it alone. So, tell me the latest."

Sonya proceeded to tell him everything she learned to that point including last night's events with Jake. She left out all the parts of her direct contact with Connor.

"This Jake Evans sounds like a piece."

"Yeah."

"While all of this is interesting conjecture, you need something solid on the guy. Yeah he could have planted the evidence, but you have a lot of questions to answer. How did he know the kid was gone that night? Why was he getting the monthly money? What does he really gain by killing his brother and family? Are there cracks in his alibi?"

Sonya groaned. "I know. I know. He's smart, Ray."

"You're smarter. Keep digging."

"I'm afraid of running out of time."

"You'll at least have raised enough questions the lawyers can run with and raise reasonable doubt with a jury. You're increasing the kid's chances of being acquitted."

Sonya couldn't stop her flare of anger. "That's not good enough. Connor will still be sitting in jail until the trial for something he didn't do. I can't let that happen."

The line became quiet on the other end. Sonya bit down on her lip knowing she screwed up. You don't use their first names.

Ray finally spoke, "If I think this case is becoming too personal for you, I will shut your investigation down as of yesterday. Even if it means you'll hate me for it."

She didn't say anything. Ray was serious and she knew he would do whatever necessary to protect her from herself.

"Sonya?"

"It's not personal."

Ray gave a short laugh. "Right. Sell that to someone who doesn't know you. Just don't do anything stupid or it's over."

Sonya rolled her eyes. Way too late for that.

"Besides, it sounds like the kid is helping you out as far as giving you time. Avoiding three captures is pretty impressive."

Sonya smiled. "He's pretty resourceful."

"I'll let you get back at it. Get that report in and keep me posted."

"I will."

After her call with Ray ended, Sonya worked on compiling all of her notes into a compelling report. Halfway through, she began to worry. While Peterson was fair, he wasn't overindulgent in detectives spending too much time on cases where they weren't showing results. Her week was nearing an end and she didn't have a lot to show for it.

Sometime later Sonya finished the report and saved it before closing the file. She planned on submitting it in the morning after rereading it with fresher eyes. She closed the window on her report and revealed the one displaying the Evans case. The page with some of the photos were up.

She clicked on the family picture. Her eyes were drawn to Madison and Connor. As she stared, the images changed and morphed until she was looking at a faded memory. The minutes ticked by and the faces from years ago became clear in her mind along with a stabbing ache. She closed her eyes and gave her head a shake before opening them. Once again she was looking at Madison and Connor.

Ray had his work cut out for him if he thought he was going to save her from herself. Sonya was shaking as she closed the tab, shut down her laptop, and stowed it once again between the side of the couch and the end table. She curled up on the cushions without bothering to take off her holster. As a tear slipped down her cheek, nothing gave her more comfort right now than the feel of her gun against her.

CHAPTER THIRTY-SIX

It was his birthday and Connor was lying on his bed waiting for his mother to call him down. He had been in his room ever since dinner ended while his parents set up the dining room.

There was a soft knock on the door and his mother poked her head in. She was smiling. "Okay, birthday boy. Come on down."

Connor leaped off the bed and followed his mother down to the dining room where his dad and Skeeter were waiting. There were balloons tied to the chairs and a paper banner hung on a wall saying "Happy Birthday Connor" that was obviously decorated by Skeeter. The table was covered in a colorful disposable tablecloth and there were three cone-shaped party hats sitting next to each place setting. Skeeter was already wearing hers.

He turned and looked at his mom's beaming face. "I'm fifteen, not five." But secretly he loved it.

"God, don't remind me." His mom wrapped her arm around him and pulled him tight to her. He was taller than her now. Something different from his last birthday.

After she let him go, he walked to the table. In the center was a large colorful sheet cake from Lydia's bakery. A closer look told him it was done in a super hero theme complete with little plastic action figures. He was so glad he didn't invite his friends over tonight. They'd tease the hell out of him for weeks.

He fought the urge to grin while he raised his eyebrows at his mom. "Super heroes? Seriously?"

She laughed and he began to grin.

"I thought super villains locked in prison would be more appropriate," his dad said.

His mom shot his dad a warning look as Connor's grin vanished. Okay. Guess his dad isn't quite over the incident from two weeks ago.

"Is it present time?" Skeeter asked.

"Yes. I think that's a good idea," his mom said quickly.

Connor looked over the small collection of gifts. He saw a large rather flat rectangular box and immediately got excited until the dimensions didn't quite match what he thought a guitar would fit into.

He had been asking for a guitar for months. It was Mike's idea to form a band. They'd been talking endlessly of being famous and rich and touring around the world. Mike, Josh, and Brett focused on the money, cars, and girls. Connor focused on seeing the world.

As per tradition, the big gift was to be last. He did a good job showing the proper enthusiasm when opening the smaller gifts, but by the time the larger gift was set in front of him it was getting harder to quell his growing disappointment. He ripped off the paper and confirmed it wasn't a guitar.

The box said Winchester. It was a gun. An M94 rifle to be precise. He lifted the lid to feign interest and saw his name engraved on the stock. Probably cost more than the guitar he wanted but he couldn't get excited. Guns were his dad's thing.

"I didn't ask for a gun." He couldn't hold back the words that fell from his lips. "I asked for a guitar."

"To do what? Form that pipe dream band you've been talking about?"

Connor glared at his dad. "Didn't know my dreams had to meet your approval."

"Well they sure as hell need to be rooted in reality. If I seriously thought for one second you wanted that guitar because you loved the idea of learning to play, you would have gotten it. I heard everything but."

"And you think this is rooted in reality?" Connor said while giving the box a shove. "This is the biggest pipe dream ever. Like I'm even interested in shooting guns, especially with you."

Connor watched his words have the desired effect. His dad's face became a stony mask before he got up to leave the room. Connor's mom let out a sharp, "Will," stopping him in his tracks. He reluctantly took his seat once again.

"Actually, it was my pipe dream. The gun was my idea."

Connor stared at his mom. She hated guns.

"I'm sorry. I thought it was a good idea. You two don't spend time with each other like you used to." She shrugged. "I thought if you learned to shoot and liked it, you and your dad could spend some weekends hunting together. Just the two of you."

He sat there and stared at the gun before pulling the box closer to him. His fingers traced the letters of his name. He swallowed hard. "That sounds good, Mom." And he meant it.

Looking back, the gun had helped a bit. His dad seemed happy in teaching him how to shoot. He didn't even seem to mind when Connor became a better shot than him. But the trips his mom envisioned for he and his dad never really materialized. There were a couple of weekends they went away together but not much more than that. It seemed like most weekends the damn cows needed his dad's attention. Yeah, he really hated cows.

Connor stretched and began to count the days that had passed in his head. He realized today was his birthday. Not just any birthday. He was eighteen. An adult. Honestly he didn't feel any different than he had yesterday. It just seemed like his life was on hold until something would give with regards to this investigation. He was getting tired of being in limbo.

He rolled over and sat on the edge of the bed. Stretching his neck, he found he was left with a dull ache in his head that was manageable. A noise outside the window drew his attention. He stood and went to the window, drawing the curtain slightly back. It was late afternoon and already quite dark out. Connor glanced about but saw and heard nothing as the rain continued to come down.

He left the room and walked down the hall. It was quiet and he wondered if Sonya was even there. Leaving the hall, he looked to his left and saw her asleep on the couch. Her blond hair was scattered across her face as if she had been tossing and turning. Her features were pinched as if in pain and her body made small jerking movements in response to what she was seeing behind her closed eyes. The movements increased and she began to make sounds, lost in the grips of a bad dream.

Connor walked around the coffee table and knelt on the floor beside Sonya's face. He carefully brushed back her hair and began calling her name. She thrashed more and Connor thought he could catch the word "no" being said over and over. He gripped her shoulder and gave her a shake.

Sonya bolted upright sending Connor sprawling backwards on the floor. In an instant her Glock was aimed at his face. She was shaking and her chest was heaving. Connor froze as he watched her struggle through her confusion. Sudden movements did not seem like a good idea right now.

He swallowed hard. "Sonya?" he said quietly.

Her eyes focused and darted around the room then back to Connor. She holstered her gun and slumped against the back of the couch. She tilted her head back and closed her eyes, still breathing hard. "Sorry," she let out on a breathy exhale.

Connor slowly stood and went to the kitchen. He retrieved two glasses and filled them with water, his hands shaking badly. Walking back to the couch he saw she hadn't moved but her breathing had calmed. He sat down next to her and said, "Here."

She opened her eyes and took the glass from him and drained half of it at one go. One hand began rubbing her face while the other held the glass tightly.

Connor took a few swallows of water before speaking again. "Does that happen often? Nightmares?"

Sonya shook her head. "It's been awhile."

"What was happening?"

Sonya stared at her glass. "I don't remember."

Connor knew she was lying but figured he wouldn't push.

She suddenly stood as if to ward off more questions even though he wasn't going to ask any. She gave him a small smile. "I was going to save my surprise till later but I desperately need some sugar right now. You wait there," she said and headed to the kitchen.

Connor sipped his water while listening to the noises Sonya was creating. He glanced towards the kitchen but she had her back to him, blocking whatever it was she was doing.

"Close your eyes," she called out.

Connor let out a short laugh. "I don't think so." He figured he should give her a hard time for scaring the shit out of him.

"I said I was sorry."

"You still wearing that gun?"

Sonya came out of the kitchen and made a show of removing her holster and draping it over a kitchen chair. "Now will you close your eyes?"

"Oh, I guess," he said, trying to make himself sound bored even though he was eager to see what her surprise was. He closed his eyes and waited. He sensed movement and heard some light clunking on the coffee table in front of him, then felt her take a seat next to him on the couch.

"Okay. Open your eyes."

He opened them and found two plates, each with a thick piece of chocolate cake. The one in front of him had a brightly lit candle.

"Happy birthday," she said. "Make a wish."

Connor stared at the flickering candle as the wax melted and dribbled down onto the frosting. So many conflicting feelings were swirling through him suddenly and he waited to see which one would take hold. As he watched the flame become distorted by the welling moisture in his eyes, he knew which one was winning.

"I'm sorry. This was a bad idea." She reached forward to take the plates.

Connor placed his hand on her arm and forced a smile. "No. It's great. Really."

Sonya let go of the plates and Connor took a breath before leaning forward and blowing out the lone candle. As it went out he realized he just wasted his birthday wish. The thing he wanted most he was never going to get. He picked up his plate and fork and Sonya did the same. "How did you know?" he asked as his fork sliced down through the cake.

"From the case file."

"Thanks for doing this. I didn't even realize it was my birthday until a little while ago." He smirked. "Been a little distracted lately."

She shrugged as she swallowed a bite of cake. "It's not much but I thought I should do something."

He gave her a grin. "This surprise is much better than the one earlier today in the bathroom."

Sonya started to laugh.

Connor gave her shoulder a playful shove. "You were so perving on me."

"Yesterday I would've felt guilty. Today not a chance. You're totally legal."

Connor laughed and shook his head before taking a big bite of his cake. Based on her comment, he began to think he should have used that candle to wish for something else.

As he finally got down to the last bite, he found she was right. The sugar and chocolate did amazing things. It emboldened him to ask about the ever present elephant. "How's the case going?"

"It's going."

Well, that was evasive. "Tell me about it."

"I'm still working on it."

"Do you have a suspect? Have you gotten some of the evidence against me gone?"

Sonya shook her head. "The evidence still implicates you in the crime."

"What about a suspect?"

As the seconds passed, he watched her demeanor become more and more like a cop. "I can't get into this with you," she finally said.

"Why not? There charging me with fucking murder, Sonya. I need to know what's going on. It's my life that will be over, not yours."

Sonya's face flashed with anger as she stood and grabbed the plates from the coffee table. "Don't even think you're the only one with everything to lose. For your information, aiding a fugitive is a career ender in this field. My career is all I have. That's my life." She turned and stormed off to the kitchen.

Connor was off the couch and hot on her heels. "Then why are you helping me?"

"You're innocent."

The answer was too quick. Too pat. His eyes narrowed. "Why are you really helping me?"

Sonya didn't answer and began rinsing the plates.

"Fine. Don't tell me anything." He turned, stalked off to the bedroom, and slammed the door.

Connor lay on the bed and stared at the ceiling. Chronologically he was eighteen. Behavior-wise? He would have picked something in the single digits based on his display about an hour ago. He sat up. Time to attempt to be an adult.

He shuffled out to the living room and found Sonya watching some television show. A closer look told him it was some sort of crime drama. Another time, it probably would have struck him as humorous. He went and sat on the couch next to her. "Sorry. I know you're trying to help me and I shouldn't have gone off on you. It seems like it doesn't take much anymore to get me shooting off in some emotional direction."

"I understand."

Her response wasn't placating. It was honest and he believed her. They sat there watching the show silently for a few minutes. "Maybe it would be better if I left," Connor said quietly.

She shook her head. "It won't change things at this point with regards to my job."

"Nobody else knows and I won't say anything. I promise."

She looked at him and he saw it in her face.

"Somebody else knows," he said.

She nodded. "Deputy Patrick. Last night I stopped him from shooting you as you escaped from your uncle's."

Connor remembered seeing someone looking down at him from the window. He remembered hearing the shot.

"I can almost guarantee he knows you're here," she said.

Connor's eyes grew wide.

"But he's not going to do anything for now," she quickly added.

"What should we do?"

"Right now? Eat dinner. Tomorrow I got to make headway on this case. It looks like both of our lives are depending on the outcome."

CHAPTER THIRTY-SEVEN

Sonya got up early, despite a not so comfortable night on the couch. and reread her report before sending it off to Ray. She tore out all her notes from her yellow legal pad that she had entered in her computer. Having no shredder readily available, she set about ripping them up into small pieces before depositing them in the wastebasket in the kitchen. Opening the fridge, she took out one of the leftover containers, heated the contents in the microwave, and wolfed down her breakfast.

She walked into the bedroom and saw Connor was still sleeping. After quietly grabbing some clothes she went into the bathroom and took a quick shower. Once dressed she sat on the edge of the bed and touched his shoulder, calling his name a few times.

His eyes fluttered open and he gave her a sleepy grin. "Hey," he said quietly, his voice roughened with sleep.

She smiled. "I'm going to be leaving to go and check some things out today."

"Where are you going?"

Her smile faded. "Connor…"

"Let me guess. You're not going to tell me."

Sonya closed her eyes and bit her lower lip briefly before answering. "I think it's better the less you know…for both of us."

He closed his eyes to her and turned his face into the pillow.

She touched his arm. "There's some breakfast in the fridge for you."

He nodded.

"I'll be back later with lunch."

He just nodded again.

Sonya let out a heavy sigh as she left the bedroom. She knew he was frustrated with being kept in the dark, but she could deal with a frustrated Connor Evans. She didn't know what she would be dealing with if he learned about some of the things she discovered.

Before leaving the apartment, she ripped a small piece of paper from her notebook, scribbled something on it, and left it on the lone take-out container in the fridge. She went down to her car, started it up and headed for the high school. She was curious about how the boys got their alcohol, particularly how Brett Aldrich got it.

Once at the school, she settled into the borrowed office and had the secretary call up Brett. After a few minutes, he came in and took a seat across from Sonya, slouching down and shoving his hands into his pockets. Unlike Connor's other two friends, this boy was smaller and seemed a bit on the timid side. He kept his eyes down on the table and seemed nervous. Sonya quickly glanced at her notes on him. He was only a junior.

"Brett Aldrich?"

He nodded.

"I'm Detective Reisler."

"Mike's told me about you," he said quietly.

"So you know I'm trying to help Connor."

He shrugged.

"I've been told you're the one who supplies alcohol to your get-togethers."

No response.

"Do you take it from home?"

"No. Everybody chips in."

"Do you buy it?"

"No."

"Somebody buys it for you?"

Brett was quiet and started biting his lower lip.

"I need to know who is buying it for you."

Brett sat up straighter and his hands came up to grip the edge of the table. "If I tell, he won't buy it for me anymore. That's the deal. I keep my mouth shut and he buys."

Sonya paused and watched Brett slouch down in his seat again. She made her tone softer. "When did you first start hanging out with Mike, Connor, and Josh?"

"About two years ago."

"When you were a freshman?"

He nodded.

"They were all sophomores, right?"

"Yeah."

"Those three have been tight for a pretty long time."

Brett nodded.

"How'd they get alcohol before you came along?"

He shrugged. "Just what they could sneak out of their houses. It wasn't much."

Sonya gave him a soft smile. "I bet they were glad you came along."

"They think I'm like a beer god," Brett said while he cracked the smallest of smiles.

"I don't want to do anything to ruin your arrangement and I'm not going to bust the guy for buying alcohol for minors. The problem is your friend Connor has no alibi for the night his parents were murdered. The sheriff isn't taking any of your statements as credible. I need to know if any beside you four knew about the get-together that night. If that person would step forward then that could help lay the groundwork in establishing a possible alibi for Connor."

Brett's brows suddenly furrowed.

"What's wrong?" Sonya asked

"If that would help with an alibi, then why hasn't he said anything?" He looked at Sonya. "Does he know it would help Connor?"

"Who?"

"Connor's Uncle Jake. He's the one who buys the beer for me." When Sonya didn't respond, Brett continued. "It's a sweet arrangement. I give him the money and tell him when I need the beer. He never rips me off and he always gets it on time as long as I let him know in advance."

"Do you talk to Jake about your plans? You know, like, where you go to meet? The time?"

"Yeah. We talk. He's pretty cool. Sometimes he even comes up with places we don't know about."

"Does he ask questions about Connor?"

"Yeah. I mean, Connor's his nephew but Jake can't see him because Connor's dad hates him. He just wants to know what's up."

148

"Did he know where you guys were the night that Connor's parents were murdered?"

"Yeah. He knew we were going to the creek."

"Did he know Connor would be there?"

Brett nodded, then his shoulders suddenly slumped. "Now I've probably fucked everything up with Jake."

"This will go a lot further in helping Connor than getting him a case of beer."

Brett shrugged. "I hope Jake helps with the alibi."

No, Sonya thought. The last thing Jake Evans wants is for Connor to have an alibi.

CHAPTER THIRTY-EIGHT

Jake had used Brett for the last two years to get information on Connor and his family. Two years is a long time to compile information and Brett was probably all too eager to spill whatever he could in his gratitude. Bottom line, Jake knew Connor was going to be out of the house that night along with other information that would help frame him.

The next place Sonya wanted to go was the clinic where Mary Evans had worked the last five years. She pulled her car in front of a small white building that had a sign reading, "Ashlin Family Clinic."

Sonya walked into the clinic and took a seat in the waiting area. In a few minutes, a woman and a young child came out of a door being held open by a middle aged woman with slightly graying brunette hair, wearing a white lab coat.

The woman smiled and said goodbye to her patients before turning to Sonya. "How may I help you?"

"I'm Detective Reisler. I was told Mary Evans worked here."

The greeting smile left as her lip began to tremble. A few tears started as the woman quickly dashed them away with a couple swipes of her hand and took a seat by Sonya. "I'm sorry. We were friends. I still can't believe she's gone."

"And your name is?"

"I'm sorry," she said as she held out her hand to Sonya, who took it. "I'm Abby Walker. I'm a nurse practitioner."

"Mary started working here five years ago?"

The woman nodded. "She was the receptionist, biller, assistant, you name it. It's a small clinic. You have to do a little of everything."

"Did she like her job?"

"She made the most of it. Would've rather been home with Maddie. She was going to get that chance. She'd turned in notice that she was quitting at the end of the month. And now ..." Abby covered her mouth as more tears fell.

Sonya waited a few minutes until Abby was in control again. "Why did Mary start working?"

Abby shifted in her seat, suddenly looking uncomfortable. "They had some expenses and needed the income."

"Did she share what they were?"

"No."

"But I take it the expenses were going to be all taken care of by the end of this month?"

Abby shrugged and shifted her eyes from Sonya's. "I guess."

"Five years ago was also around the time when Jake Evans showed up. Any coincidence?"

"I don't know."

"She also turned in her resignation the same month Connor turns eighteen. Another coincidence?"

"I ... I don't know."

"Actually, I think you know more about a lot of these things. The truth is I know about some of Mary's secrets like you do. More importantly, I'm trying to find the person responsible for killing her."

"You don't think Connor did it?" Abby asked quietly.

"No. Do you?"

Abby paused, then shook her head. "No. Mary loved that boy."

"Like he was her own."

Abby's eyes grew large.

"I know Mary and Will adopted him," Sonya said quietly.

Abby nodded and exhaled. "She told me about three years ago. She was upset. Connor had gotten into a fight with Will, then went out and got into trouble." She shrugged. "She needed to talk and it kind of came out that Connor was adopted."

"She told you who his father is, didn't she?"

"Yes. Jake Evans."

"I know they were paying Jake a sum of money every month. Do you know why?"

"She told me that Jake was not informed of the adoption. It was done while he was in jail. He threatened to take a paternity test and take them to court to be granted custody of Connor, or at least get visitation rights. She was scared he would take Connor away and with the trouble Connor started getting into, she was afraid the courts might find them unfit and reinstate some of Jake's parental rights. They agreed to giving him money every month if he stayed away."

"Connor doesn't know Jake is his dad, does he?"

"No. That was also part of the agreement."

"Was she quitting this month because Connor is turning eighteen?"

"Yes. They figured Jake legally couldn't do anything. He really only wanted the money anyways. He never really wanted Connor."

"But he could've still told Connor that he's his dad."

"They were planning on telling him. They figured Connor would be old enough to handle the knowledge and it'd be better to hear it from them instead of Jake."

"What about the military school talk?"

"Mainly talk. They really couldn't afford something like that. The place in Texas they were checking out was thirty-five thousand a year." Abby shrugged. "Will was at his wits end with Connor's behavior. He wasn't happy the sheriff never let those boys get the full consequences of their actions. The boys knew they were safe, in a way, and did whatever they wanted around here. I guess he thought the military school threat would rein him in. It seemed like it was working too."

"How so?"

"The last four months had been good as far as not getting picked up by the sheriff. They still suspected he was sneaking out and meeting up with his friends to drink, but he wasn't getting in trouble."

"So nothing that would possibly lead to his dad upping the military school threat?"

"Nothing that Mary told me about."

"Thanks for your time, Abby. If you think of anything else that might be important, let me know."

"I will."

Sonya handed her a card and then walked to the door. As she exited, she saw a bright red pickup parked out front and its driver had gotten out and was shutting the door.

Jake turned, and upon seeing Sonya, gave her a slight smirk. "We seem to cross paths often, Detective."

"Does it make you uncomfortable?"

"The only thing causing me discomfort is my back, which is why I'm here. You being here? Don't really care."

"How'd you hurt your back? Was it from the other night when you tried to get your son arrested?"

He shook his head and chuckled. "Actually, it's work related. Harris sent me over here." Jake paused, his smirk growing. "As for the other night, I was doing my civic duty by capturing a wanted man. Guess I'm doing your job."

"My job is to find evidence to link the real killer to the crime, not fall for some well-crafted framing of an innocent kid."

"Well, you might not be doing that job for much longer."

"How so?"

"As far as backs goes, I'd be watching yours."

Sonya raised an eyebrow. "Are you threatening me?"

"Not at all. Just giving you a friendly warning."

"And why would I need a warning?"

"You may represent the law, but you're not above it. As far as I reckon, hiding a fugitive is frowned upon by your kind. Can get you in all sorts of hot water." Jake shook his head and clucked his tongue. "Closing your curtains was good. Telling the boy not to peek through them would've been better." He made an exaggerated show of looking at his watch. "I figure by now Sheriff Bennett is already at your place poking around." He then looked at Sonya. "Starting to feel the heat?"

CHAPTER THIRTY-NINE

Connor was having a hard time with the lock. Part of it was the fact he only somewhat knew what he was doing, but the larger part was nerves. Breaking into the high school was a step up from the normal stunts they pulled and he was unsure of what the consequences would be if they got caught. But Mike wanted to make their mark as freshmen at this school and was eager to put to use Connor's newly developing skill.

"What's taking so long?" Mike grumbled.

Connor turned and glared at him. "You want to do it?"

"It didn't take you this long at Lydia's."

"It's a different kind of lock. It's gonna take me longer." He turned back to his task at hand and tried to concentrate.

"This is going to be so awesome," Josh said while looking at the nearly two gallons of concentrated yellow food coloring he was holding.

Mike laughed. "You know it. I would love to see their faces. Everyone will be talking about it."

Connor rolled his eyes. It probably wasn't even going to work. Tomorrow was the start of the swimming unit in P.E. and Mike had this idea of turning the pool water yellow. Connor felt like kicking himself after he opened his big mouth and suggested food coloring. Mike jumped on the idea and now here they were, attempting to perform their second break-in of the evening. The bakery was easy. This not so much.

After a couple more minutes, he felt the lock start to give and it began to turn. When the door opened, Mike grabbed his shoulders and rocked him around a bit. "You are the man," he said before he and Josh hurried in.

Connor made sure the door was unlocked from the inside in case they needed to make a quick getaway, then ran after his friends. He noticed the floors had some wet streaks like they were mopped not too long ago. His eyes darted around and he had a bad feeling the school wasn't as empty as they thought.

He finally caught up to Mike and Josh at the door leading to the pool. It was the same kind of lock he had just picked, so it went quicker this time and soon they were standing at the edge of the pool. The water was circulating and Connor suggested they pour in the coloring at the water outlet. The thick liquid-like gel poured slowly out of the jugs and was whisked away by the water pressure from the outlet. Slowly the water transformed into a pale yellowy green. Not dark but definitely enough to notice. They rinsed the jugs out with pool water to get every last bit of coloring they could.

Mike gave a final appraising look and said, "Nice." The three headed out, ditching the jugs in the trash. They were talking about what people would say tomorrow and if swimming would be cancelled as they approached the back door they'd entered. They opened the door and suddenly saw flashing red and blue lights coming from a sheriff's car parked on the street by the fence. A deputy was already over the fence and halfway to the door.

"Halt," he yelled.

The boys turned around and ran back into the school. The deputy gave chase. Connor brought up the rear as they tore through the hallways. He hadn't seen this young blond deputy before. A quick glance over his shoulder revealed this deputy was fast. Definitely faster than Moore or Cleary and he was gaining.

The layout of the halls was a big square and Connor could tell Josh was leading the group back to the door. If they could get out and over the fence, they could disappear in the corn field across the street. Turning the last corner, Connor's feet began to slide out from under him causing him to stumble and lose valuable seconds.

By the time Connor burst through the doors he saw Josh had already finished scaling the fence and was running across the street to the corn field. Mike was at the top and dropped to the ground on the other side and began to run. Connor leaped and hooked his fingers into the chain link and began scrambling up. He felt his leg being grabbed and kicked out as he pulled himself to the top. His foot connected and he heard the deputy curse as he too began scaling the fence. Connor cleared the top and dropped down to the other side. He got two steps into his run when a massive weight fell on him sending him to the ground, pinning him.

With all the breath he could muster, he yelled, "Mike!" while he felt the deputy's knee jam into his lower back and his arms were wrenched behind him. As the cuffs were snapped into place he heard a whistle being given by Mike in the near distance. Connor was hauled to his feet and escorted to the nearby patrol car. He saw Mike and Josh coming out of the cornfield and heading to the patrol car. Connor smiled.

The deputy seemed surprised by the sight of the two boys coming back and quickly shoved Connor in the back of the car. He drew his gun and ordered Mike and Josh to the ground, face down. After securing their hands with zip ties, he led them to the patrol car, stuffed them in back with Connor, and began the drive back to the station.

The boys watched as the new deputy busily typed away at his report. This Deputy Patrick was serious. He even fingerprinted them. They looked up as a very tired sheriff entered the building. He took one look at them, pursed his lips and shook his head. "What did they get picked up for this time, Kerry?"

"They broke into the high school and vandalized the pool."

Sheriff Bennett turned to the boys. "What the hell did you do to the pool?"

Mike grinned. "Turned the water piss yellow."

The sheriff shook his head again. "I bet you did."

"It was food coloring, Sheriff," Kerry said. "With the charges of breaking and entering, vandalism, and resisting arrest, I figured they should be booked and..."

"Whoa there, Deputy. You're getting a little carried away."

"Between my report and the janitor being an eyewitness there should be no problem..."

The sheriff held up his hand and effectively silenced the deputy. He turned to the boys. "Have your folks been called yet?" They shook their heads. He lifted his chin towards the reception desk phone. "Start dialing."

Connor was waiting his turn to use the phone and watched as the sheriff pulled Deputy Patrick to the side. The deputy looked none too happy with what the sheriff was telling him. "So that's it? They just go home?" The deputy's voice had risen in volume. "All because one of them is a deputy's kid?"

"Look. I know you're new to law enforcement, but the first rule is we look out for each other. Now don't worry. I'll talk with Principal Stanfield and he'll make sure they have consequences."

"What about my report?"

"I'm sure it's fine. Just finish it up and make sure the wording says they were detained. They were not arrested." The sheriff clapped the deputy on the shoulder. "I'm going into my office to sleep until it becomes a decent hour."

After the sheriff left for his office and Josh and Mike were picked up, Connor was left alone with Deputy Patrick. He felt the deputy glaring at him from time to time. He knew part of it was the new deputy learning how the laws in Ashlin worked with regards to Mike Traynor and part of it was probably the darkening red mark on the deputy's forehead resulting from the kick he received.

Connor did feel kind of bad about kicking the deputy and figured it wouldn't hurt to try and improve his standing with him. "Hey, Deputy Patrick. Sorry about your head."

The glare grew more fierce. "Save it, kid. One day the immunity your friend Mike provides you and your other friend will be gone and I hope I'm the one who is lucky enough to be there to bust you good."

Connor looked away and scowled. There was going to be no improving anything with this deputy.

Cops. It seemed to Connor they took it upon themselves to determine how much they wanted to follow the laws. In some ways Sonya was no different. She was not arresting him like she should, but then she wasn't sharing with him what she was learning through her investigation. He hated not knowing what was going on. So frustrating.

He got out of bed and dressed before wandering to the kitchen. Opening the fridge, he saw the lone take out container sitting on the top shelf. There was a note setting on it. It said, "Soon." He plucked it off of the container and stuck it in his front pocket. He guessed he was suppose to be content in knowing she wanted to tell him.

Connor heated the omelet and hash browns in the microwave, then sat at the table to eat it. It was too quiet in the apartment and just magnified the fact he was alone. After a couple of bites, he took his food to the couch and turned on the TV in an attempt to drown out the silence. He flipped through the channels, then paused when he saw his own face staring back at him from the screen along with that of a female news anchor.

"Authorities still have no leads on the whereabouts of eighteen year old Connor Evans. Evans is charged with the shooting deaths of his parents, William and Mary Evans, and the shooting of his six year old sister that left her critically injured. While there have been confirmed sightings in the Ashlin area, Connor Evans has eluded authorities and still remains at large. Anyone seeing Connor Evans is asked to call the Ashlin Sheriff's Department."

The camera panned out to show the male newscaster looking serious and shaking his head. "What a terrible tragedy. Let's hope authorities get a lucky break and catch him soon." The female anchor nodded her head and looked equally serious as he continued, "Thanks for the update, Andrea." Suddenly they both broke into smiles as he said, "What do you get when you let loose a dozen kids armed with hoses, buckets, and soap? A whole lot of…"

Connor flipped off the television. Silence wasn't so bad after all. He finished eating and got up to throw away the empty container. He lifted the lid of the wastebasket, tossed the container in, and let the lid fall back down. He immediately lifted it up again and moved his container out of the way to look at the yellow pieces of paper that caught his attention. They were small torn squares of yellow legal pad paper. He fished quite a few out and looked at them. They had writing on them.

He grabbed as many as he could that weren't too soiled and brought them back to the coffee table and spread them out. Quickly he realized these were pieces of Sonya's case notes that she had ripped up and thrown away. He spent quite a few minutes shuffling them around to try and gain some sense from them. Many pieces were missing but he made out his name on a couple, as well as Jake's and his parent's. He also saw "Dandrid…" and "Karen Un…" There was something about a will, inheritance, and "birth cer," which he took to mean birth certificate.

He sat back and thought about the fragmented words. "Dandrid…" probably meant Dandridge and Dandridge, the local law office. Sonya must have went there during her investigation and they probably handled the wills for his family. He scowled as he looked at the piece with "Karen Un…" written on it. He didn't know of any Karen and never heard his family mention a Karen.

Connor heard a noise at the front door. Thinking Sonya was back already, he quickly swept the scraps of paper into his palm and shoved them in his pocket. He stood as the door opened and suddenly his heart was hammering out of control.

Deputy Patrick stood there, hand at the ready to pull his gun. Kerry closed the door behind him with his foot, all the while keeping his eyes on Connor. "Listen to me carefully. Sheriff Bennett received a tip from Jake that you're hiding out here and is on his way over. You need to get the hell out of here. Any trace of you being here has to be gone. Your clothes…whatever you can think of."

Connor stood there staring at the deputy, trying to process everything the last few seconds threw at him.

"Now!" Kerry shouted and Connor moved to action. He ran to the bedroom and tossed on his sweatshirt and jammed his feet into his sneakers. He gathered all his dirty clothes, which he hadn't been too neat about, and the few clean ones he had in the room and scooped them into a pile. Kerry entered the room with a trash bag and together they shoved the clothes in.

"Anything else you got here?"

Connor shook his head. "I…I don't think so."

"Go out the window and stash the bag behind the building. I'll collect it later after the sheriff leaves," Kerry said.

Connor pulled back the curtains and lifted the window. Before he stepped out, he looked at the deputy. "Thanks."

Kerry glared at him. "Don't flatter yourself. I'm only doing this to save Sonya's ass. If I see you anywhere outside of this apartment, I will arrest you."

Connor had no doubt and backed out the window.

"One more thing," Kerry said. "Don't dare come back here. If you care anything about her, then stay away." With that he slammed the window shut and Connor was left out in the open on a bright sunny mid-morning.

CHAPTER FORTY

As Sonya drove up in front of Ashlin Tool and Hardware, she could already see two sheriff vehicles parked and her apartment door wide open. Already shaking from what Jake told her, it increased tenfold when she saw he wasn't lying. She took the steps two at a time to reach the landing. Kerry and Sheriff Bennett were looking around the living room.

"What the hell are you doing here?" Her words were strong and steady even though she wasn't.

Kerry quickly turned and held his hand in front of him to signal her to stop. He quickly mouthed the words, "It's okay."

Sonya looked at him knowing she wasn't doing anything to mask the fear she was feeling.

He mouthed the words, "He's gone," as Sheriff Bennett began to respond to her question.

"We received a tip that you may be hiding Connor Evans in your apartment here," the sheriff said.

"You don't see him here, do you?" Sonya said as she got herself together.

"Doesn't mean he wasn't."

"Let me guess. Jake Evans supplied the tip,"

"Doesn't matter who supplied it. I've got an obligation to check it out. You don't mind do you?"

Sonya threw a quick glance at Kerry who gave her a nod. She took a deep breath. "I don't mind at all. Knock yourself out."

Sheriff Bennett went to the kitchen and looked around. He lifted the trash can lid. "Looks like quite a few take out containers."

"Girl's gotta eat and I was never planning on cooking during this trip."

He set the lid back and headed down the hall to the bedroom. The sheriff walked into the bathroom and looked at the counter. There were two toothbrushes laying next to each other. "Now why would a person need two toothbrushes?"

Sonya shrugged. "I like using two different types of bristles. The green one is soft and the blue is extra soft."

"Uh-huh," he said, not sounding the least bit convinced and spent a few more minutes looking around. He walked out into the bedroom and began walking around as his eyes roamed over the unmade bed and nightstand.

The sheriff got on the floor and looked under the bed. After a couple seconds he started to get up, then paused. "Well, what's this?" he said while reaching between the bed and nightstand. He pulled out something wadded up, stood, and held up the item. It was a pair of boxer shorts.

He chuckled. "I don't care how big of balls you attempt to swing, Detective, but I sure know you ain't holding them in these." He turned to Kerry. "Bag these, the toothbrushes, the food containers, and wipe down the shower for any hairs."

Kerry began to look sheepish. "Uh, Sheriff," he said while reaching for the boxers. "Those are mine. And...and the toothbrush too."

The triumphant expression on the sheriff's face soured.

"Jake must have seen me here when I, uh, visited."

The sheriff thrust the pair of boxers into Kerry's waiting hand. "Good Lord, Kerry," he said as he glanced at Sonya and started shaking his head. "I know the pickings are slim around here, but still..." Suddenly the two-way crackled, hailing the sheriff. He grabbed the device off his belt. "This is Bennett."

"We got a call from the hospital in Scottsbluff. Madison Evans has regained consciousness."

162

"Alright. I'm on my way." He turned to Kerry. "Grab the video equipment from the station and meet me over there."

"Yes, sir," he said while tossing the boxers on the bed.

The sheriff walked out with Kerry and Sonya trailing behind. Kerry leaned toward Sonya. "Ride with me," he said quietly.

Sonya nodded and followed him to his car. As soon as they were both in and had shut the doors, Sonya asked, "Where is he?"

"Gone," Kerry said flatly while starting the car.

"Kerry!"

"I don't know where he is and I don't really care. He's out of your place. That's all that matters." As he pulled out he threw her an irritated look. "Oh, and you're welcome."

They rode in silence to the station and Sonya waited in the car while Kerry ran in to get the video equipment. After stowing it in the trunk, they started the drive to Scottsbluff.

"How did you know?" Sonya asked.

"I was on my way out when Jake came in and wanted to talk to the sheriff. Decided to wait a little bit and see what was up. Good thing. I ended up getting to your place ahead of Bennett and got the kid out."

"Thanks, Kerry."

"Yeah, yeah," he said with only a hint of his former irritation.

As they drove through Ashlin, Sonya couldn't help but scan the roads and sidewalks for Connor. She didn't expect to see him but it didn't stop her from looking.

"Have you made any more headway?" Kerry asked once they had cleared the Hennessey Reservoir.

"Some. Jake was threatening Will and Mary that he would take a paternity test and take them to court to get some of his parental rights reinstated. They paid him to stay away from Connor."

"How's that related to the murders?"

"The money was ending this month when Connor turned eighteen. Will and Mary were going to tell him Jake's his father. Legally Jake couldn't do anything anymore."

"So you think he knew this and found another way to get money by murdering his brother?"

"I think this thing has been in the works for awhile. I found out Jake has had an in with Connor's group of friends for the last two years. Brett Aldrich."

"Brett?"

"He's the one who supplies alcohol to the group and Jake's been the one buying it for him. They've been pretty chummy and Brett has inadvertently been giving him information about Connor and his family. Jake knew Connor would be gone that night."

"So it's likely he knew about the relationship between Connor and Will, the military school talk, the gun in the house that was Connor's… enough to stage a convincing framing."

Sonya nodded.

"So where's the money in this?"

"I still don't know."

"Maybe this trip to the hospital will put an end to this."

"Maybe. If Madison can identify Jake."

"Or Connor."

Sonya glared at Kerry. "He didn't do it."

"So you say."

"So you know. If you really thought he was guilty you wouldn't have helped him."

"I wasn't helping him," he gritted out.

"By helping me you're helping him."

"And just how much are you helping him?" he snapped.

"What's that suppose to mean?"

"Nothing," he muttered while focusing on the road.

"Obviously there's something. Just say it."

"The boxers…"

"Seriously? You're going there?"

"At least I could understand that. This case? You latched onto it the first day you stepped foot in the station. Why?"

"I need to solve this case."

Kerry shook his head. "It's become an albatross, Sonya. Cut it loose before you get so god damned entangled you get hung by it."

Sonya turned and looked out the window. "I can't."

Kerry let out a sigh. "I know and that's what I don't understand."

CHAPTER FORTY-ONE

Connor pulled his hood up and kept his head down as he made his way through downtown Ashlin. He felt exposed and vulnerable and it fueled his steady stream of curses directed toward his uncle. What the hell had he done for this man to have it in for him so bad? It just didn't make any sense for Jake to go out of his way to have him busted. What was worse was Sonya had come close to getting busted as well and Connor knew it would have been his fault, even though he would love to blame Jake.

Deputy Patrick was right. He needed to stay clear of Sonya's place which left him with limited options. The only idea he had at the moment was getting to the high school, but it was quite a few blocks away and mid-morning was a busy time in town, increasing his chances of being seen. He often crossed the street if someone was heading down the sidewalk toward him or turn and look at a storefront if a car was driving by.

It was during one of these times he found himself in front of Dandridge and Dandridge. The posted hours stenciled on the door told him they were closed today. Looking down the street, he could see the high school coming into view but a new idea was forming in his mind. Sonya had gathered some information about the case during her visit here and he was tired of being in the dark.

Connor walked along the side of the building and saw two windows. The first one was part of the front reception area. The second one was set further back and had blinds blocking the view to the inside. He continued walking until he was behind the building. At the back there was a door. The lock was part of a regular home door knob set that had a matching dead bolt as well. Not a big deal.

He walked back around the corner to check out the window. Connor studied the window and saw on the inside, mounted to the sill, was a little white piece of plastic that butted up against a matching one on the window frame. This was a big deal. The place had an alarm system, meaning the back door was a no go.

Connor walked back to the front of the building. The windows facing the street had no blinds and would offer an unobstructed view of the reception area. Reaching the corner, he glanced around. Being on the edge of the main downtown area meant significantly less foot traffic, but it was still on a main street people used to get in and out of town. A car was coming so he knelt down on the sidewalk in front of the nearest window and pretended to tie his shoelace. He glanced up and focused on the corners of the room near the ceiling. Connor didn't see any motion sensors in the reception area and figured the rest of the place didn't have any either.

He went back to the side of the building, taking off his sweatshirt as he went. He pulled out his wallet, opened one of the compartments, and pulled out a thin little rectangle of metal. Placing it between his lips to hold onto it, he put his wallet back, and loosely folded his sweatshirt. He gave a quick glance of his surroundings before putting his back to the window. His left arm crossed over his body to hold the sweatshirt over the lower half of the window. Three hard jabs of his right elbow caused the glass to crack and give way.

Reaching inside, he quickly slipped the thin metal in between the little magnetic alarm sensors, then reached up and turned the window latch. He slowly raised the window making sure the metal stayed attached to the lower sensor. One more glance around and then he was pushing the blinds out of the way as he stepped through the open window.

Connor found himself in an office. A really nice one. There was a dark wood desk with a large leather chair behind it on one end of the room and a leather couch and coffee table towards the other. Built in book shelves and paintings gave the place a look of class and money. He walked over to the desk and saw a file cabinet against the wall. Trying a drawer, he found it was locked. Within a few seconds he had it open.

He saw a couple different file folders with the name Evans, pulled them out, and brought them over to the desk. One of the folders had his grandfather's name and the other had his dad's and mom's. He reached into his pocket, pulled out the yellow bits of paper, and laid them out on the desk top before taking a seat in the large leather chair. There was some note about inheritance so he looked through his grandfather's folder first and found his will. After flipping through the pages it looked like his dad had gotten everything. There was no mention of Jake, which led Connor to believe he didn't get along well Grandpa Evans either. There was also no mention of this Karen person Sonya had written notes about.

After a few more minutes, Connor switched to the folder of his parents. Within a few seconds of scanning the first couple pages he came across the word "adoption." He sat up straighter and began from the beginning, reading every line no matter how convoluted the wording was. His heart beat faster and his breathing more shallow with every passing second. They were adopting a baby. They were adopting him.

His hands began to shake as he felt like a rug had suddenly been pulled out from beneath him, leaving him falling. They weren't really his mom and dad. Everything he grew up thinking was real was instantly stripped away from him. He desperately kept reading to see if somehow he was wrong and then he saw the name…Karen Unger. She was down on the documents as his birth mother.

He stared at the name and felt an odd empty feeling. This was his mother. Not Mary Evans. Not the woman he grew up thinking was his mother. After long minutes, he began searching for another name. There was no mention of who his biological father was. He looked through the paperwork and found a copy of a birth certificate. No father was recorded.

Underneath this paperwork was more court paperwork and beyond that was a thin file folder. Connor pulled it out and saw sheets of hand written notes. The writing was difficult to read but he gathered that Karen had been living with Will and Mary while she was pregnant and after she gave birth. They weren't living in Ashlin at the time.

Will had contacted the lawyer before Karen gave birth and there was discussion about whether or not to list the father's name on the birth certificate due to the potential adoption. Connor kept searching through the written notes. They knew who the father was. His finger traced line by line until it froze under a name. In this line it was advised that Jake's name not be put on the certificate due to him needing to agree to the adoption and Will was concerned his brother wouldn't.

Connor couldn't see the papers sitting in front of him anymore. Jake was his father. He grabbed the file folder and flung it away from him, papers scattering in every direction. His emotions spiraled out of control as he grabbed anything he could get his hands on. A desktop pen and pencil set was hurled across the room, crashing into the door. A decorative paper weight was sent flying and took out a lamp by the leather sofa. The crystal clock hurtled through the air knocking a painting off the wall.

As Connor grabbed the phone and hoisted it above his head, he took in the devastation he was causing. He paused, panting heavily, and then set the phone back down. He slumped back into the chair, laid his head on the desk and just cried.

CHAPTER FORTY-TWO

Sonya was pacing in front of Madison's door. The doctors wanted no more than two people in at a time and for no more than thirty minutes. She could have taken issue with the sheriff and went in instead of Kerry, but memories of her last time here played on her and the last thing she needed was another breakdown. Knowing Kerry was in there made her feel a bit better.

She looked at her phone. It had been twelve minutes. Two since the last time she looked. If the little girl could identify Jake then it would be over. If she couldn't... Sonya didn't want to go there.

The door suddenly opened and Sheriff Bennett stepped out looking rather frustrated.

"Well?" Sonya asked.

"Madison's not talking. Keeps asking for her mom and dad." He paused, then seemed to grow uncomfortable. "Kerry was thinking you might have better luck. You, uh, being female and all."

Oh, this was killing him and Sonya fought to control the grin tugging at her mouth. "Are you asking for my help, Sheriff?"

His eyes narrowed. "Actually, it seems I'm helping you by allowing you a shot at her. If you're bent on pissing me off, I'm more than happy to wait for them to send up some child psychologist. That could take days. I can wait. I don't think you can."

Sonya's grin faded. Bennett was right. She didn't have time to needle him and needed to play nice. "I'll see what I can do."

An irritating smirk appeared as he nodded. "Much better, Detective." Then he stepped aside and waved his hand toward the door.

Sonya entered the room and saw Kerry had the video camera set up at the foot of the bed. Madison was curled up in a ball with her covers pulled up tight. Sonya felt a tightness in her chest and she began to feel like she couldn't get enough air. Closing her eyes, she focused on relaxing. After half a minute she opened her eyes and made her way to the bed.

"Hey, Skeeter."

The little girl's head lifted a bit at the sound of the familiar nickname, she rolled over a little, and her eyes curiously took in Sonya.

Bolstered by the small response, Sonya took a seat on the edge of her bed. "I was in a hospital once." She began pulling the bottom edge of her t-shirt out of her jeans, then lifted it enough for Madison to see the round scar on her abdomen.

The little girl turned toward Sonya. Her hand snaked out from under the blanket and touched the raised pink puckered skin. "Did it hurt?" she asked in a voice barely above a whisper.

Sonya nodded. "Lots."

"Did you cry?"

Sonya nodded again.

"Did they put a band-aid on it?"

"Yes. A big one like yours."

"Did your mommy come to the hospital?"

"No," Sonya said as she shook her head. "She couldn't come."

"My mommy can't come either."

Sonya wasn't sure how much the staff had told Madison about her parents, so she didn't pursue the subject. "I want to ask you some questions. Is that okay?"

Madison nodded and Sonya signaled Kerry to start the video camera.

"Do you remember the night you were hurt?"

She nodded.

"Tell me about it."

"Daddy and Connor were shooting guns in the house."

"How do you know they were shooting guns?"

"Because the bangs. I don't like the guns. They scare me. Mommy's going to be mad they were shooting in the house."

"What did you do when you heard the bangs?"

"I hid."

"Where did you hide?"

"In my closet."

"Did you see who came into your room."

Madison shook her head.

"How come you didn't see?"

"I was hiding under my blanket."

"Did you peek even a little bit?"

Madison shook her head. After a pause, she asked, "Is he going to get in trouble?"

"Who?"

"Connor."

Sonya couldn't help but tense. She had a bad feeling she should have signaled Kerry to stop the tape a couple questions back. "Why do you think Connor will get in trouble?"

"It was an accident."

"What was an accident?"

"He didn't know I was there. He didn't mean to shoot me."

Sonya kept her voice steady. "Why do you think he shot you?"

Madison pulled out a now slightly crumpled purple paper crane. "He brought me this and said he was sorry."

CHAPTER FORTY-THREE

Connor lifted his head from the desk. He didn't know how long he had been laying there, but it must have been awhile. His tears had long dried. The little scraps of yellow paper caught his attention once again. He pushed the ones that had anything to do with what he already knew to the side and focused on what was left.

One piece had a partial "4" next to "Ave. B, Kim..." The rest was lost but Connor was willing to bet it was an address in Kimball County. Another scrap had "...en Har..." with a cut off letter that could be a "p."

Connor stared at the scraps and his hand drifted toward the phone, his fingers hovering for long seconds as his thoughts battled each other. He snatched the phone from its cradle and quickly dialed, feeling he was balancing on the edge of a knife. Part of him wished it would go to voicemail. If it did, it would give him time to think about what he was planning to do. A few seconds later, though, he heard a familiar, "Yo," and his decision was made.

"Hey, Mike. I need you to ditch and pick me up."

"Connor?" It came out in a whispered hiss.

"Yeah."

"Where you at?"

"Dandridge and Dandridge."

"The law office? What the hell you doing there?"

"Just come get me."

"I'll be there in five."

"Park between Dandridge's office and Taylor's Appliances. I'll meet you."

"You got it." There was a pause. "Are you okay?"

"Yeah."

"You don't sound…"

Connor hung up before Mike's words were finished, then went to the window to wait. In less than five minutes he heard the familiar rumble of his friend's truck, then he pushed back the blinds and stepped through the open window. He walked swiftly to the truck and once inside, simply said, "Head towards Kimball County."

Mike just nodded, made a u-turn in the street, and started driving without a word.

Connor picked up Mike's phone that was setting in a cup holder and got on the internet. He began to plug in the bits of information he had. Nothing came up for Karen Unger. He entered Karen Harp, Ave. B, and Kimball County. After a few tries on various sites something popped up for a Karen Harper, 1684 Ave. B in Kimball County.

He reached behind him for Mike's backpack and pulled out a notebook and pen. He ripped out a piece of paper and his hand shook as he wrote down the address and looked up directions. Once finished writing everything down, he handed Mike the paper. "I need to go here," he said quietly.

Mike looked at the paper briefly. "Yeah. No problem." As he drove down the open highway, Mike kept giving him sidelong glances but made no attempt to talk to him.

Connor turned his head to avoid the glances and stared out the passenger window. The rolling fields covered with dried brown stalks from the last harvest of the season lay waiting for the blanketing snow that was on its way. The sky was clouding up again and the temperature was dropping. Not enough for snow, but enough to let you know it was coming and soon. His time was running out. The weather, if nothing else, would see to that.

Once in Kimball County and coming up on the county seat, Mike started looking at the paper more closely, making sure he knew what street names he was looking for. "Is this a business, a home, or what?"

"I don't know. A home, I think."

Since he got a response to the question, Mike braved another. "Who is this Karen Harper?"

Connor's stomach clenched suddenly. He shrugged and went back to looking out the window.

Mike let out a disgruntled, "Right," and lapsed back into silence.

The directions took them out of the populated area and set them driving once again through rolling fields. They drove for another twenty minutes as the sky continued to darken. Drops began to intermittently hit the windshield as they peered out to catch numbers on the widely spaced mailboxes.

Mike suddenly stopped the truck and left it idling in front of the dirt drive. "This is it. Do you want me to pull in?"

Connor shook his head as he looked down the drive toward the dilapidated light blue and white mobile home. A small, thin woman was hurriedly trying to take laundry off the line as more drops began to fall and barely gave the truck a glance. Her hair was pulled back in a messy ponytail and a toddler hanging onto her leg was slowing her progress. She pushed the toddler away and began yelling toward the mobile.

Two older kids emerged, a boy and a girl. The girl began lugging the screaming toddler away while the boy tried helping to take down the laundry but was too short to reach the clothes pins. The woman finally thrust the nearly full laundry basket at the boy and gave him a shove toward the mobile.

Connor got out of the truck and began walking down the drive. Rain was starting to fall harder and the woman was losing the battle in saving the rest of the laundry. Hearing his approach, she turned as she was still attempting to rescue one more sheet from the line. The wind had picked up and the sheet flapped up, obscuring her view of Connor.

"Can I help you?" she asked while batting down the sheet so she could get a better view of the approaching person.

Connor didn't respond as he came to a stop outside of the reach of the flapping sheet, just a few feet away from the woman. Having grabbed the loose edges, she held them down as she focused her attention on the person in front of her. The irritated questioning look was replaced by narrowed eyes that roved his face. After a moment, her eyes widened and her mouth dropped open.

He wanted to say something to her but he hadn't thought this far ahead. They just stared at each other, vaguely aware of a screen door slamming and the approach of the boy. "Who's that, Mama?" he asked.

The words seemed to break the trance and she blinked a few times. Her voice was unemotional as she never broke eye contact with Connor. "Nobody. He's nobody."

Connor couldn't breathe.

She looked down at the boy standing next to her as the sky let loose. "Get back in the house," she told him. She gave Connor one more brief glance before hurrying after the boy.

Connor stood there watching her leave as the rain began to soak his clothes. She made it to the door and stepped inside. He saw her watching him through the screen door until he heard Mike shout his name from the truck, then she quickly shut the door.

Vaguely he became aware of someone shaking his shoulders and calling his name. Connor turned and saw Mike standing next to him, concern deeply etched on his features. "Come back to the truck, Connor."

Connor didn't move until Mike physically turned him around, grabbed his shoulders, and forced him toward the truck. Somehow Connor got his legs to work enough to make the trek back.

Once in the truck, Mike cranked the heater on high as drops fell from his wet dark hair. He removed his soaked sweatshirt then turned in his seat to face Connor, his patience gone. "What the fuck is going on? I've played along with this little road trip of yours and now I want some fucking answers. Who the hell was that? Was that Karen Harper?"

Connor began to shake as he opened his mouth but no words came.

Mike's anger ebbed and his voice fell lower. "Who is she?"

Connor knew he had to say the words even though he was afraid of what would happen when he did. He looked at Mike and drew in a shuddering breath. "Dandridge's. I found I was adopted. She's…she's my mother." Connor only caught a glimpse of the confusion on Mike's face before his eyes closed. He wanted all this to go away. It was stupid of him to come. What did he expect to happen? This on top of everything else was just becoming too much. His body shook more as he felt himself falling apart.

He heard Mike curse then felt his friend's arm wrap around him. He offered no resistance as he was pulled against Mike's chest. Without giving a second thought to his pride, Connor clutched his friend's shirt and proceeded to soak it more than what the rain had already done.

CHAPTER FORTY-FOUR

Sonya was quiet as Kerry began the drive back to Ashlin. Dark clouds had rolled in and she watched the wipers make their measured passes on the windshield. She hated to admit she was counting on Madison to remember something from the night that would've been helpful. Not seeing who shot her and thinking it was Connor was worse than getting absolutely nothing.

Kerry glanced at her. "I think you really need to think about throwing the towel in on this one, Sonya."

"Just because Madison can't identify Jake as the guy doesn't mean it's over."

"All that videotape succeeded in doing was to link Connor's name to the crime. At this point you're actually making negative progress, if that's at all possible. The only thing worse would've been if he was actually stupid enough to go to the hospital."

Sonya closed her eyes and pinched the bridge of her nose.

Kerry caught her response. "Jesus. You've got to be kidding me." He shook his head. "If they run the hospital's security footage and see him even on the premises it's going to look bad."

Sonya tossed her head back and let out a humorless chuckle. "Oh, imagine how going in her room will look."

"How the hell...? Never mind. I don't want to know."

"This still isn't over. Tomorrow I'm going to follow up on the alibi."

"Yeah, about that..." Kerry's lips pressed into a hard line.

Sonya was afraid to ask. "What?"

"I talked with Dr. Veckle again. He insists he saw Jake that night at his house making a delivery. Jake's alibi still stands."

"Damn," Sonya said while slumping in her seat.

"The hard evidence still implicates Connor. The stuff you have so far could be pure coincidence. It's time you start to face the fact you aren't going to get him off. It won't be long before he figures that out for himself."

"He doesn't know anything about the case."

"Maybe. But if I were in his shoes I'd start taking matters into my own hands. Especially if I felt you knew stuff and weren't sharing. He's smart enough to get himself in trouble. Obviously. And it's only a matter of time before he gets in trouble again."

Sonya remained silent.

Kerry let out a drawn out sigh. "I get you want to solve this case. I get that it is important enough to you to risk your career. I don't understand any of it, but I get it. But is it worth risking Connor's safety?" Kerry added quietly, " You need to arrest him, Sonya."

Sonya fell silent, then finally muttered, "I don't even know where he is."

Kerry let out a soft snort. "I have a feeling he'll make his way back to you even though I told him to stay the hell away." He shook his head. "You two are a pair to draw to. The detective and the delinquent."

Sonya's phone rang and displayed a number she didn't recognize. "Detective Reisler," she answered.

"Hello, Detective Reisler. This is Thomas Dandridge."

"How can I help you, Mr. Dandridge?"

"My office was broken into sometime today. Well, my father's office to be exact. I wanted to call you before I called the sheriff. I'm pretty sure it was Connor Evans."

Sonya closed her eyes and took in a steadying breath. "What makes you think so?"

"Two file folders with the name Evans on them were removed from the file cabinet. The one held information about his grandfather's will but the other had all the adoption paperwork."

"I'm about thirty minutes outside of Ashlin. Can you hold off on the call till I get there? I have a deputy with me."

"Sure. I'll be here."

"Thanks," she said and hung up. Immediately a slew of curses streamed from her mouth.

Kerry glanced over and raised an eyebrow. "I take that as not being a good phone call."

"I need you to take me to Dandridge and Dandridge."

"Why?"

"His office was broken into."

"Connor?"

Sonya rubbed her temple in slow circles. "More than likely." Kerry started opening his mouth but Sonya cut him off. "Don't even say anything." Her warning tone was enough to keep him silent but did nothing to keep him from shaking his head in an irritating "I told you so" kind of way.

They arrived at the law office after a rather silent drive and were greeted by Thomas Dandridge. He led Sonya and Kerry back to his father's office. Once through the door, Kerry let out a long low whistle.

Sonya's chest tightened as she took in the damage as she walked around the office. This wasn't Connor. At least the one she knew.

"He came in through the window," Thomas said.

Sonya and Kerry walked over to the open window. "Looks like the window was alarmed. Was the system turned on?" Kerry asked Thomas.

"Yes, it was."

Sonya looked at the lower magnetic sensor and removed a thin metal strip. "He bypassed it."

Kerry took the metal piece from Sonya. "Why would he come here?"

Sonya wandered over to the desk and some yellow pieces of paper caught her attention. She instantly recognized them. "Oh, God."

Kerry looked at the pieces of torn paper and smattering of words.

"They're my case notes. He came to find answers I wouldn't give him."

"From the looks of the place, I think he found some of them." Kerry continued looking over the scraps of paper. "This was about the adoption, wasn't it?"

Sonya walked around the desk, knelt down, and was looking over the papers scattered on the floor. "He shouldn't have found out like this."

"But he did and racked up more charges to boot. Sonya…"

"I know. I know." She took one more glance of the office. "I'm going to go, Kerry."

"Call if you need anything."

Sonya nodded and headed for the front. Stepping out of the building, she saw the rain had stopped. She'd gone a few yards when a truck pulled up alongside her and the window rolled down. Sonya looked over and saw it was Mike.

"Can we talk?" he asked.

Sonya climbed into his truck. "What's up?"

"Connor had me drive him to Kimball County."

"Oh, my God," Sonya said as her hand went to her head. "Did he see Karen Harper? Did he try talking to her?"

Mike nodded. "She wouldn't talk to him. He said she's his mother. Is that true?"

"Yeah," Sonya said. "Where is he now?"

"That's what I want to tell you. We got into town and I'm at a stop and he just opens the door and gets out. Just starts walking down the street. Not caring who's around. Not caring if he's seen. I tried to park and go after him but I couldn't find him." Mike paused. "I've never seen him like this. I'm worried about him, Sonya."

Sonya's eyes made a sweeping glance of the darkening streets. "Me too."

CHAPTER FORTY-FIVE

Mike dropped Sonya off at her apartment. As she was unlocking the door her phone began to ring. Opening the door, she looked at the screen.

"Hi, Ray," she answered as she stepped in, closed the door behind her, and leaned against it.

"You don't sound too happy."

"I'm not. I just got back from the hospital. The little girl can't identify the shooter."

"Then what I'm going to tell you next isn't going to help your mood."

Sonya braced herself.

"Peterson reviewed what you sent in. He says you need to produce something solid by end of day tomorrow or you're coming home."

"Tomorrow? You said I had a week."

"Tomorrow is day six already and Peterson is over me. It's his call."

Closing her eyes, she bit down hard on her lower lip to keep herself from going off.

"Listen. You catch a break tomorrow, and it's something you can sell him, you can probably get a few more days."

"I don't know where else to look, Ray."

"What about Jake Evans' alibi?"

"A deputy double checked it for me. The alibi still stands."

He paused. "I'm sorry, Sonya."

Sonya appreciated the simplicity of his words. He knew better than to give her the "we can't win them all" bullshit, but she still wasn't in the mood to be consoled. "I'm going to go."

"Okay. Just remember no…"

"No drinking. I know the drill, Ray," she snapped and promptly disconnected the call. She let her head thud once against the door before pushing off from it and headed to the couch. Sonya set her notebook on the coffee table, then promptly picked it up and threw it across the room with a yell.

"Sounds like I'm not the only one having a crappy day."

Sonya's hand immediately went for her gun but was stilled as she recognized the voice emanating from the kitchen. She cautiously rounded the corner of cabinets and saw Connor sitting on the floor with his back against the wall. A soaked sweatshirt was balled up next to him and his hair was sticking out at odd angles as if recently rubbed in an attempt to get it dry.

"But I'd still be willing to bet mine was crappier," he said.

"Probably."

His eyes locked with hers. "How long have you known?"

"A few days."

"Why didn't you tell me?"

"Because I didn't think you would handle it too well right now."

He let out a wry chuckle. "Guess you're right on that one. How does one handle having his whole world ripped from him? Not just once but twice. That everyone has lied to me. Making me think I'm someone when I'm not. My real parents want nothing to do with me while the ones I thought were my parents are both dead. And the best part in all this is finding out that fucking saying about apples and trees is true. How do you handle all that because I'm not doing a great job."

His volume had slowly risen and Sonya watched the different emotions play across his face as he fought to control them. "Will and Mary were your real parents and they loved you. Skeeter still loves you," she said softly. "That's the truth in all of this. That's all that matters when everything is said and done."

Connor pushed himself up from the floor and stood, his expression unreadable. "All I know, right now, is that I'm done."

Sonya's brows drew together. "What do you mean?"

"I'm tired. Tired of running. Tired of hiding. That's why I came back." He slowly walked towards her, reached out, and removed the set of handcuffs from her belt. He held them out to her. "I want you to arrest me. I need this to be over."

Sonya just stared at him, making no move to take the cuffs.

After a few seconds, Connor shrugged, withdrew the cuffs, and snapped one onto his wrist, then turned and placed both hands behind his back. "Do it, Sonya. You know it needs to be done."

Sonya stepped behind him and took hold of the empty cuff dangling from his wrist. She held it but made no attempt at securing it to his other wrist. She dropped her head until it rested between his shoulder blades. "This isn't the answer."

Connor spun around and glared at her. "What is the answer, Sonya? From what I overheard, it sounds like you haven't come up with one. This investigation isn't going to go on past tomorrow and I don't think I can handle you digging up any more secrets about my life. I don't even know who the fuck I am anymore."

She focused her eyes on his. "You're not Jake Evans." She watched his anger and composure crumble at her words.

"I...I don't know that."

"Yes, you do," Sonya said and reached out, laying her hand against the side of his face. He closed his eyes and pressed his cheek against her palm. She felt him trembling. Before she thought about what she was doing, she drew her face closer to his and kissed him.

His response was immediate as he brought his hands up to hold her face to his and moved his lips against hers.

The better part of her knew this wasn't a good idea for either of them and she withdrew from him.

Connor leaned forward and rested his forehead on hers. "Don't stop. God, please don't stop."

The desperation and need in his plea had her resolve collapsing faster than a house of cards and she began to kiss him again. He matched her kisses and they quickly became deep and heated. As she pulled his shirt up and over his head, she made it clear she had no intention of stopping anything.

CHAPTER FORTY-SIX

Connor watched his fingers trace over the scar on Sonya's abdomen, then travel over her skin to touch the one on her chest. The handcuff trailed behind over the path his fingers took. He wasn't sure if it was his touch or the cold metal that caused her to shiver, but she didn't stop him from his curious exploration.

He felt calm and a certain sense of peace as he felt Sonya's warm skin beneath his fingers. Tomorrow wasn't completely absent from his thoughts, but for now he was more than happy to be lying here with Sonya.

Recognizing the scars for what they were, he looked into her eyes. "Tell me."

Sonya stiffened, then shrugged and looked away from him. "Not much to tell."

A moment ago he would have been willing to bet she got shot while making a bust and was trying to be low-key about it, but something was off. He brought his hand up alongside her cheek, turning her so she was looking at him again. "Someone put two bullets in you. There's plenty to tell."

She stayed silent but Connor wouldn't let her escape his gaze. "Tell me," he said softly.

She swallowed once and her face became a mask devoid of any emotion. "I was eight."

Connor's brows drew together. He really wanted to know the story but those first three words left him feeling unsure this was a good idea.

Sonya continued without missing a beat leaving him no option but to listen. "My parents were meth dealers. We lived in a mobile out in Cheyenne County. It was pretty remote. Better the chances of their lab not being discovered. I hid a lot... from the fights...the strangers who'd come to buy."

Sonya closed her eyes to him. "One of their customers showed up sounding angry. I hid under my bed. I covered my ears but it didn't help. They were all yelling then suddenly it got quiet. There were two loud bangs. My mother started screaming and then there were two more bangs. It was so quiet, then I heard his footsteps coming toward my room. I tried not to breathe but he found me. He took hold of my leg and dragged me out. He stood over me and pointed the gun. 'Sorry, kid,' was all he said before he shot me twice. I remember seeing him walk out of my room, then hearing the screen door slam."

She opened her eyes and looked at Connor. "Another one of their customers found me and called the police. He didn't want to be busted so after he made the call he left me there, alone, to wait for them to come. They got me to the hospital in time." She grew silent, her story over for now.

Connor didn't know how to respond. She was completely detached, reporting it like it was someone else's life, not hers. What bothered him more was her face remained devoid of emotion as she stared back at him. There was nothing he trusted himself to say at this moment, so he kissed her.

He worried when she didn't kiss him back but slowly he began to feel her returning to him. Soon she was right there with him, kissing him with an urgency as if he could fill some emptiness the story left behind. Connor felt her pulling him on top of her as her legs drew up alongside his hips. She broke the kiss long enough to let out a breathy, "Need you."

The words and look heated him and he took the lead in their coming together. Through every kiss and touch, he gave her everything he could of himself and hoped she understood how much he needed her too.

CHAPTER FORTY-SEVEN

Sonya stirred from her sleep. She opened her eyes and took in a soundly sleeping Connor Evans. She carefully got out of bed so as not to disturb him and made her way to the dresser, dodging various pieces of clothing that had been hastily discarded last night. She quietly opened drawers, pulled some things out, and dressed quickly, deciding she would shower later. She needed to get out of there for awhile.

Morning afters were not something Sonya hung around to experience and she was an expert at making stealthy escapes. This time she was doing it more out of habit. After all, Connor was in her bed and he wasn't going anywhere.

She left a note on her pillow for Connor telling him she would be back soon and headed out of the apartment, locking the door behind her. It was chilly this morning with a light layer of frost covering vehicles and roofs. She zipped up her leather jacket and set out at a brisk pace down the sidewalk, texting Mike as she went to let him know Connor was with her and safe. In a few minutes she arrived at Lydia's Bakery.

She opened the door, setting off the jingling bells, and immediately was comforted by the smell of coffee and doughnuts. Lydia came out from the back and smiled at her. "What can I get for you this morning?"

Sonya smiled back at her. "I'll let you take a guess."

"Custard doughnut and a large coffee?"

"You got it, but make it two of each and I'll take it to go."

"Coming right up." Then Lydia gave her a wink. "You take Kerry up on his offer of trying to break you of your doughnut eating habit?"

"I think it will take him more than two doughnuts."

Lydia laughed. "I'm sure he's more than willing to keep trying."

A low rumble started to grow outside of the shop. Sonya looked out the window and soon saw two large heavy-looking vehicles lumber down the street. They were followed by three pickup trucks and two jeeps. They all had an insignia with the words "Landmark Oil" on their doors.

Lydia was shaking her head as she was putting the doughnuts in a small box. "Lord, not those vibrator trucks again."

Sonya looked at her questioningly.

"Seeing them means another ranch is thinking of selling out."

"To Landmark Oil?"

Lydia nodded and began pouring the coffee. "Started a few years back. The company came in and started offering free oil surveys for ranchers interested in maybe selling out. They find potential for oil, then they make an offer. Usually they pay out two to three times what the land is worth. They've bought up about four large spreads around here."

Sonya became quiet as she absorbed the information. At length she asked, "Was Will Evans interested in selling?"

"Don't really know," Lydia said as she placed the coffee cups in a cardboard carrier.

Sonya tossed quite a few creamers and packs of sugars into the empty spots in the carrier. "You said Landmark buys ranches. They don't buy farms?"

"Ranch land is cheap by comparison. It's usually not suitable for farming. More rocky, hilly, and such. I suppose it would take larger offers to get farmers interested in selling."

Sonya handed Lydia some money. "Thanks, Lydia. For the goodies and the info."

"You have a good day, honey," she said, handing Sonya the change.

"You, too," Sonya said as she left the shop. She mulled this bit of news over in her mind until she reached Ashlin Tool and Hardware. Her steps slowed as she eyed the stairs leading to the apartment. She took a deep breath before climbing them. No escaping what happened last night.

She let herself back in and went to the kitchen. She set the coffee and small box on the table, then removed her jacket, draping it on the back of a chair. A noise made her look up.

A still sleepy looking Connor, wearing only boxers and a t-shirt, came shuffling out of the hall. The handcuff was still dangling from his wrist. His eyes briefly met hers and he gave her a soft, "Hey."

Sonya mirrored his greeting as she opened the box with the doughnuts and removed the two cups of coffee from the holder.

Connor pulled out a chair and sat at the table. He seemed quiet and cautious, not sure of how to handle this morning after either it seemed.

She came over to him with the handcuff key and he quirked his eyebrows at her. "I have till the end of the day before I have to arrest you," she said as she tapped the table top with her fingers. He brought his hand up and set his wrist on the table. She unlocked the cuff and saw the reddened and bruised skin underneath. She gave it a light touch before putting the cuffs back on her belt.

He gave a small smirk as he rubbed his wrist. "No big deal. I've had worse."

Sonya went and set a coffee and a couple of napkins in front of him. "I know this isn't much of a breakfast, but I felt like sugar and caffeine this morning."

"Works for me," he said. Leaning forward, he peered into the doughnut box and began to smile. He lifted one of the custard doughnuts out and immediately flipped it upside down.

Sonya smiled as she took a seat and watched as he pulled a piece of the bottom off and put it in his mouth.

He looked up and saw her watching him. "I know this looks weird."

Sonya shook her head as she turned her doughnut over. "I eat them that way, too."

He smiled at her and they slipped into silence as they ate their doughnuts and sipped on coffee. Once the doughnuts were gone, she began thinking about what Lydia told her. "What do you know about Landmark Oil?"

Connor shrugged as he swirled his coffee around. "They've bought a few ranches in the last three or four years. The ranch next to ours sold out to them a couple years ago."

"Did your dad ever express interest in selling?"

"No way. He tried to talk Bernbauer out of selling but the offer was too good. They even contacted my dad quite a few times to set up a survey. He always said no."

Sonya grew quiet as she thought about this.

Connor raised an eyebrow. "Do you think you might have found something?"

"Maybe."

He leaned back in his chair. "You're not going to tell me anything, are you?"

Sonya shook her head. "Not yet," she said quietly.

Connor didn't look too happy with her response, but didn't press the issue. After a time his face became serious from whatever thoughts he was having and Sonya grew nervous. He opened his mouth to say something but she beat him to it.

"I'd better get ready," she said as she stood. "I want to get some things checked out today."

He nodded, remained silent, and started cleaning off the table.

Sonya went back to the bedroom, once again stepping around the scattered clothing items. She picked up quite a few as she went, as if it would help erase what happened last night, and dumped them into the closet. Turning to the bed, she was finishing straightening the sheets when Connor entered the bedroom. He looked like he definitely had something on his mind and Sonya was sure she didn't want to know what it was.

"Last night…" His voice came across tentative. "Was it because you didn't want me to turn myself in?"

Sonya looked away from him. This wasn't a conversation she wanted to have, and was exactly why she never hung around after sleeping with someone.

He came closer to her. "I just want to know if last night was about me or was it just about the case?"

She closed her eyes to block him out. *It's the case. Just tell him it's the case and be done with it.* But the words wouldn't come. Sensing him coming even closer, she began to tremble when his fingers touched her face. Then she felt his lips on hers and he began to kiss her.

Sonya began kissing him back knowing she was answering his question whether she really wanted to or not. The floor once again became littered with their discarded clothes before they fell onto the bed. As the sheets twisted around them, Sonya knew the case was becoming the lesser of her problems right now.

CHAPTER FORTY-EIGHT

After she and Connor got out of bed for the second time that morning and showered, Sonya made quick progress on tracking down the ranch Landmark was surveying today. Connor was familiar with the place and sketched out a map and directions for her. Before she left, he had promised to stay put and told her he was ready for what the end of the day would bring. As she got into her car, she found she was not feeling the same and was hoping this would turn into the break she desperately needed.

As she drew closer, Sonya saw a large number of cattle grazing on the open land of the ranch she was heading for. In the distance she saw some of Landmark's vehicles and heard a large boom. The cows bolted in the opposite direction of the noise. She slowed down her car and watched as they banged into each other in their frantic escape. She remembered what Connor said about spooked cows not caring what was in their way.

Sonya parked her car at an open section of fence and began her trek toward the vehicles congregated on the property, a couple hundred yards away from the road. As she walked she noticed blue metal discs set in the ground every hundred feet or so with wires strung between them, connecting them to each other. She saw a green portable canopy and started heading toward it.

The closer she got she saw a table where a guy was seated and busily working on his laptop. He looked fairly young, late twenties maybe. His thin build, round glasses, and lengthy brown hair curling out from the sides of the hardhat he wore made him look more computer geek than oil worker.

He glanced up, then left his seat, hurrying towards her. "Hey, Miss, I'm going to have to ask you to leave. You can't be in this area without a hardhat."

Sonya held up her badge. "Maybe you can give me one."

The man glanced between her and the badge a couple times before motioning her to follow him. He walked over to the pickup, lifted the lid off of a tool box, reached in, and plucked out a hard hat. He handed it to her and she placed it on her head.

"We have all the necessary permits. I can show you them. They're right inside the truck," he said while grabbing the door handle.

"That's okay. I believe you."

He looked at her skeptically. "You here to inspect something?"

"Actually I'm conducting an investigation and I wanted some information on your company."

"Alright, but would you mind if I finish taking readings of this area first? It should only be another fifteen minutes. Then we'll be moving and setting up in another area and I'll have time to talk."

"Sure."

He smiled. "Thanks."

He went back over to the portable table and Sonya followed. He sat in front of his computer and signaled the driver of the large truck. Soon Sonya felt the ground shake beneath her feet. She watched the flurry of activity on the computer screen. After ten or so minutes went by, he signaled again and the truck stopped.

One of the other men came up to the guy at the computer. "How'd it look?"

"Good. We can move to the next spot."

The man turned and began calling out orders and a flurry of activity ensued. Men began disassembling the surveying tripods and coiling up the hundreds of yards of wires that connected all the blue discs. Some men began pulling up the blue discs and Sonya could see they were actually fancy-looking metal stakes.

The man at the computer turned to Sonya. "Sorry. I didn't introduce myself. I'm Brent. Brent Davis," he said while pushing his glasses further up on his nose.

"Detective Reisler," Sonya replied.

"We only have two days to get this done so I got to keep it moving. Each spot takes two hours or so to set up and this is a large property."

"So what exactly are you doing?"

"Conducting a seismic survey that will get converted into a 3-D seismic image." He chuckled at Sonya's expression, then tapped a few keys on his laptop. He turned it toward Sonya so she could see the colorful 3-D image. "I map what the underground looks like."

"That finds oil?"

"Well, it finds if the conditions are good to *maybe* find oil."

"What do you look for?"

"Certain types of rocks that form structural traps for oil deposits. The vibrations produced by the truck travel through the earth and bounce off the rocks and are picked up by the sensors we've placed around the area. The faster or slower they travel gives me a picture of what's underground."

"I take it Landmark Oil has been liking your pictures."

He smiled while giving his glasses another push. "This area has been very good for the company. Large areas of limestone capped by shale."

"Meaning a good amount of oil?"

Brent nodded. "The properties they bought have been producing well."

"I heard they pay two to three times the property value to those looking to sell."

"Usually two. The company wants to maintain a good profit margin."

"Does that include the Bernbauer ranch?"

"That is one of the better ones. Landmark paid him three times the value."

"Why?"

"The anticline formations are great." He once again laughed at the look she threw him. "It's like an upside down bowl trapping all the oil. Not only that but we've had positive signs of layering. That means when one layer taps out we can drill down to another."

"I've heard only one in ten wells yield oil."

"Our average is better than that in this area. We got it at about one in three. But there are still times where we miss. In fact, on one edge of the Bernbauer property, we detected the start of an extremely large anticline formation. We tried drilling into it by getting as close to the property line as we could, but no luck. Couldn't tap into it. Frustrating as hell being so close."

"So you would need the other property to drill into this supposed gold mine."

"Exactly. We've been trying for two years to get it, but the owner hasn't been interested. Don't know why. Landmark tentatively offered to pay four times the market value."

Sonya's eyebrows raised. "That's a lot of money."

Brent nodded. "A little over a million dollars."

"Wow," Sonya said. "But you said, 'tentatively.'"

"Nothing is firm until the survey comes back. But, I think we're making progress with the guy."

"How's that?"

"He finally allowed us to do a survey in September."

Sonya's brows suddenly furrowed. "Did it happen over the Labor Day weekend?"

"Yeah. Not an ideal time but we jumped on the opportunity. He said it was best his wife didn't know and they were heading out of town that weekend."

She asked the question even though she knew the answer. "Who owns the ranch?"

"William Evans."

CHAPTER FORTY-NINE

Sonya got the name and number of the man at Landmark who was responsible for property acquisitions from Brent. She swung by her place to drop some lunch off for Connor and to pick up her laptop. She told him she would be gone most of the afternoon following up on what she learned. He just nodded in response and didn't ask any questions.

With Connor staying at her place, she had no choice but to head to the sheriff's station to do her work. Deputy Moore didn't pay much attention to her as she set up her stuff on the far empty desk. Glancing around, he seemed to be the only one in the station besides the temporary receptionist who was busy making a fresh pot of coffee.

After getting set up, she pulled out her cell phone. She scrolled through her contacts and paused before tapping the one she wanted. She bit her bottom lip as it rang.

After a couple of rings the call was picked up. "Decided you're talking to me today?" Ray only sounded slightly miffed even though he had every right to be a few clicks beyond miffed.

"Sorry about yesterday. It wasn't a good day."

He let out a soft humph. "This one looking better?"

"Maybe. I might have gotten a break on finding a motive. A company called Landmark Oil has been doing free oil surveys in this area and making offers on ranches they think will be good producers. They usually pay two to three times the market value."

"Tell me more."

"The ranch next to the Evans' sold two years ago for triple market value. Landmark contacted William Evans several times to do a survey, but he always said no. I spoke to this guy who runs the surveys and he says that William Evans asked them to do a survey over Labor Day weekend while they were out of town. Said he didn't want the wife to know. The survey came back good and Landmark is willing to pay a little over a million dollars for the property."

"Sounds like the money got too good to pass up and Will was planning to sell."

"But that's just it. Will would never sell. He's personally invested in that place. For two years he turned down the survey requests and then suddenly he okays one a month before his death? I think Jake knew the family would be out of town and contacted Landmark posing as Will."

"Don't you think that's a bit of a stretch?"

"No it's not. This whole thing has been in the works for at least two years. He works at Harris's Feed and Farm Supply. Plenty of opportunity to hear what Landmark is doing with what ranches. He conveniently became the alcohol supplier to Connor's group of friends and became chummy with one of them so he could get information on the family and Connor's comings and goings. He has been flying under the radar here in town. Not been in a lick of trouble since moving here so no eyes would fall on him as a suspect. Having it look like Connor killed his family would look more realistic than the whole family being killed by some mysterious stranger. Connor wouldn't be able to inherit anything if convicted leaving Jake free to while away the time until probate would give him the ranch."

"Why take the risk of posing as Will and the risk of authorizing a survey?"

"No offers are guaranteed without a survey. He had to make sure the money was going to be there before committing murder."

"He's not going to get anything with the little girl alive."

"He still needs Connor to take the fall to keep himself free and clear to be able to try again."

"You think he will go after the little girl in the future?"

"Definitely. He's patient, smart, and she's in the way."

There was a pause. "What do you need me to do?"

"I need you to get warrants for the phone records of William and Jake. I want to see if either of them were calling Landmark. I'm hoping I can tie Jake to requesting the survey."

"I'll get on it."

"I'm going to call Landmark and see what other information I can get out of them."

"I'll send the records as soon as I get them and you let me know how that call goes, good or bad."

"I will and thanks."

As soon as she got off the phone with Ray she pulled out the number Brent had given her and tapped the numbers in.

Quite a few rings later she got a man's voice. "Adam Kendall."

"Good afternoon, Mr. Kendall. This is Detective Reisler with the Nebraska State Patrol. I'm investigating the murder of William Evans. Your company was interested in purchasing his property."

"Still are, but very unfortunate about Mr. Evans."

"How did you find out about his death?"

"It was quite the news story, but I also got a call from his brother, Jacob. He said that he would be the one to go through now. He made it clear he was interested in going through with the offer and would contact us when the transition of title was finalized."

"When did he call?"

"A few days after his brother's passing."

"Brent Davis said Landmark was willing to pay three to four times market value for the Evans' ranch."

"Ends up being four. Will wouldn't take less and the survey came back good. Really good. We weren't going to quibble over the price."

"Did you ever meet with him in person?"

"Once when we were out at the ranch next to his. That was a couple years ago. We asked then if he was interested in a survey."

"What was his response?"

"A resounding no."

"What made him change his mind?"

"Said he got thinking about the money and wanted to get out of ranching."

"Why did he want the survey done on Labor Day weekend?"

"He said his wife wasn't keen on selling and he wanted to wait for a firm offer from us. Figured seeing the actual dollar amount would sway her."

"You don't think it odd he changed his mind?"

"Not particularly. That's why we keep in contact. More often than not people see we're offering them an easier way of making money. It just ends up making sense."

"So all this contact with William Evans was by phone?"

"Yes. He first contacted us at the end of July. Insisted we call the number he provided. No calls to the house or anything mailed that the wife would pick up on."

"Do you happen to have that number you used?"

"Give me a few seconds to look it up." There was a brief pause. "Here it is." He read off the number while Sonya copied it down.

"Did he have to sign any documents regarding the survey?"

"Yes. Release of Liability forms and such."

"How'd you get them to him?"

"Mailed them to a P.O. Box, if I remember correctly."

"Didn't you think the secrecy and arrangements odd?"

Adam gave a short chuckle. "My job is to acquire properties. If he wanted them delivered via singing telegram, I would've dressed in drag and belted out, 'Man I Feel Like a Woman,' if he wanted."

Sonya couldn't help but roll her eyes. "Could I get the P.O. Box address?"

"Yeah. Hang on a sec." Adam came back in a minute later and read off the address. It was in Ashlin.

"I would also like a copy of those documents he signed. Could you scan and email them to me?"

"Sure."

"Also, would it be possible to get phone records for your company dating from July to now?"

"I'll have to contact admin so it might take awhile, but I'll get it out to you."

Sonya gave him her email address and thanked him for the information.

While waiting for Adam's email to come in, Sonya called Thomas Dandridge and asked him to scan and send her Will's signature page from his will. He said he would do that. Sonya looked at the phone number Adam had provided her. She dialed it and was immediately greeted with a message saying the number was no longer in service.

Soon her email popped up with an attachment from Thomas and, shortly after that, one came in from Adam. Sonya pulled both documents up to compare the signatures. They were similar. Not enough difference to make forgery glaringly obvious. Sonya forwarded both documents to Ray to have him get the signatures analyzed.

Since she had to wait anyways for the phone records to come in from Ray and Adam, Sonya headed over to the post office. When she entered there were a couple people ahead of her being waited on by a slender middle-aged man wearing dark grey pants and a light blue shirt with United States Postal Service embroidered on it.

When it was finally Sonya's turn, he greeted her with a warm smile which looked natural on his face. "How can I help you?"

She showed him her badge. "I'm Detective Reisler and I would like to know who is renting box thirty-four."

The man turned to a computer and started tapping. "Looks like no one."

"Can you tell me when it was last rented?"

"Looks like it was rented for three months. July, August, and September of this year."

"Who rented it?"

"Jesse Aldrich."

The last name piqued Sonya's interest. "Do you know where I can find him or her?"

"It's a him and I can give you his home address. He still lives with his folks. Probably why he got the box."

"What do you mean?"

The man glanced at the screen and started writing on a piece of paper as he responded. "I get some young people come in sometimes to get a box if they want to get packages their parents wouldn't approve of. Three months is the minimum so usually they go in on it with some friends." He slid the paper over to her. "He seems like a nice kid. He's not in any kind of trouble is he? "

"I hope not," Sonya said as she took the piece of paper.

CHAPTER FIFTY

Sonya drove to the address that the postal worker gave her and found Jesse wasn't home. Speaking with Jesse's dad, she learned Jesse was at work. He worked at none other than Harris's Feed and Farm Supply.

She was about to head over there when her phone alerted her to a new email from Ray. He had gotten the phone records. Sonya opted to go back to the station to look over the records. If Jesse was involved it was probably unwittingly. She figured she would learn no more from him than what she already surmised — Jake used Jesse's P.O. Box to get the documents.

Once back at the station, she went through the phone records for both Will and Jake and found absolutely nothing. Neither made calls to Landmark and the number Adam provided did not match the Evans' home phone, either Will's or Mary's cell phones, or Jake's cell. The number probably belonged to a burner phone and it would require some time to track it and link it to the purchaser. Her immediate hope was to wait and see what Landmark's phone records could tell her.

Not too long into her work on updating the case report, the email from Adam finally came in. He sent an attachment of the phone records. It was countless pages long documenting hundreds of phone calls made from the company's main office and calls made from cell phones the company had accounts for. Sonya drew in a deep breath, got up from the desk, and headed over to the coffee machine. This was going to take awhile.

Two cups into her search she found a couple of hits in August and another in the latter half of September where Landmark had called the number. The calls were made from Adam's office phone. Another cup of coffee later she saw the phone number pop up once more in the beginning of September. This call came from one of the company's cells.

Sonya looked at the date. It was made the Saturday morning of Labor Day weekend. She dialed the number. It rang quite a few times before it was picked up.

"This is Brent."

Sonya's eyebrows raised. "Brent Davis?"

"Yeah."

"This is Detective Reisler. I met with you this morning."

"Sure. I remember."

"You made a call to Will Evans on the Saturday morning of Labor Day weekend. You were surveying his property that day, right?"

"I was out there Saturday and Sunday."

"What was the call regarding?"

"We were working in an area that quite a few of his cattle were grazing in. They got startled when we started the survey and took out some fencing. We're not responsible for livestock or property damage but I wanted to give him at least a heads up about it."

"Did you speak with him in person or leave a message?"

"In person. He thanked me and said he'd take care of it when he got back in town."

"Thanks, Brent."

"Sure."

Shortly after getting off the phone with Brent a text came in from Ray asking about the phone records. Sonya reluctantly texted back telling him the phone records revealed nothing directly linking Jake but one phone call made to Will while he was on vacation was worth checking into. She also mentioned the P.O. Box address that was given to Landmark to mail documents to. While it wasn't in Jake's name, it should be followed up on. Ray texted back saying he was going to meet with Peterson now and he'd let her know what the final word would be.

Sonya let out a long sigh and packed up her laptop. She swung by Lori's and ordered four meals to go before heading back to her place. The apartment was dark when she entered. After turning on the lights she saw Connor coming out of the hall.

His eyes avoided hers and focused on the bag. "Last meal?"

"Don't know yet," she said while heading for the kitchen. "I'm waiting for a call."

Connor followed her. "I meant what I said earlier," he said. "If you get the call that it's over, I'm okay with that."

Sonya nodded and took the containers out, setting them on the counter.

He leaned over and looked at the writing on the four containers. He opened one and saw the contents were breakfast. He quirked an eyebrow at her.

Sonya looked away and shrugged. "I'm being optimistic."

"Thanks," he said quietly.

Sonya's gaze returned to him. Connor looked like he was keeping it together just barely. "You ready to eat?" she asked, hoping food could be a distraction while they waited for Ray to call.

"Can we eat on the couch?"

"Sure."

They put their food on their respective plates, grabbed some silverware, and headed to the couch. Once seated, Connor spread his legs slightly so his knee was touching Sonya's. She didn't move hers out of the way, seeming to sense he needed the contact right now. He took the remote and turned on the television, keeping the volume low but enough to where potential silence would be covered.

They started eating, paying minimal attention to whatever was on the screen. Connor spent more time moving his food around on his plate than eating and, after a few minutes watching him, Sonya felt the need to talk about the Labor Day weekend phone call. "Where in Colorado did you and your family go over Labor Day?"

Connor gave a slight start at the sudden conversation starter and set his fork on his plate before responding. "White River National Forest."

"Is there cell coverage in that area?"

"Not really. Especially where we were camping. My mom told us all to be careful because we couldn't call for help if we got hurt."

"Were you in your campsite Saturday morning?"

"Close by. Me, my dad, and Skeeter were fishing."

"Was your dad there the whole time?"

Connor nodded. "He was fly fishing. Once he gets in the water, he stays for hours." His brows suddenly furrowed. "Or would...or did...or used to..." He finally gave up and closed his eyes, uttering a barely audible, "Shit."

Sonya slipped her hand into his hand, giving it a squeeze.

He opened his eyes, gave a tight lipped attempt of a smile, and squeezed her hand back.

"He never received a call Saturday morning, did he?"

Connor shook his head. "Phone, keys, wallet...everything was left on shore."

"When did you get home?"

"Late Monday night."

"When did he find the broken fence and injured cattle?"

"Tuesday early afternoon. I had to help him separate out and treat the injured ones. The fence he started repairing Wednesday and I helped him finish it after school."

"If he would have known about the cattle being injured, he would've done something about it first thing Tuesday morning, wouldn't he?"

Connor gave a humorless chuckle. "If he'd found out about it during the trip we would've had to pack it in and come home."

Sonya's phone started buzzing. Connor let go of her hand as she looked at the screen and saw it was Ray. She swallowed before picking it up and tried to steady her voice. "What did Peterson say?"

"It's going to be a few days before we get the handwriting analyzed and with nothing solid turning up in the phone records... He wants you coming home first thing tomorrow. Doesn't mean the investigation is dead," he added hurriedly, "but he doesn't want you out there sitting and waiting. Whatever work that can be done on the case can be done from here now."

"Okay."

Ray paused. "That's it? That's your response? Did you understand what I just said?

"I understand."

"So ... you're fine with coming home?"

"Yeah."

"Like hell you are. What's going on?"

"Nothing. I'll call you tomorrow."

"Call me? What the hell is that suppose to mean? You should be saying you'll be seeing me tomorrow. I swear to God, if you..."

Sonya closed her eyes. "Bye, Ray." She hung up and promptly turned off her phone.

"Well?" Connor's voice was barely above a whisper.

She turned and saw he was strung taut as a bow, trembling and eyes large as he waited for her response. Despite his assurances that he was okay with the decision he looked scared shitless.

It was the look her face would've had if she wasn't forcing a smile. "We got another day."

CHAPTER FIFTY-ONE

Sonya stirred from her sleep. It was still dark out, so hard to tell exactly what time it was. She felt Connor's soft breathing fall warm against the back of her neck. His arms were around her holding her close to his chest. She lay there for a few minutes enjoying the heat and comfort, trying to stay lost in it before she fully awoke. Thoughts about Ray, the case, and what she needed to accomplish today intruded into the peace she felt and she began to tense.

Her slight movement caused Connor to stir. His arms tightened more drawing her closer to him. He dropped a kiss on her neck. "Morning," he said softly.

The word surprised her. She hadn't woken up with someone in a very long time. Not since Ray. "Morning," she said back, hoping it came across somewhat natural. She was about to pull away from him when she felt his fingers slide over her skin and began tracing the scar on her abdomen.

"Did they ever catch the guy who shot you?" he asked.

"No," Sonya said softly.

"If you saw him, would you recognize him?"

"Yes," she barely breathed out.

There was a long pause. "Does it get easier? You know, knowing the guy got away with it? Do you eventually forget thinking about it all the time?"

Sonya turned in Connor's arms and looked at him. She knew he was asking just as much for himself as for her. "No. It doesn't get easier. I have thought about it every day since it happened or spent my days getting wasted so I wouldn't have to think." She watched his face fall. "But that's my story. It's not going to be yours. I'm going to get the person who did this to you and your sister. He's not going to get away with it."

"Sounds like you know who did it."

"I just have to prove it."

Connor began to open his mouth and Sonya swiftly placed her fingers over his lips. "Please don't ask me about the case," she said.

He took hold of her wrist, removed her fingers from his mouth, then rolled, pulling her on top of him. "I can think of a way you can shut me up and get me to the point where I can't even remember my own name let alone the case."

Sonya smirked and raised an eyebrow. "I'm that good, huh?"

"Definitely."

She suddenly fixed him a grin. "If I remember right, you're not so bad yourself."

Connor tried to keep from smiling as he gave a mock gasp. "*If* you remember?"

Sonya's grin grew. "Well, it has been a few hours. Perhaps you need to remind me."

Connor's fingers slipped into her hair, took hold, and gently tilted her head back, exposing her neck. Placing his lips at the hollow of her throat he began slowly working his way up.

The feel of soft lips and the light scrape of stubble along her sensitive skin made her breath catch. "Oh, yeah. It's starting to come back to me."

She felt him smile against her neck. "Does that mean I should stop?"

"Do you really want to?" she said as her fingers worked their way into his hair.

He continued kissing up her neck. "No," he breathed into her ear causing her to shudder. "Do you?" he asked before nipping her earlobe.

She moaned softly. "Hell, no."

Sonya was sure Jake was the murderer and that meant there was no way he could have an alibi. First thing this morning was to talk to Dr. Veckle in person. She called the number for him and found it was his home number. His wife answered and said he was out on an early call delivering a calf at a local dairy. The woman provided her his cell phone number and directions to the dairy. Sonya tried the cell phone and got no answer. She decided to head on over to the dairy with the hopes of catching the veterinarian.

After driving for a good hour, Sonya pulled into Carson Dairy and went down a long dirt drive. She drove past the house and continued on to what looked like the main dairy operations. She saw a pickup with Dr. Veckle's name on the side parked next to a long building. She pulled alongside it, got out, and walked up to a set of large doors already open.

Looking down the long corridor flanked by pipe rail stalls, Sonya saw a couple men by a hose. Heading toward them she passed by a large cow licking a newborn calf only minutes old. One of the men, wearing what looked like black rubber waders, was stripped down to his waist and was vigorously scrubbing his arms while animatedly talking and laughing with a slightly younger man who was holding the hose for him. The hose was soon turned off and a towel was handed to the older man.

"Dr. Veckle?" Sonya asked.

"Yes, ma'am. What can I do for you?" the older man said while toweling off.

"My name is Detective Reisler with the Nebraska State Patrol. I'm investigating the Evans murder case. I'd like to talk to you about a statement you gave to the Ashlin sheriff's department."

The younger man quickly said, "I'll go up to the house and get your money, Doc," then departed after giving a nod to Sonya.

Dr. Veckle began pushing the waders down before taking a seat on a bench. He removed a large pair of black rubber boots, then finished pulling off the waders. He stood while pulling a shirt over his head and looked at Sonya. "I thought the investigation was over."

"Not quite."

"I just spoke with a deputy a couple days back," he said while tucking in his shirt.

"I know. I'm just following up."

Dr. Veckle shook his head while chuckling. "Every time you folks talk to me you get the same thing."

"I know, but I would like to go over it one more time."

The man gave a shrug and said, "Okay."

"You told them Jake Evans made a delivery to you at eleven-thirty the night his brother and sister-in-law were murdered. That seems kind of late."

"Yeah. Normally I would just put off getting it till the next delivery, but I really needed the stuff."

"What was the stuff?"

"Cattle de-wormer. I had an appointment with a rancher the next day to de-worm his entire herd. I was shorted three boxes on my delivery that day. I would have rescheduled but the rancher already hired extra help for the day. Jake was good enough to bring it out."

"What time was your earlier delivery?"

"I'd say about four-thirty."

"Who brought the delivery?"

"It was Jake. He actually suggested I go through the order and make sure it was all there since someone else had gotten it together. We found it was short three boxes and he offered to bring it by. Asked me if I would mind if it was late since he had to finish work and grab dinner and such. Told him no problem. Just leave the stuff on the porch if it was past ten."

"Why ten?"

"I usually head off for bed around that time."

Sonya's brows drew together. "Did you actually see Jake that evening?"

"Yeah. Eleven-thirty comes and I hear this horn honk a few times. I look out my bedroom window and see his truck. I give him a wave and he waves back."

"You sure it was Jake?"

Dr. Veckle let out a short laugh. "Can't miss that red truck of his."

"Was he in or out of the truck?"

"In the truck."

"So you saw only an arm waving. Did you actually see him?" Sonya pressed.

The doctor let out an exasperated breath. "Well, I guess I didn't *actually* see him. But I know it was him because he would never let anybody else touch that truck."

CHAPTER FIFTY-TWO

Dr. Veckle was none too happy to learn he was going to have to drive into Ashlin to revise his statement after he admitted he only thought it was Jake sitting inside the truck. The only thing he knew he saw for sure was a hand waving. Sonya uncovered the much needed crack in Jake's alibi and was hoping the next person she was planning to see would shatter it completely. The person who she was willing to bet the hand belonged to.

Sometime later she pulled into Harris's Feed and Farm Supply. She walked in and asked the owner if she could speak with Jesse. He directed her to the loading dock. She walked through the back doors and saw a familiar young man tossing fifty pound feed sacks onto the flatbed parked up against the dock.

"Jess?"

The young man finished tossing a sack and turned to Sonya. "Yeah, that's me." Then he paused, giving her a better look. "You're that detective that was here a few days ago."

"For the record, what's your full name?"

He paused before answering, looking unsure. "Jesse Aldrich."

Sonya's brows drew together. "You related to Brett Aldrich?"

"Yeah. He's my little brother."

"I want to talk to you about a P.O. Box you rented at the post office."

Jesse scowled. "How'd you know about that?"

Sonya showed him her badge. "Detective. Remember?"

210

"I don't have it anymore," he muttered.

"I know. Why'd you get it?"

"I wanted to get some things mailed to me without my parents knowing."

"What kind of things?"

Jesse's face began to flush. "Personal stuff."

"Did Jake Evans ever use your box?"

"No."

"He never asked if he could have something sent to it?"

"No."

Sonya paused as she watched Jesse. "How often did you go to your box?"

"I never really had to go."

"You didn't order whatever it was you wanted?"

"No... I mean yes." He shook his head in confusion. "I mean my girlfriend and I both got stuff but I never had to pick it up."

"She picked it up?"

"No. Jake would check my box while he was picking up Harris's mail. Since he always had to go to the post office regular anyways, he offered."

"So he knew about your box?"

"Yeah. He actually gave me the idea when I told him what I wanted to get."

"I also want to talk to you about what you were doing on the night Will and Mary Evans were murdered."

Jesse shifted his weight as he asked a cautious, "Why?"

Sonya saw his growing nervousness and decided to rattle him even more. "I'm expanding the list of possible suspects and you're on the list."

Jesse's eyes grew wide. "I ... I was at home."

Sonya's face became stern to aid her bluff. "Someone can verify this? Because I just spoke to your parents..."

"Alright, alright, I wasn't at home."

"Where were you?"

"Listen. I was doing someone a favor, okay?"

"Was that person Jake Evans?"

"Yeah. He screwed up a delivery and I covered for him."

"Why'd he need you to cover?"

"He had this date. He'd been talking about it for days. Didn't want to cancel it at the last minute."

"Someone here in town?"

211

"I think he said the next county over."

"Did he offer you anything to cover for him?"

Jesse nodded. "A hundred bucks."

"Anything else?"

"He said I could use his truck to run out there. My car has a lot of miles on it."

"Did you use his truck?"

"Yeah."

"How'd Jake get to his date?"

"I said he could use my car."

"Did he give you any special instructions for the delivery?"

Jesse shrugged. "Just leave the boxes on the doorstep, then honk the horn before I left to let Dr. Veckle know the stuff was there."

"Did Dr. Veckle see you?"

"Yeah. He saw me."

"He saw you or did he think he saw Jake?"

"Well, Jake kinda wanted me to make the doc think it was him."

"Why?"

"Jake was afraid Harris would find out he put the delivery off on me. I'm not suppose to make deliveries. I'm not insured."

Sonya didn't say anything right away.

Jesse grew more nervous. "You can verify this with Jake if you need too."

"I don't think I'll need to do that," Sonya told him.

He raised his eyebrows. "Does this mean I'm not a suspect?"

Sonya gave him a smile. "You just got ruled out, but I'm going to need you to go over to the sheriff's station when you're done here and give Deputy Patrick a statement of everything you told me."

Jesse closed his eyes and blew out a breath in relief. "Anything you want."

"Speaking of Jake, is he around?'

"Nah," Jesse said while shaking his head. "He's had to take the last couple of days off because of his back. He's been over at the hospital in Scottsbluff visiting his niece now that he's got the time and she's awake and all."

Sonya felt her stomach give an unpleasant lurch. "He has?"

"Yeah. He leaves pretty early and comes back late. I've been covering his shifts. Getting lots of overtime doing it."

"How many more days are you covering for him?"

"The doc gave him a note for a week, so five more days including today."

"Thanks, Jesse."

"Sure," he said as he turned and grabbed another feed sack to toss onto the flatbed.

Sonya hurried to her car and started heading for the sheriff's station. Jake was spending an awful lot of time at the hospital and she was sure it wasn't being spent all visiting. He was casing the place and Madison was in danger.

CHAPTER FIFTY-THREE

Shortly after Sonya left, Connor began to feel restless. It wasn't being holed up alone in her apartment that was causing the feeling, but rather the fact that Sonya knew the identity of the killer and he didn't. The answers he wanted were so close yet purposely put out of his reach.

That was part of it. The other part was he couldn't help but feel Sonya was hiding something else. She had kept her phone off since her call to her partner had ended last night. When she turned on her phone to call the vet she was going to see, Connor caught a glimpse of her screen showing an obscene number of missed texts and calls. All were from a Ray Boone. What was more suspicious was she didn't look at the texts or listen to the voice mails. Something was up and he had a feeling it wasn't good.

He plopped himself on the couch and looked at the television. He needed a distraction and quickly reached over for the remote on the end table. In his haste, he misjudged and his fingertips struck the end of the remote sending it sliding across the surface and off the back end of the table. Connor turned and got on his knees on the couch cushion to look behind the end table for the remote. Propped up between the side of the couch and the end table was a black bag. It was Sonya's laptop case.

Remote forgotten, he pulled out her bag. Unzipping it, a quick glance told him her laptop was inside. He pulled it out, set it on the coffee table, and opened it. Connor hit the power button and the screen immediately displayed her password page. He smiled as he recognized the operating system. He pressed the window key at the same time he pushed the 'r' button. Suddenly a cursor flashed in a new display box. He typed in the required code and clicked "OK." Password screen was now disabled.

On her desktop screen he clicked the documents icon to see what was there. A long list flashed on the screen. He scanned it until he found a folder with the name "Evans." He clicked on it and it revealed a few things that were part of its contents. One of the items was a large PDF titled "Case File." He opened that first. There was a table of contents that he read the headings of. The one titled "Crime Scene Photos" was something to be avoided. He made a click on one of the other headings and settled into going through the thing page by page.

He realized this is what the sheriff department had put together with regards to the murders. After a couple hours of reading, the file almost made him believe he was guilty. The evidence was pretty convincing and there was a lot of it. Connor sat back as the realization hit him. This wasn't some random crime committed by some random person. The evidence was too specific. It all pointed to him. He was purposely framed. But why?

Connor closed this document knowing it wasn't going to answer his question. He clicked on another titled "Evans Investigative Report." Once opened, he saw this was something Sonya had prepared. It was only a matter of a minute when the name leaped off the page and left him feeling like he'd been kicked in the stomach. Jake Evans.

Anger and adrenaline took over as Connor launched himself from the couch and ran to the bedroom. He hurriedly tossed on a sweatshirt all the while feeling like his legs were going to give out on him from how badly he was shaking. Finding his shoes nearby, he sat on the edge of the bed to stave off collapsing while putting them on. He cursed as his fingers fumbled with the laces. Once his shoes were on, he ran to the front door, twisted the knob, and flung it open.

A gust of cold air caught him, momentarily cooling his heated skin, and stopping him in his tracks. He glanced down at the street and saw a few people ambling down the sidewalks on either side and a couple cars pass by. What was he going to accomplish by leaving? Confronting Jake would only succeed in getting himself arrested. He was the one the police wanted. Not Jake. At least not until Sonya could get the proof she needed.

Connor slowly closed the door and rested his head against it until he felt marginally calmer. Questions began to form in his mind that he needed answers to, the main one being *why?* He turned and went back to the laptop and Sonya's report.

Sitting back down on the couch he took a deep breath before reading the report. Very quickly he realized it was about money. A company called Landmark Oil was interested in the ranch and would pay more than a million dollars to get it. Would Jake really be willing to commit murder to get that kind of money? Sonya seemed to think so.

Connor was unclear on what probate meant and how Jake could get the ranch. He went on the internet and researched probate laws. The more he read the more things began to make sense. If he was framed it would look more convincing than a random crime and if he was convicted then he couldn't inherit the ranch. It also made him convinced Skeeter was suppose to die when his parents did. With her being alive, how does that change things? Jake can't get the ranch with Skeeter alive even if he were convicted of the crime. Connor began to get a gnawing feeling. Jake went to all this trouble to get the million dollars. Connor doubted he would just give up. Would he try to kill Skeeter again? Connor swallowed hard. Yeah. Jake would try again at some point in time.

Connor needed information to at least calm his growing fear. He quickly set up an email account in Sonya's name. His was probably being watched. After set up was complete he quickly began typing.

Hey Mike. It's C.

It took less than a minute and his email was returned. *Damn. I thought it was a hot detective demanding to interrogate me. Been fantasizing about her good cop bad cop routine. More about her as bad cop.* There was a winky emoticon at the end.

Connor rolled his eyes and typed, *Sorry to disappoint.*

LOL. Just joking. We're going to see Walter tonight. Haven't been out since that night. Can you come? Miss hanging with you. Brett scored some beer.

Walter was code for the old water tower. Mike came up with people names for their regular haunts after the one time his dad got a hold of his phone and had a deputy waiting for them when they arrived at their destination. The creek was Keith, the high school football field was Frank, and so on.

I don't think she who must not be named would like me going out.

The next message was accompanied by a laughing emoticon. *You're so whipped.*

Better than being arrested.

True.

Connor was ready to get to the point of why he emailed. *I need to know if Jake has been working at the feed store as usual.*

Okay. Give me a few.

Connor waited and went ahead and deleted the recent emails. After quite a few long minutes Mike's email came in. *Brett says Jake's taken a few days off. Been in Scottsbluff at the hospital.*

Connor's fingers shook as he typed. *Is today one of those days?*

A couple minutes pass. *Yeah. Problem?*

Connor's fingers hovered above the keys as he debated asking Mike to pick him up. He quickly typed back, *Nah. I'll talk to you later.* He deleted the rest of his emails and quickly jumped off the couch. What he was planning would be easier with Mike, but if it went wrong he didn't want Mike getting caught up in the fallout.

Connor went to the kitchen and looked in the cupboard under the sink. Behind the cleaning products looked like a small tool caddy. He lifted it out and began to look through it, pausing to remove a Phillips and a slot headed screwdriver before slipping them into his back pocket. Connor saw a couple pair of pliers and selected the needle nose with built in wire cutters and stuck those in his pocket as well. He also saw a pair of rubber gloves which he rolled up and stuffed in his front pocket.

He then went to the bedroom closet and began looking at the selection of hangars. Most of Sonya's clothes were hung on plastic hangars but off to the side, shoved to the very end, were a few wire hangers. Connor took them out and began looking them over. He selected the one with the heaviest gauge wire and began unwinding the end that was twisted around the neck of the hangar. He spent a few minutes reshaping the wire into what he needed. He inspected his finished product. It wasn't going to be as good as the one he normally would use but it would work.

Connor went to the front door of the apartment, opened it, and stepped out on the landing. He pulled his sweatshirt hood up before closing the door, then slowly headed down the stairs, surveying the cars parked in front of Ashlin Tool and Hardware. He spied one in particular that was near the end of the group. It was an older model Toyota not directly parked in front of the storefront window and was partially obstructed from view by a larger pickup parked next to it.

Once off the stairs, Connor strode swiftly to the driver's side of the little tan sedan. He gave a quick glance around while shoving his wire between the window and its seal. After fishing around a few seconds, Connor found the locking armature and gave a pull. The locked popped up. Connor removed the wire, opened the door, and took a seat behind the wheel.

He pulled the screwdrivers and pliers out of his pocket and placed them, and the rubber gloves, on the passenger seat. Taking the Phillips screwdriver, he scrunched down and located the screws attaching the plastic cover to the steering column and began removing them. Once free, he tossed the lower cover into the backseat and put on the rubber gloves before grabbing the pliers. After a quick examination of the exposed wires, Connor quickly snipped through two brown ones, stripped the plastic off the ends, then twisted the exposed ends together. Next came the two red wires. After stripping them, he touched the two ends together and the car came to life. He quickly twisted them together and was in the process of pushing them out of his way so they wouldn't touch his leg while driving when he heard a voice.

"Hey! What are you doing in my car?"

Connor jerked his head up and saw a man standing in front of the hood with his hands full of purchases from the hardware store. Bags were immediately dropped as the man quickly rounded the hood toward the driver's side door. Connor slammed his hand down on the door lock just as the man grabbed the door handle. When the door wouldn't open, the man began banging on the glass, yelling the whole time.

Connor tried the steering wheel but it was locked in place. He quickly grabbed the slot head screwdriver and jammed it between the steering wheel and steering column. He frantically pushed down and wiggled the screwdriver as the window banging stopped. A quick glance told Connor logic was replacing the man's shock as he began fumbling in his pockets.

Connor redoubled his efforts as the man produced his car keys and another person came into view at the front of the hood. Finally he felt a snap, flung the screwdriver away, and threw the car into reverse. He gunned the motor a couple times and it was enough to get the owner to back away from the door before Connor peeled out of the parking space. Connor saw a few more curious people stepping out on the street but before they could even think of blocking his path he slammed the car into drive and stomped on the accelerator and took off like a shot down the street.

CHAPTER FIFTY-FOUR

Sonya walked into the station and looked around for Sheriff Bennett. She didn't have time to put everything together for an arrest warrant and she didn't have time to wait for it to come in. What she needed right now was for the sheriff to send a deputy with her to pick up Jake Evans for questioning. It was going to be a tough sell but she was ready to do battle if it came down to it. Not readily seeing him sent her rushing toward his office.

Suddenly Kerry strode over to her and headed her off. He leaned close to her. "Sonya, do you know where your boy is?"

Sonya glared at him, impatient with the delay. "Why are you asking me that?" she hissed.

"A call came in about a half hour ago. A report of a stolen car."

"Shit," Sonya swore and turned on her heels to hurry back the way she had came.

Kerry took hold of her arm, stopping her in her tracks. "What's going on, Sonya?'

"I don't have time to explain," she said as she shook loose from his grip and began to run to her car, her original plans ditched with this piece of news. She heard Kerry call out after her but she never looked back.

She drove to Ashlin Tool and Hardware, bringing her car to a screeching halt in front, then bolted up the stairs to her apartment. A quick check of the place told her Connor was gone. On the coffee table her laptop was left open. Not a good sign. She swiped the touch pad. It went directly to her desktop. No password screen. He had access to everything. She went on the internet and checked out recent searches. Numerous sites regarding probate were visited. She was sure Connor figured out Skeeter was in the way of Jake getting the ranch and the money, but something else must have set him off.

Sonya saw an email had come in. She looked at her phone but it didn't show she had one. A few clicks later on her computer showed she now had two email accounts. She swore as she clicked on the email from the new account. It was from Mike. All it said was, *Later.* Any messages leading up to that one were deleted.

Sonya grabbed her laptop, went back down to her car, got in, and tossed the laptop onto the passenger seat. She started the engine before scrolling and tapping on her phone.

Mike answered on the first ring. "Hey, Sonya."

Sonya tore a tight u-turn and started heading out of town as fast as she could. "What was Connor emailing you about?"

"He just wanted to make sure Jake was working today."

"What did you tell him?"

"I didn't know so I asked Brett."

Sonya groaned. "And Brett said he's been in Scottsbluff at the hospital the last two days."

"Yeah. That's exactly what he said."

Sonya let out a loud expletive.

"Uh, I take it that wasn't a good thing for him to know."

"No, Mike. Not at all. He just stole a car and is on his way to Scottsbluff."

"Oh, fuck."

"Exactly. I'm on my way to find him."

"Anything I can do?"

"Nothing right now. Just let me know if he contacts you again."

"Okay and, hey, sorry about that."

"I'm more sorry. I left him with my damn laptop. Talk to you later, Mike."

"Kay."

Sonya ended her call with him and scrolled to another contact and tapped the screen while making sure her car stayed on the road. After a few seconds, she said, "Kerry, I need a description of that stolen car."

CHAPTER FIFTY-FIVE

Connor looked at the waiting room clock. It was just after three p.m., nearly twelve hours after his father woke him up saying it was time to go to the hospital. He was bored. He'd long read through his books he brought and flipped through every magazine no matter what the topic was. He'd grown tired of the TV and just plain sitting around. Even the walks to the cafeteria had grown tiresome. Connor scowled. How long does it take to have a baby for crying out loud?

His dad would come out every so often to check on him and tell him everything was fine. But the last time Connor saw his mother, which was hours ago, she didn't look fine. It scared him and left him wondering why anyone would want a baby.

Suddenly his dad appeared in the waiting room. He was smiling. "Your mom had the baby."

Connor smiled with relief. "What is it?"

"You have a sister. They're going to clean her up a bit and then I'll come and get you so you can see her." His dad turned and left.

Connor slumped in his seat. A girl. All this time waiting and it was a girl.

It was another half hour before his dad came and led him to his mother's room. When they entered, Connor saw his mother sitting up in bed holding a small blanketed bundle in her arms. She looked tired as she smiled at him. "Come see your sister." His dad steered him to the side of his mother's bed. "Hold out your arms," she said as she passed the bundle to him.

Connor froze as his dad helped him position his arms to hold the newborn baby. Little bright eyes peaked out from under a pink knit cap and stared into his. "What's her name?" he asked.

"Madison Parker Evans," his mom said.

Connor grinned a little. He wanted the name Parker for a brother but it worked as a middle name. "She's so small."

He felt his dad's hands on his shoulders. "You're officially a big brother now. That role comes with a lot of responsibility. She's going to look up to you. Depend on you. You need to watch after her and protect her, especially if we aren't close by. Will you promise to do that?"

Connor took his finger and brushed it lightly over her little hand. Tiny fingers gripped his large one and he smiled. "I promise."

Connor pushed the little Toyota about as fast as it would go, but the drive to the hospital was unbearably long. When he finally arrived, he parked in the middle of the lot and pulled apart the red wires to kill the engine. Reaching into his back pocket, he pulled out his hospital ID badge and slung the lanyard around his neck. Connor stepped out of the car and looked around before heading to the entrance. He really had no plan. His only thought was to get Skeeter as far away from Jake as possible.

Once inside, Connor swiftly headed for the elevators and went to the fifth floor. Everything seemed to go smoothly as he entered the empty changing room, got into a locker, and changed into a set of scrubs. He was even able to find a near empty laundry cart. Where before it only functioned as a prop, now it was a necessity.

He entered an elevator and rode it down to the third floor. Connor exited and began pushing the cart toward the hallway Skeeter's room was located. Before turning he cautiously peered around the corner and his breath caught. Jake was leaning against the nurse's station talking to one of the nurses while she worked.

Connor looked around then, pulling the cart after him, pushed open a door, and ducked into the room that had a view of the entire corridor. A quick glance told him the patient occupying the room was sleeping. Connor positioned himself by the door and left it open enough where he could keep an eye on Jake.

It wasn't long before Jake left the station and started heading down the hall toward the room Connor was hiding in. Connor let the door close and waited a few seconds before opening it to peek out. He saw Jake had turned the corner and was heading for the elevators. Connor waited until Jake was out of sight before leaving the sleeping patient's room.

He pushed the cart at a casual pace and waited until the nurse had her back to him before going past the nurse's station. A guard was on duty outside of Skeeter's room. Much to Connor's relief, it was still only hospital security. As he drew closer the guard was suddenly hailed on his radio, and then he entered Skeeter's room. Connor paused with the cart as his brows furrowed. Seconds later the guard emerged, talking into his radio and positioned himself back outside the door.

Connor pushed the cart once again heading towards Skeeter's room. He lifted his picture ID card hanging from the lanyard around his neck for the guard to see. After a quick glance, the guard gave him a nod and opened the door. Connor nodded back and pushed the cart through, then closed the door behind him. He drew the cart alongside Skeeter's bed and saw she was sleeping. She was also still hooked up to the IV that he would have to deal with.

Taking a seat on the edge of the bed, Connor began to gently brush her cheek with the backs of his fingers until her eyes fluttered open. Her surprised sleepy look quickly transformed into a large open mouth smile.

Connor put a finger to his lips before leaning over to hug her. "God, I missed you Skeeter girl," he whispered into her hair. He backed off so she could see his face. "You got to be real quiet, okay?"

She nodded.

"I'm going to get you out of here but we got to be sneaky about it. They don't want me taking you so I'm going to hide you in this cart," he said while pointing to it.

Skeeter looked past him to the cart, nodded her head, and gave him a smile.

"You gotta promise me you'll be really quiet. No noise or they'll catch us."

"I promise," she whispered.

Connor looked over the infusion pump Skeeter's IV line was running through. He hit a button to turn the pump off, then opened the cover of the side her line was strung through and took it out. He noticed the chamber below the bag now showed the fluid running too fast. He looked at the line and saw a white plastic piece with a small plastic wheel. He thumbed the wheel until the fluid began to drip slowly once again.

Connor quickly pulled the extra sheets out of the cart and laid them on her bed, then grabbed a couple of pillows to stuff into the bottom. He pulled back her covers. "I know you're sore so I'm going to try hard not to hurt you. Just keep really quiet."

She nodded again as he scooped her up, causing her to stifle a small noise that tried to escape.

"Sorry," Connor said as he lowered her into the cart and settled her onto the pillows. "Try to scrunch up as much as you can."

Skeeter adjusted herself carefully and Connor could tell she was trying hard not to make noise. She was trembling a bit and Connor began to worry this was going to be too much for her. Once she was settled he grabbed the height adjusting knob on the IV pole and began turning it. When loose, he pulled the top half of the pole free from the bottom and propped it up within the tall laundry cart, making sure it was wedged tightly enough not to fall on his sister.

He took the extra sheets, shook them out, and started rumpling them up. He looked down at Skeeter. "Now I'm going to cover you up so they don't see you, okay?"

"Okay," she said softly.

He began to loosely drape the sheet over her and the pole. Before covering her head, he smiled at her and said, "Time to go for a ride. No noise till I say it's okay."

She smiled back while placing a finger over her lips, then disappeared as the sheet fell over her.

He bunched up the other sheet and put it and some pillows on her bed before throwing the blanket over them. Connor pushed the cart to the door, took in a couple of deep breaths to steady his nerves before opening it. Stepping through the doorway, he pulled the cart after him, letting the door shut behind it. He gave the guard a parting nod and began pushing the cart down the hall.

Connor came up on the nurse's station and cautiously looked around. There was no sign of Jake. As he passed by, a nurse took a tray and began heading down the hall Connor had just come from. He picked up his pace. It was going to be close in seeing if he could get Skeeter and himself out of the hospital before the nurse discovered she was missing.

He passed by a doorway just as a nurse with short dark hair was emerging. Connor recognized her as the same nurse he had seen on his last visit to this floor and quickly cast his eyes away before she caught his, praying she didn't recognize him or worse, need his help. He silently counted to himself knowing if he made it past three he would be safe. *One ... two ...*

"Hey there. Wait up."

Connor's knuckles turned white as he kept pushing the cart. He heard the squeak of rubber soled shoes against the linoleum tile coming up behind him quickly, then a hand latched onto the cart bringing him to a stop.

She was smiling at him. "I was hoping I'd see you again. I was trying to get you assigned to this floor but I must have got your name wrong. I thought you said, 'Mason,' but personnel said there is no one by that first name on record."

Connor couldn't get his mouth to work and his eyes kept darting beyond the nurse toward where he had come from.

She lifted his badge hanging from the lanyard around his neck and studied it. "I was right. It is 'Mason.'" Her brows furrowed. "Now why would they go and tell me no one ..."

Suddenly commotion erupted down the hall and Connor began to shake. The nurse glanced in the direction of the shouts and back at Connor. Guilt must have been rolling off of him in palpable waves because her eyes suddenly narrowed and her grip on his badge tightened. At the same time the sheets in the cart shifted catching both of their attention. With her free hand she reached toward the sheets. Connor grabbed her wrist.

The nurse began yelling, "Security," at the top of her lungs. Connor let go of her and tried to push the cart. Her grip on his badge was tight and the lanyard bit into his neck as he strained to get away. He swiftly ducked and tucked his head down so the lanyard slipped off, freeing him to begin pushing the cart at breakneck speed toward the elevator.

CHAPTER FIFTY-SIX

Sonya immediately parked her cruiser near the hospital entrance in a spot marked with a "Reserved" sign attached to a metal post planted in the sidewalk. She didn't bother to look for the Toyota Kerry gave her a description of, but went straight inside. She was sure Connor was here.

Just past the sliding automatic doors Sonya saw a security officer. She showed her badge as she approached him. "I need you to call up to the guard stationed outside of Madison Evans' room. Have him peek in and see that she's okay."

"Sure," the guard responded and immediately radioed up. After some brief back and forth the guard turned back to Sonya. "He says everything is okay up there."

Sonya relaxed a bit at the news about Skeeter but needed to find Connor. "I'm looking for a couple of men who might be inside the hospital. Is there a place where the security footage is viewed?"

"The security office is on the first floor here. I'll show you."

"Thanks," Sonya replied and began following the guard.

"Are these guys dangerous?" the guard asked over his shoulder.

"One of them might be."

The guard looked a little uneasy. "Should we do a lockdown or something?"

"I need to see the footage first," Sonya said as they reached the door marked "Security."

The guard opened the door to a room that was little more than a glorified closet. Two men wearing security uniforms seated in the cramped quarters facing a bank of small screens looked up as Sonya entered. "This is Joe and Don," the guard who escorted Sonya said. "And this is …"

"Detective Reisler. Nebraska State Patrol."

"She's here to look over the feeds. She's looking for a couple of guys. You two see anything unusual happening?"

The one guy shook his head. "Quiet as usual."

"Well, I got to get back. Good luck finding them, Detective." He backed out of the room and closed the door.

"Any place in particular you want to see first?"

"Show me the feeds for the third floor."

"We got about six feeds for that floor on these monitors here," Joe said while pointing to a few upper screens.

Sonya studied the monitors and didn't see Jake or Connor at the present. "Can you back these up time-wise?"

"Sure. How far you want to go back?"

"About an hour."

"You want all of them?"

"If you can give me the ones that show me the hallway for room 320, that would be great."

"That would be two. One does a long view of the corridor and the other is from behind the nurse's station. Do you want it to play in real time or fast forward?"

"Fast. I should be able to recognize who I'm looking for."

The recordings started and after a couple minutes Sonya called out, "Stop. Play it in real time." An image of Jake popped up on the recording from the nurse's station. The camera was positioned on the wall behind the desk. The time stamp showed it was only about half an hour ago. He was smiling and seemed to be chatting up one of the nurses really good, if her returned smiles and laughter were any indication. She seemed to be in the middle of preparing a med tray that was set next to the computer on the desk top. She would refer to the computer and then turn and prepare a syringe which she would attach a label and set it on the tray. When the nurse's back was turned to the tray, it would temporarily block it from the view of the camera. The action would also block most of Jake's body but never his face. Sonya watched as Jake's eyes would drop down to the tray every time the nurse's back was turned.

Sonya took in the scene that played out over the span of a few minutes. "Wait," she said suddenly. "Back it up for me."

"How far?"

"Three minutes."

Joe took the recording back and Sonya leaned in closer to the monitor, watching the tray. The scene rolled forward again. "Stop," Sonya said. "Take it back thirty seconds and pause."

"You seeing something?"

"I think so." She pointed at the screen. "How many syringes do you see?"

"Looks like five."

"Start it up again." They watched as the nurse turned, blocked the view of the tray while preparing another syringe, then turned around and laid it on the tray. "Okay ... Pause. Now how many do you see?"

"Looks like seven." Joe paused. "There's an extra syringe."

Sonya nodded. "Play it forward." They watched the same thing unfold as the nurse went about making up another syringe and turned to lay it on the tray. "Stop. Now how many do you see?"

"There are six on the tray now. The seventh is in her hand. You think that guy is messing with the meds?"

"I'm pretty sure."

Before Joe could comment, Don interrupted. "Hey, I think I see something on a different feed same floor. Some sort of altercation between an orderly and a nurse."

Sonya looked at the screen and immediately recognized Connor. He was holding the nurse's wrist while she had a firm hold on his ID badge. Suddenly he broke free and started hurrying away with a laundry cart. "Is this a recording or current feed?"

"Current," Don said just as his radio came to life.

"This is Sam from the third floor. Patient by the name of Madison Evans is missing. Nurse just went to treat her and she's gone. The only one who has been in her room since I last saw her was an orderly with a laundry cart."

"We got a visual on the suspect and we're going to call for a lockdown."

"You know we don't have enough guys to cover everything."

"I know, but lock what doors you can and at least position yourself by the main exits."

"Got it."

Don immediately radioed all security personnel of the situation and ordered them to execute a lockdown of the facility.

While Don was busy, Sonya turned to Joe. "Can we track him?"

"Yeah, there he is," he said, pointing to one of the screens. "He's getting on an elevator." Joe pointed to a different monitor and Sonya could see the inside of the elevator and Connor. "Looks like he pushed '1.' He's coming to us."

Sonya reached for the door handle to the room.

"Wait," Joe called out. "looks like it's stopping at two." They watched as the elevator stopped at the second floor and the doors opened to pick up someone. Sonya's face blanched as the camera revealed the person.

"Hey, isn't that the guy who was messing with the med tray?" Joe said.

Sonya watched as Jake quickly positioned himself to keep the door from closing. Connor made a move toward Jake but suddenly stopped. His eyes kept glancing at something Jake must've had but from the positioning of the two Sonya couldn't tell what it was. Then Connor took hold of the cart and pulled it out of the elevator like Jake directed him to do. Joe pointed to a different screen getting the hall shot of that floor. It looked like they were going to get into the other elevator.

"No, no, not that one," Joe groaned.

"Why? What's wrong with that one?"

"The camera's busted in that one. We won't know where they are going."

Sonya figured that was exactly why Jake wanted that particular elevator. She and the two security guards watched all the elevator hall feeds for every floor but never saw them emerge. After lengthy minutes Sonya felt something was wrong. "Where are they?" she growled. "They can't just disappear."

The guard paused. "They could if they were heading for the roof."

Sonya was out of the room like a shot.

CHAPTER FIFTY-SEVEN

Connor fled from the hall and hurried towards the elevators. He was trying not to jostle Skeeter around too much in his haste. Just as he reached the elevators, one of them dinged and the doors opened letting a couple people out. Connor maneuvered the cart in and pushed the button for the first floor, exhaling as the door closed.

He knew his chances for getting out of the hospital were gone at this point. He reached into the cart and lifted the sheet back a little, exposing Skeeter's head. She looked at him, her eyes big and unsure. He grinned and gave her a wink, drawing a smile from her before he covered her again. If he could get someone to listen to him and keep Skeeter safe it would be worth getting arrested.

The elevator slowed, coming to a stop at the second floor. The door slid open and Connor gave a start as a man stepped partway in, blocking the door from closing.

"You got the hospital in quite the uproar now," Jake said.

Anger eclipsed the initial shock and Connor made a move toward Jake.

"Uh-uh," Jake said sharply. "Look at my pocket, boy."

Connor stopped and glanced at the pocket of the jacket he was wearing. Jake's hand was inside holding something that was stiffly pushing against the fabric. Connor easily believed the object could be a gun and instinctively positioned himself between Jake and the cart, causing Jake to smirk.

"You're going to push that cart out of this elevator and into the one next door unless you want me to put a few holes in all that laundry."

Connor took a firm hold of the cart and pulled it after him as he got out of the elevator. Jake could be bullshitting big time, but he couldn't take the chance. Not with Skeeter. He pushed the cart into the empty waiting elevator as Jake quickly followed him in and pushed a button. The doors closed and Connor felt the elevator taking them up. "Where are we going?"

"Since you shot to hell the plan that took me days to put together, I came up with a new one. If nothing else, I am adaptable and might even enjoy this one more."

Connor didn't like the sounds of this at all. He glanced around the elevator and focused on the little security camera in the corner.

Jake must have seen where his eyes went to warrant his comment of, "Don't bother. Camera's busted in this one."

At least that answered Connor's question of why they changed elevators. He felt the elevator slow to a stop and a ding sounded before the doors slid open. Immediately the cool evening air hit him. They were on the roof.

"Out you go," Jake said, now motioning with a very real gun.

Connor pushed the cart out and Jake followed behind. The sky was a deep dusky rose color, the sun nearly completely set. The lights set around the edge of the heliport were glowing brightly. "Why are we up here? You could've shot us in the elevator."

"Not the plan. See, you're going to take your own life and your sister's."

Connor stopped pushing the cart and turned, glaring at Jake. "Why the hell would I do that?"

Jake grinned at Connor. "Why, the running and guilt became too much. So you snatched your sister and decided to jump with her in your arms."

"I'm not jumping."

"It's either jump or I shoot her and leave you very much alive." He waved the gun again. "Keep pushing."

Connor had no choice but to turn around and begin to push the cart again. He had no doubt Jake was serious. The man had already put a bullet into Skeeter once and would not hesitate to do so again. Connor's mind began to race in trying to figure out how to get out of this as the edge of the building drew closer.

"Okay, that's good right there. Get her out of the cart."

Connor looked over his shoulder at Jake. "Sonya knows everything. She knows you did it and why."

"Knowing and proving are two different things."

233

"She's got the proof." Connor said it more as a hope than actual fact. "Landmark Oil, right? You killed them and tried to frame me to get the ranch." He gritted his teeth to control the trembles racking his body. "You killed them for some goddamned money that you're never gonna get."

Jake eyed Connor for a moment as his smug look faltered ever so slightly. The cocky smirk swiftly returned as he said, "If your lady detective had this so-called proof, then things would be looking a lot more different for you right about now. Now get her out of the cart."

Connor turned around and bent over the cart. He saw the metal IV pole and quickly started calculating. The top half of the pole was about three feet in length and his arm would reach out another two or two and a half. That would give him about a good five foot reach. He tried to remember where Jake was standing. It didn't matter. This was his only idea and time was up.

He thumbed the clamp on Skeeter's IV line to turn it off, then carefully unhooked the IV bag from the metal pole, and laid it down on the pile of sheets at the bottom. Taking a deep breath, he took hold of the bottom of the metal pole. He had only one shot to get this right. Slowly he straightened, drawing the pole with him, keeping it tight against his chest.

"Get a move on, boy, and get her out of…"

Before Jake could finish, Connor spun, reaching out with the metal pole. The end struck Jake's hand and the follow through of the hard swing Connor delivered sent the gun skittering across the roof.

As Jake was still reeling from the blow, Connor was already sprinting for the gun that lay a few yards away. Jake recovered quickly and made for the gun as well. Connor was getting closer when a heavy weight fell against his legs sending him crashing down to the rooftop. He tried to kick out but Jake kept his full weight on his legs and began to work his way higher up Connor's body. Connor twisted frantically as he felt himself being more and more pinned by the larger man. With a heavy jerk, he brought his elbow up and around, catching Jake in the face. It was enough to cause Jake to shift allowing Connor to shimmy out from under him and make a mad scramble for the gun a few feet away. Connor lunged and felt his fingers touch the handle of the pistol.

He grabbed the gun, rolled onto his back, brought himself up in a half crunch, and aimed the gun between his knees. "Stay the fuck away from me," Connor yelled, "or I swear to God I'll kill you."

Jake froze then slowly stood, keeping his hands in front of him the whole time. Connor quickly got to his feet, keeping the gun trained on him the whole time. His hands were shaking causing the gun to waver slightly.

"You're thinking about it, aren't you?" Jake said. "Thinking about how good it would feel to put a bullet in me. I see it in your face. I know the look. I've had it myself. We're a lot alike, you and me."

Connor heard his name called and took a quick glance past Jake and saw Skeeter's head over the top of the laundry cart. She was crying and scared as she reached her arms out toward him. Connor began to make a wide skirt of Jake.

"You're right. I'm thinking about it. But we're nothing alike. As much as I'd love to pull this trigger and watch what would happen, I'm thinking about my sister more."

Jake smirked as Connor continued to back away from him. "She's only a cousin at best to you."

Connor felt the sting in the words as he continued to back away from Jake and draw closer to the laundry cart. "Pick up your bag Skeeter," he told her as he reached the side of the cart. Once she had hold of her fluids bag, Connor leaned sideways and her free arm circled his neck in a death grip. He wrapped his one arm around her waist and lifted her from the cart as he continued to keep the gun trained on Jake. Once out of the cart, Skeeter wrapped her legs around Connor and buried her head in his neck as she continued to cry.

Connor hurried to the door marked "Stairs," not wanting to chance waiting for the elevators if they were on other floors. He threw the door open, cast one more glance at Jake, and began his hurried descent. He cleared one floor, then heard numerous footfalls pounding up the stairs from the floor below. He made the landing and turned to head down the next flight when he saw two security guards at the bottom of the steps. They immediately drew their weapons and started yelling, "Drop the gun. Drop the gun now!"

Connor kept the gun in plain sight as he half squatted and dropped it at his feet. He heard another set of footsteps heading up the stairs as the guards slowly came toward him, weapons still trained on him. One retrieved the gun off the floor while the other said, "Hand us the girl nice and slow."

Skeeter began to shriek as she felt the guard's hand touch her and clung even tighter to Connor.

"I'll handle this one," came a loud call from behind the guards. "You two go see if the other suspect is still on the roof."

The guards glanced behind them then rushed past Connor, leaving him face to face with Sonya.

His relief at seeing her was tempered by the expression on her face. He couldn't tell exactly what emotion was wrapped up in the look. "I'm sorry," Connor began. "I thought Skeeter was in danger. I had…" His words were cut off as she swiftly went to him, put her hand on the back of his head, and slammed her lips against his. The kiss wasn't gentle and Connor groaned into it as all the emotions of the day came flooding out as Sonya's mouth warred with his own.

When the kiss finally ended, Sonya gripped his chin firmly, forcing him to look at her. She tried to appear stern but it was undermined by the fear in her eyes. "I should be royally pissed off with you after everything today."

"But?"

She let go of his chin as her look softened. "But, I'm not." She turned to Skeeter, who was watching both of them curiously, and ran her fingers lightly down her arm. "You were right on this one. She was in danger."

"Now what's going to happen?"

"I think I finally got what I need on Jake to bring charges against him."

"So…it's over?"

Before Sonya could answer, they heard one of the guards coming down the stairs. "We've searched the roof and there's no sign of the suspect."

CHAPTER FIFTY-EIGHT

Sonya fell exhausted into one of the chairs in Skeeter's room, watching as Connor continued to stroke his sister's hair even though she was sound asleep. Once back in her room, the doctor had given her a full examination and, despite all the jostling about, determined she was fine, but decided a sedative would do her good.

While Connor stayed with Skeeter, Sonya had spent the last three hours working with Scottsbluff police who had been called to the hospital and tried to tie up the case. The locals quickly put out an APB on Jake so he could be picked up for questioning and left Connor in Sonya's custody. She knew Sheriff Bennett would be notified of what went down at the hospital and knew he would make an appearance at some point, probably sooner than later.

She spent a good amount of the time pouring over video footage from the hospital to track Jake's movements over the last couple days. Sonya saw where he swiped the empty labeled syringe. It took place yesterday with the same nurse he had been chatting up tonight. He used the same technique and the recording showed the nurse briefly looking around the tray for the missing empty syringe before shrugging and getting another one.

Later footage showed him hanging around the emergency treatment room. He made his move when the view to the door was obstructed by a large shelved cart. Sonya examined the room and found vials of morphine of varying concentrations. She was willing to bet Jake had filled Skeeter's syringe with a lethal concentration. Tests run on the syringe taken into evidence should confirm her hunch.

Then it was a matter of forwarding everything she had to the DA. Kerry came through with the two new statements from Jesse and Dr. Veckle, and with all the hospital footage and statements from Connor and the nurse, Sonya felt she had enough to request an arrest warrant be issued for Jake Evans and that charges against Connor Evans be dropped. She doubted she would hear anything until tomorrow, and it would still take days to finalize all the evidence, but for now it was over. At least this part of it.

At some point she would have to face Ray. The day had passed with no contact from him. That worried her. With all the shit she's pulled, Sonya wouldn't have been surprised if Ray finally had enough. She pulled out her phone and looked at the screen showing the numerous calls and texts he had made last night. Biting her lower lip, she pulled up the last voicemail and decided to listen to it. It was left at one-thirty-seven in the morning.

"Okay. I'm a little slow but I take it that after leaving you a dozen messages you're not going to talk to me tonight. Probably got your damn phone turned off, but I know you're going to listen to this at some point. In fact, if I know you, this is probably going to be the first one you listen to and that's probably a good thing. You know me well enough that you should probably just erase the others."

Sonya heard a large exhale that bordered on a sigh before the message continued.

"Listen, I have a deposition taking place mid-morning tomorrow, oh hell, make that today. I don't know when it will finish but as soon as it does I'm heading out there. I realize I should've been out there days ago and not going was a bad call on my part. This was supposed to be a simple paperwork thing but with you nothing is ever simple. I should know that by now.

"I'm worried about you. I want to make sure you're okay. Scratch that. I need to make sure you're okay. I'll think of something to tell Peterson about your delay in getting back. Wouldn't want him to think you were defying a direct order now, would we? Call me when you're ready to talk otherwise I'll see you tomorrow. Love you, Sonya. Always. Bye."

For several seconds after the message ended, Sonya tapped her phone against her chin. Then she brought her phone down and swiped the screen. It was time to call Ray. Before she could put the call through, her phone began buzzing with an incoming call.

Connor glanced up at the sound and Sonya looked at the display of her phone before answering. She smiled at Connor and put it on speaker. "Hey, Mike."

"Hey yourself, Detective."

Sonya's stomach took a sickening drop. "Jake?"

"You sound surprised. You and Connor didn't really think the final hand was played, did ya?"

"How'd you get Mike's phone?"

"He's letting me borrow it. I gotta surprise of my own when I found he has your direct number. Simplifies things since you're the one I want to talk to."

"Is he okay?"

Jake let out a low chuckle. "I know a thing or two about catching a fish. It's best done with live bait."

"I want to talk to him."

"Sure." There was a somewhat lengthy pause and some indistinguishable sounds coming through.

"Guess Martin's is a no go tonight." The voice came across as more of a labored grunt but easily recognized as Mike's. Then it was gone as more background sounds were heard.

"Convinced?" Jake asked after a brief pause.

"Yes."

"Good. I figure it's time you and I finished that dance we started. Best get yourself paper and pen. I'm going to tell you exactly what to do and you will follow it to the letter if you want this boy around to see the sunrise."

Sonya took in the stricken look on Connor's face while pulling out a notepad and pen from her jacket, then switched the phone off of speaker. "I'm listening."

CHAPTER FIFTY-NINE

Connor watched Sonya leave Madison's room. He was out of the room short seconds later following her down the hospital corridors as she walked at a brisk clip, writing down everything Jake was telling her she needed to do. As she got to the elevators the call ended and she slammed her hand against the down button.

Connor shook his head trying to make sense of the last few minutes. "I don't get it. Mike was out with Brett and Josh tonight. How could Jake just take him?"

Sonya was glaring at the elevator number display. Neither one was near their floor so she took off for the stairs. "Was Brett bringing alcohol?"

"Yeah."

"Then Jake knew the plans. He's been the one buying the alcohol for Brett."

"What are we going to do?" Connor asked.

"*We* are doing nothing," she gritted out as she banged open the door leading to the stairs and began her hurried descent. "I'm going to finish this."

"I'm not letting you go alone," Connor huffed as he matched her step for step.

Sonya didn't respond as she reached the first floor and pushed open the door. Her pace quickened into a run as she headed for the exit. Impatient with the slowness of the automatic doors, she turned sideways and slipped through the narrow opening leaving Connor to wait a few seconds longer. She ran to her car and began opening the door when Connor's hand slammed against it, closing it once more.

Sonya whirled around and shoved him. "Back off. You're staying here."

Connor grabbed her arm as she tried opening her door again. "You can't keep me in the dark this time. I know where you're going. They're at the abandoned meat packing plant."

Sonya turned to face Connor. "How do you know that?"

"Mike said 'Martin.' We have code names for all the places we hang out. The old meat packing plant in Westbrook is Martin."

Sonya paused, the heat draining from her face. She took out the notepad from her jacket pocket, opened it, and placed it on the hood of her car. "These are the directions he gave me."

Connor stood next to her and studied the piece of paper. "Yeah. That's the place." His finger followed the directions as he read. "The way he has you coming in he'll be able to see you approaching. He'll know exactly where you are and there is only one entrance on that side."

"Is there a better way?" she asked while handing him a pen.

Connor took the pen and began to sketch on the sheet of paper. "Yeah. Cutting over on Bannock and parking instead of using Claymore like he wants you to. There is a blocked dirt road that leads to the back of the building. It's a bit of a hike but he won't be able to see anyone approaching."

"Is there a way to get in?"

"Other than the front, just a couple." He began to sketch the back of the building. "There's a ramp leading to a large door and to the right of it there are some busted out bricks at ground level that drops you into the basement. Part of the roof is gone so that is another way we can get in."

Her jaw tightened. "There is no 'we.'"

"I'm going with you."

Sonya shook her head. "Connor…"

"If you don't take me with you I'll just go there anyway and you know it."

Her eyes flicked over his face, seemingly gauging his determination. "You're not giving me much of a choice," she finally conceded.

Connor shook his head. "Not this time. I'm not sitting around while Jake tries to take more people I love away from me. Not happening."

Sonya's expression softened as she placed her hand on top of Connor's. "I will get Mike back."

"It's not just Mike." His eyes fixed on hers and a tremble ran through him. "He wants you. It's all a set up to get you." He slammed his hand down on the hood of the car. "This shouldn't even be happening. I had the chance to take him out."

"Listen to me. This is not your fault. Nothing is going to happen to Mike or me."

"You of all people know you can't make a promise like that to me."

Sonya's expression was unreadable, then her hand slipped behind his neck as she pulled him to her. He readily went and put his lips on hers. It was a slow thorough kiss, something in it Connor couldn't quite decipher.

When they parted, her brows were driven together as if struggling with something but a second later it was gone, replaced by a small tight lipped smile. "We'd better get going." She nodded her head in the direction of the passenger side of the car as she took the notepad with the directions and put it in her jacket pocket. "Get in."

Connor nodded, turned, and took a step to round the front corner of her patrol car. He suddenly felt his shoulders gripped tightly, then a sharp blow delivered to the back of his knee sent him sprawling to the ground. Out of the corner of his eye he caught the flash of metal as a handcuff was snapped onto his wrist and his arm yanked forward so the other end of the cuff could snap around the metal post of the "Reserved" parking sign setting in front of the car.

His mind began to catch up to what was happening and launched into full panic as he felt Sonya remove his wallet from his back pocket. "No," he yelled as he rolled over and made a lunge for her but was stopped as the metal bit into his wrist. She was just beyond the reach of his outstretched hand.

Sonya slowly stood, gripping his wallet tightly before putting it in her jacket pocket. "I'm sorry," she said, devoid of any emotion as she backed away toward the driver's side.

Connor scrambled to his feet as she opened her driver's door and got into her car. He strained against the metal holding him back from reaching her. "Sonya," he yelled before she shut the car door. He suddenly was awash with air rushing out from under her car as she started the engine and blinded by the headlights coming on as she tore out of the parking space.

He watched as the taillights faded once she hit the main road then turned back to the sign and gave it a couple of good yanks. It didn't budge. He squatted down and began looking at how it was attached at the base. Whispered curses began to fall from his lips when an answer to his predicament wasn't readily apparent. His eyes roved the post and began to focus on the attachments holding the sign. There was movement to his left but he ignored it as his fingers tested the tightness of a couple of nuts.

"Well, well, well. Looks like Christmas came early."

His head whipped around at the sound of the familiar voice. Sheriff Bennett was watching him, a smug smile on his face, hand resting on the handle of his pistol. Connor instantly sank to the ground and closed his eyes. *Fuck.*

"Connor Evans, you have the right to remain silent."

CHAPTER SIXTY

Connor gave up trying to get comfortable in the back of Sheriff Bennett's patrol car. His hands were cuffed behind him and his frustration kept him shifting restlessly in his seat. Earlier, after many long minutes, he also had given up on trying to explain everything to the sheriff. He wasn't listening to any of it and threatened to gag Connor if he uttered one more word. Not doubting the sheriff, and deciding he needed his mouth to work when the time came he found someone who would listen, he elected to shut up. They were heading back to the sheriff station in Ashlin and Connor prayed Mike's dad or Deputy Patrick were on duty.

Almost as if his prayer was being answered, a voice came through the two-way. "Sheriff Bennett? It's Kerry."

The sheriff picked up the hand set and, as soon as he pushed the button, Connor leaned forward and yelled, "Sonya's in danger."

The sheriff immediately dropped the hand set, gripped the steering wheel, and stomped on the brakes. Connor was thrown forward and his face slammed into the divider screen. The sheriff swerved and parked along the shoulder of the road. Connor slumped back into his seat, feeling blood start to trickle from his nose.

The sheriff had exited the vehicle and was rummaging in the trunk, all the while Kerry continued to try and hail him. The sheriff came around and opened the backseat door next to Connor. He was holding a roll of gauze. "I warned you, boy," he said as he made several passes around Connor's head and mouth, then tied the ends tightly together. He got back into the driver's seat and pulled back out onto the road before picking up the hand set. "Sorry about that, Kerry. Had a little trouble with my cargo. Go ahead."

"Was that Connor?"

"Picked him up at the hospital and bringing him in now. ETA of thirty minutes."

"What was he saying about Sonya?"

"Nothing important."

"Did you see her at the hospital?"

"No."

A voice Connor didn't recognize suddenly came through the two-way. "This is Detective Ray Boone with the Nebraska State Patrol. I want to speak with the Evans boy."

"You can speak to him when I get him back to the station."

"If he has information concerning my partner, I want to know it."

"Then you best be at the station when I get there."

"Now you listen…"

Sheriff Bennett had no intention of listening any further as he turned off the radio.

Connor's nose was starting to swell making it difficult to breathe and the gag wasn't allowing him to suck in enough air either. The harder he tried the more he felt like he was choking. He laid down on his side across the backseat and tried to slow his breathing, taking comfort in the fact his message was heard. It was hard to relax, though. Sonya had a good twenty minute lead on everyone at this point and it would probably grow to more by the time Connor could tell her partner where she'd gone. A lot can happen in that amount of time.

About fifteen or so minutes further into their drive Connor felt the car start to slow.

"What in Sam Hill…" The rest trailed off in indistinguishable mutterings.

Connor slowly sat up and saw an Ashlin sheriff vehicle parked sideways in the middle of the two lane highway, effectively forming a roadblock, and a dark grey sedan parked off to the side of the road. Standing outside the vehicle, illuminated by the sheriff's headlights were Deputy Patrick and a tall dark haired man wearing a suit.

Sheriff Bennett brought his car to a stop a few feet from the men and got out, leaving his door open. "What's the meaning of this, Kerry?"

Kerry gave a nod toward the man in the suit who was already making his way around the sheriff. "Detective Boone ordered the roadblock. He needs to talk to Connor."

The tall dark haired detective wasted no time in making his way to the backseat door of the sheriff's patrol car. Yanking open the door, he reached in, grabbed a fistful of Connor's shirt, and pulled him from the car. As Connor leaned back against the car, the detective pulled the gauze from his mouth and down over his chin. "Where's Detective Reisler?"

Connor's eyes moved past Ray's shoulder, saw Kerry, and directed his words more toward him. "Jake took Mike and is threatening to kill him unless Sonya comes." He looked at Ray. "She went to meet Jake."

Ray once again took hold of Connor's shirt. "Where is she?"

Despite the control the man was showing, Connor could tell her partner was on the verge of losing it. His next move was risky but the location of the meat packing plant was the only card he had and he couldn't waste it. "I'll only tell you if you take me with."

The result was immediate as Connor was turned and roughly slammed down on the trunk of the patrol car. A large hand gripped his head and pressed the side of his face down against the cold metal. He felt her partner press against him. "You think this is a game?"

"I'm the only one who knows where she is. Just uncuff me and take me the fuck with you."

Connor felt himself lifted from the trunk of the car only to be slammed down once again with the full weight of Ray on his back. His breath was knocked out of him in one large grunt.

Connor felt someone struggling with Ray, then heard Kerry say, "We're wasting time. You can trust him. He'll take us to her."

"Why the hell should I trust him?" Ray growled.

"Because Sonya does."

Suddenly the pressure was gone and Connor slid off the car and onto the ground. As Kerry moved behind him and pulled his wrists up to unlock the cuffs, Connor glanced over at Ray. His one hand was over his eyes, thumb and fingers applying pressure to his temples. The other hand was intermittently gripping the handle of his still holstered gun. Connor knew he just painted a target on himself that might end up too tempting for the dark haired detective right about now.

"How much of a lead does she have on us?" Kerry asked him as one wrist slipped free and then the other.

"About thirty minutes now," Connor said as Kerry hauled him to his feet.

Kerry pursed his lips and shook his head. "Too much time. We gotta get our asses moving."

"Now just a minute there, Kerry," Sheriff Bennett said. "That boy is in my custody. I say what is done with him and right now I want him back inside my car."

Ray got in between Kerry and the sheriff. "Consider yourself relieved of the responsibility. Connor Evans is now in the custody of the Nebraska State Patrol and I'm taking him and your deputy to go get my partner." Ray gave a nod indicating Kerry should head to his vehicle. Kerry put a hand on Connor's shoulder and directed him toward his cruiser.

"This is my case," the sheriff gritted out. "I arrested him. You think I'm going to let you and the Patrol take credit for all of it?"

"Credit? You think I want credit for your two bit case? The only thing I want is finding my partner and that Mike person safe. If anything happens to them I'll make it my mission to see you're finished."

"I'm willing to bet this is all a lie he concocted to delay the inevitable, but if the boy is telling the truth I won't be the only one worrying about being finished. If I were you, Detective, I'd be wondering how he got that kind of information and, more importantly, how he happens to be on a first name basis with your partner. Should make for some interesting conversation."

Connor waited for Ray's response but instead all he heard were swift footsteps approaching. Suddenly a hand clamped painfully on the back of his neck as he was steered away from Kerry towards the dark grey sedan. "The kid is going with me, Deputy." Ray said. "Follow me in your car."

"You got it," Kerry said as he got in and started his car.

Connor struggled against the hold Ray had on his neck as they drew closer to the grey sedan.

"You even think of running and I'll shoot you," Ray hissed as he gave Connor a shove before he let go. He started to open the back door.

"Hell no. I'm riding in front." Connor didn't even look at Ray as he walked around the car to the passenger side, opened the door, and got in.

Ray quickly slid in and started the car, glaring at Connor the whole time. "Start talking," he growled.

"Start driving," Connor growled right back as he pointed behind him. "Fast."

CHAPTER SIXTY-ONE

Sonya killed the lights as she spotted the dirt road branching off of Bannock. She turned off the engine and stared up the rise. There was a nearly full moon casting a silvery light over the tall scrubby brush covering the open land. She couldn't readily see the old slaughter house building from her position.

Sonya got out of her car. She closed the door quietly, stepped over the chain strung between two metal posts, and began walking up the dirt road, skirting the brush that had taken root and was working to reclaim the unused path. A shiver ran through her. It was cold, the temperature hovering near freezing. As she watched her breath come out in a little cloudy puff and fought off another tremor, she knew it wasn't just the cold causing her to be tense. Walking toward the unknown without backup was not the brightest thing to do.

She didn't know the layout of the building and had no idea where Mike was being held. More importantly, she wasn't sure if Jake was armed. He lost the gun he had brought to the hospital but that didn't mean he didn't have another one.

What she did know was he didn't want her having one. The instructions he gave her were clear. When she arrived her gun was to be placed on the roof of her car along with her belt, shoulder holster, and jacket. Pant legs were to be rolled up and pockets turned out.

She also knew Jake had given her an hour and now forty minutes of it were gone. This didn't leave her much time and she was taking his time frame seriously. He knew the gig was up. This was all about revenge. When already facing two charges of premeditated murder, there was nothing to dissuade you from adding more. One death penalty is the same as four when you came right down to it.

Sonya crested the hill and was looking down at the decaying brick and wood structure. She ducked off the dirt trail and stepped in amongst the taller brush to get the lay of the area. The building was dark and it was quiet. Up near the roof was a line of rectangular windows that were mostly busted out. They were high enough where Sonya felt confident Jake would not see her approaching. She recognized the ramp and door Connor described and a darker area at ground level she assumed to be the opening leading into the basement.

She winced as she thought about Connor but pushed it aside. She would deal with the fallout later. Right now she needed to get into the building and find Mike. A quick glance of her phone told her she had less than twelve minutes before Jake would start getting suspicious. She pocketed the device and started toward the abandoned building. Staying close to as many stray outcroppings of brush as she could, she angled her way down the gentle slope, then scurried across the flat open ground surrounding the back.

Sonya came up on the hole. A few bricks were scattered in the dirt around the opening but the angle of some that were loosened indicated most had been kicked in from the outside. She knelt on the ground and peered into the opening. It was very dark with no windows to let in the moonlight from the outside. Right below the opening Sonya could see the top of a wooden crate. It was about five feet below the opening and looked to be set on top of other wooden crates. The basement itself appeared deep, about twenty feet.

Entering backwards through the opening, Sonya slid until her waist was at the edge. She extended her leg downward to try and find the crate. She lowered herself more until her toe scraped the top. She paused as she got both feet situated under her and put more of her weight on the crate. Suddenly it shifted causing Sonya to grab the bricks at the bottom edge of the opening while she repositioned her feet to get better balance. She tested her weight carefully once again and found the crate stable.

Carefully squatting, she peered down to get a better idea of what she was standing on top of and found it to be a collection of dilapidated crates, wood planks, what appeared to be a broken old desk, and god knows what else. Definitely the efforts of teenage boys who showed little regard toward physics or keeping their necks intact. The precarious pyramid did nothing to bolster Sonya's confidence in getting Mike out without Jake knowing. She was having doubts she could scramble down unheard and unscathed.

She stepped down to the next crate. The wood creaked but remained stable. Slowly she descended watching so her foot wouldn't slip between open slats or missing boards. Finally stepping off what appeared to be part of an old office chair, she reached the bottom, her foot making a small slap sound as she stepped into a puddle of water. The dim light glinted off numerous little pools of water on the concrete floor formed from all the recent rain that leaked into the old building. Bricks lay scattered from where they had rained down from above as the opening was enlarged over time by the boys or nature.

She drew her gun, and peered through the darkness. The area was open with metal beam support columns every dozen feet or so. The far ends of the large expanse disappeared into the inky dark. Near the center was a set of stairs illuminated partly by moonlight coming from the floor above. As her eyes grew accustomed to the dark she made out more relatively indistinguishable items scattered throughout the space. A particularly large object at the base of one of the support pillars directly in line with the stairs caught her attention. There seemed to be more light filtering through from the floor above but not enough to make out fully what or who it was.

Sonya glanced at the stairs, fairly certain Jake was waiting up top, keeping a watch for her arrival. She had a few minutes left before the deadline to find Mike and get out. Keeping close to the wall, she made her way toward the pillar, hoping the mass at the bottom was him. A cold drop of water hit her face causing her to glance up. There seemed to be some sort of track suspended from the ceiling by long metal rods. Every so often a hook could be seen still connected to the track. Each one a good foot in length and stout enough to hoist up a full size steer. Most were now scattered on the floor, rusted but still wicked looking. Sonya carefully stepped around them not wanting to accidentally send the metal clattering across the concrete.

As she drew closer to the pillar, she began to make out that it was a person sitting at the base with their hands secured behind it. Sonya could see light making its way through a large hole in the floor above where boards had rotted and given way. At the right angle, a person standing near the hole could have a clear view of the pillar. She'd have to take the chance Jake's attention was elsewhere.

She crept up, knelt down next to Mike, laid her gun on the wet concrete floor, and gently lifted his head. His eyes began to flutter then he jerked away from the touch and began to struggle.

"Mike, it's okay. It's me," Sonya whispered.

He became still as his eyes squinted in the dim light. They closed once again and his head dropped down as if the effort was too great to maintain his focus. "Sonya," came out as a slurred whisper.

Sonya scowled. He seemed out of it. "Are you hurt?"

"Uh-uh."

"Drunk?"

Mike shook his head. "Just two beers."

"Then what's…"

"Shot me with something."

"Shot like a syringe?"

Mike nodded.

Sonya cursed under her breath. The damn morphine syringe he switched out at the hospital. Not enough to harm Mike but enough that getting him out of here was going to be more of a challenge than it already was.

"Listen to me," she said while placing her hands on the sides of his face to make him focus on her. He felt cold and was shivering. "We've got to get out of here." He nodded before she took out a knife from a compartment on her belt. She went behind Mike, pushed a button on the handle to eject the blade, and cut through the ropes binding his hands.

She stowed her knife before picking up her gun. Mike struggled to get to his feet. The drugs, alcohol, cold, and wet doing nothing to aid him in his efforts. Sonya, unwilling to holster her gun, did her best to help him with her free hand. Once upright, he leaned heavily against her as they made their way back to the way out.

"I'm not feeling so great," Mike whispered.

"I know. You just got to hold it together for a little while longer," she said as she steered him around the scattered hooks littering the floor, waiting for errant steps. "When you get out, I want you to run. Just run. My car is parked on Bannock."

Sonya slowed as they passed by the stairs, listening carefully for any sign of Jake. It was eerily silent except for the various drips coming from the ceiling. She continued guiding Mike towards the collection of piled junk. Once at the base, she said, "Take it slow. We're going for quiet, not speed."

Mike nodded and set his foot on the broken chair. He wavered as he pulled himself up and Sonya did her best to steady him while maintaining a firm grip on her gun. A step higher, a crate creaked as he put his weight on it, but it held. Sonya followed close behind, steadying him as needed. Every time Mike went up another level she held her breath. He was panting and growing more unsteady. She found her hands constantly on him, putting her own balance at risk. The opening drew closer.

No sooner than she dared to breathe again, a board splintered under Mike's foot. He grabbed a crate in front of him just as his foot broke through the board. He tried to pull his foot out but it was stuck. Sonya was reaching to try and see if she could guide his foot out when he kicked out. His foot came free but not before the crate he had stepped through was yanked out of position and knocked Sonya's gun out of her hand. She watched in horror as it and the crate went crashing to the floor below.

"Hurry," Sonya yelled and Mike pulled himself onto the box situated below the opening. She glanced over her shoulder and saw Jake coming down the stairs. She looked back to Mike who took hold of the bricks lining the bottom edge of the opening and was pulling himself up. "Once you're out you run. You hear me?"

"But…"

"You run, Mike."

Mike disappeared through the opening and Sonya scrambled onto the last crate. It shifted and began to tilt. She thrust herself toward the wall and grabbed hold of the bricks as the crate toppled and left her dangling.

She looked behind her and saw Jake coming up the pile of crates. In his hand was one of the discarded meat hooks. Sonya dug her toes into the wall and began to pull herself up.

"Oh no you don't," Jake grunted from right below her.

She turned to see his arm completing the arc of his swing. A scream tore out of her as the hook sank deep into her thigh.

CHAPTER SIXTY-TWO

Jake let go of the hook as the crate he was standing on began to splinter and give way. He clawed at Sonya and grabbed the bottom edge of her jacket to keep himself from going down. The bricks she was clutching began to break loose from the crumbling mortar. Jake's feet found purchase once again on the rickety wood and he began to tug on her jacket. The bricks beneath her fingers start twisting inward and she knew she was going down. She pushed off hard from the bricks to catch Jake by surprise and take him down with her.

His reflexes were quick as he shifted to avoid an impact with her, but he still received a hard glancing blow. The sound of splintering wood was heard as Jake's weight caused more crates to shift and give way, sending him to follow Sonya to the ground.

Sonya hit first, her full weight landing on her already injured leg. She felt a snap as a fresh searing jolt of pain ripped through her. Any sound died on her lips as her breath was knocked from her. Jake landed with a thud next to her and was still. Sonya slowly began to gulp in air and started to sit up. Every little move set her leg on fire. She gritted her teeth as she shifted herself. The lower part of her leg was at an odd angle and a protrusion could be seen beneath the denim fabric of her jeans. Despite the hard landing, the meat hook had stayed firmly implanted in her thigh, a darkening stain radiating out from the point of entry. As she moved, the metal end scraped against the concrete sending painful little vibrations rocketing up and down the metal deep in her thigh.

Sonya grasped the hook and began to pull on it but the pain caused her to cry out and abandon the attempt. She had a bad feeling it was imbedded in the bone. Taking in deep breaths, she began to assess her immediate situation. Jake was softly groaning. He was incapacitated for now but for how long he would be out, Sonya could only guess. She needed to put as much distance between her and him as she could.

Placing her hands behind her on the concrete floor and drawing her good leg up and planting her heel firmly on the floor she began to slide herself backwards toward the stairs. As she reached the bottom of the stairs, she was breathing hard and couldn't control the whimpers escaping with every exhale. One by one she pulled herself up the stairs biting back cries as her injured leg bumped against each step. She was only a third of the way up when she heard Jake beginning to stir. Ignoring the pain as best she could, she took the steps faster and began to shake from the effort.

When she reached the top, she looked around. It appeared to be what was once the processing part of the operation. A long line of wooden tables held remnants of rusted metal machines, most stripped of their parts. Bolted to the table legs was a metal shelf about a foot off the ground. At the far end was a wall with an open door probably leading to smaller rooms which could offer a place to hide if she could get there. Broken glass, torn out light fixtures, metal debris, and countless pieces of junk littered the floor. There was also the large hole she had viewed while in the basement that she would need to pass by.

Sonya heard Jake curse as he stumbled around in the basement and hoped he thought she was still down there. It might buy her the time she needed, but only if she got moving. Planting her hands behind her, she started dragging herself backwards toward the far end of the room trying to be as quiet as possible. Her attention was split between watching where she was going and watching the stairs, though she still heard him thrashing about below.

The floor began to feel wet and rather slimy under her hands, the dampness seeping into the seat of her jeans. She looked up and saw a large section of the corrugated metal roof was gone, no longer protecting the interior from the elements. Sliding herself farther along, she noticed a growing perceptible tilt as if everything was being funneled towards the large opening.

While watching the hole draw closer, her back struck an object behind her. It toppled and sent a couple metal light fixture hoods thudding to the floor. They rolled toward the opening, gaining speed until they fell through, and landed with a loud clatter onto the basement floor below. Then there was silence.

Sonya cursed silently to herself and frantically looked around. There really wasn't anywhere to hide. The table next to her was her only option. She slid over to it, lay down, and pulled herself under the metal tray. Silence stretched until she heard the crunch of a footstep on broken glass.

Memories began to take over as Sonya lay still in the small cramped space. She was once again under her bed, listening to the footsteps, waiting to be found. She shook her head to clear her thoughts. "Not this time," she whispered as her hand slipped to a compartment on her belt and snapped it open.

The footsteps stopped and she felt a hand grip her ankle. "Gotcha, Detective," Jake said as he gave a yank.

Sonya grabbed the leg of the table with one hand while her other hand took hold the item she wanted. The metal hook dragged along the floor sending jolts of pain up and down the length of bone as Jake tried pulling her out, causing her to shriek. A final tug was given and Sonya lost her grip on the leg of the wooden table. She came sliding out and Jake was immediately on top of her, drawing his face close.

"Any last words, Detective?" he said as he trailed a finger slowly down her cheek.

"Yeah," she said before a soft snick was heard, drawing his attention to a glinting metal blade. "Goodbye, Jake."

CHAPTER SIXTY-THREE

Ray didn't seem to have a problem understanding the concept of fast. He was pushing the cruiser as if demons from hell were nipping at the tires. Connor was hopeful they could gain some time on Sonya and help her face the very real one waiting for her at the meat packing plant.

He glanced in the side mirror and saw Kerry keeping up just barely. He had spent the last few minutes answering his questions about Jake and Mike over the radio. The lack of follow-up questions on Kerry's part told Connor he was up to speed on Sonya's work on the case. It appeared Ray was the least informed of the three of them and it was not setting well with him.

They were on an open desolate stretch of road and Ray was pushing his speed even more. "When?" he gritted out between clenched teeth.

Connor glanced at him. "When what?"

"When did this whole thing start?"

"The night before she was suppose to leave I asked her to stay."

"Why didn't she arrest your ass?"

Connor paused before answering. "She wasn't really in a position to do that."

"Explain."

"Uh-uh." Connor didn't think telling Ray he had a gun, albeit an empty one, pointed at his partner would go over too well. "I'd like us to arrive in one piece so I think I'll hold off on that."

Ray let out a, "Humph," then asked, "When did the deputy know she was helping you?"

"I suppose when she stopped him from shooting me."

"Jesus," Ray muttered.

Connor looked at the mirror again and saw a pair of headlights trailing far behind them. "We're losing Kerry."

Ray glanced at his rearview. "How much farther?"

"Not too much. We're going to make a turn, though. He may not be able to tell where we went."

Ray nodded and kept his speed the same.

Connor took in the familiar landmarks and a couple minutes later he was telling Ray to start slowing down. "There," Connor said while pointing out the windshield to the right. "That's the road we want."

Ray slowed and took in the street sign, then grabbed the handset to the radio. "Hey, Kerry, we're turning right on a road called Bannock."

He completed the turn when Kerry responded. "Bannock? I know where they're at."

Connor could just make out Sonya's car in the headlights and before Kerry could tell Ray anything more, he undid his seatbelt, opened the passenger door, and dove out of the moving car.

Ray yelled and slammed on the brakes as Connor tumbled to a stop. Connor quickly scrambled to his feet, disregarding the sting of the road rash he was starting to feel, and took off in a run, crossing behind the cruiser and disappearing into the tall brush. Ray wasn't familiar with the area and Connor was banking on this. Ray would wait for Kerry instead of following him, not wanting to risk getting lost and losing more time.

Cutting a diagonal path to the right, Connor weaved between the clumps, trying to get to the dirt path that led to the packing plant. Ahead of him he heard a noise followed by the sounds of someone throwing up. He slowed his pace a bit and made out a person bent over and coughing. It was Mike.

Connor ran over to him. Mike started and stumbled a couple of steps backwards before he recognized his friend. Connor looked around. "Where's Sonya?"

"I don't know," Mike panted as he struggled with his balance. "She told me to run. I heard her scream." His legs gave way as he collapsed to his knees. "I…I couldn't help her. Wanted to … just too sick."

Connor gripped Mike's shoulder. "You wait here. Kerry and another officer are coming. I'm going to get her."

Mike nodded. "Basement. We were in the basement. Be careful. He's crazy."

Connor took off running once again and didn't stop until he reached the opening. He knelt down and looked into the opening. The crate was gone. Straining his eyes against the darkness he could tell the whole arrangement had gone crashing down.

"Shit," he said as he jerked himself off the ground. So much for the back door. He ran around to the front of the building and saw Jake's truck, but no sign of anyone. Connor grabbed the handle of the rusted metal door and pulled. The weathered hinges creaked and groaned in protest as the door began to swing outward.

Before stepping inside, Connor listened for sounds so he had a better idea of where they were. Off to his right, hidden from view, he heard Sonya let out a shriek and that was all it took for him to rush in. Stumbling over the scattered debris, he careened around the large metal tables and saw them. Jake had Sonya pinned to the ground. Suddenly the man reared up and roared in pain as she made a swipe at him.

Connor dove for Jake and the impact was hard enough to knock him off of Sonya. The momentum sent them landing a couple feet away from her and closer to the gaping hole. Connor was on top of Jake for only seconds before a hard jab to his chest sent him rolling off.

Slowly sliding toward the opening in the floor, he looked to see Jake crawling toward Sonya. She was propped up on one elbow and there was a glint coming off of the knife in her hand. He was wondering why she hadn't gotten up, run away, or done something. Then he saw her leg.

He flipped over on his knees, dug the toes of his sneakers into the wet slick wood, and made a lunge for Jake. He grabbed hold of his pant leg and gave a yank as his toes slipped out from under him. They slid faster as the pitch of the floor became steeper. As his feet hit open air he let go of Jake and scrambled to find something to hold onto. There was nothing.

Jake was sliding faster and latched onto Connor's legs before going over the edge. Connor felt the sharp tug and heard Sonya scream his name. Out of the corner of his eye he saw a long stout piece of metal hanging down from the sagging floor joist. It was one of many used to suspend the track from the basement ceiling. While its paired partner had long ago broken free from the wood, this one held tight to the joist and half of the track.

As Connor slipped over the edge he grabbed it and hung on tight with both hands. He groaned as Jake continued to cling to him. Connor wasn't going to be able to hang on for long. Hearing Sonya call his name again he looked up. His breath caught as he watched Sonya drag herself closer to the opening, then take her knife and plunge it into the rotting floor boards.

She lowered herself, using the knife as an anchor. While her left hand gripped the knife, her other hand went down to the hook still in her leg. She took hold of the metal, gritted her teeth, and gave it a sharp yank. A scream tore out of her as it was pulled free.

"Connor," she cried as she lowered the hook toward him.

It wasn't going to come close enough for him to grab it. He looked at her and gave a nod. She let go of the hook and it began sliding toward him. He removed one of his hands from the metal rod and thrust it up as the hook came sliding to the edge. He grabbed the end of it, twisted his body, and swung downwards.

The pointed end sunk into Jake's shoulder, causing the man to howl in agony. Connor savagely ripped it out and was ready to strike again when Jake lost his gripped, fell to the basement floor, and lay still. Connor's concern with him ended at that point when he heard Sonya call to him.

He swung the hook over his head and sunk it into the floor boards and began to pull himself up over the edge. Sonya was reaching for him and he took her hand. She didn't have the strength to pull him up but kept him steady as he pulled the hook out of the wood and plunged it in higher up.

Suddenly her grip slipped from the knife, her strength giving out, and she began to slide. Connor swiftly placed a hand firmly under her ass and pushed her back up until she was more level so he could reset the hook. Once he was able to get a better purchase on the floor he dragged Sonya far enough away where there was no longer any danger, then rolled on his back to catch his breath.

"Jake? Is he…" Sonya began.

"I don't know." Once his breathing had calmed he turned to look her over. "Oh, shit, Sonya," Connor said as blood oozed steadily from the wound in her thigh.

He started unbuckling her belt, then pulled it free and discarded the few compartments attached to it. He slipped it under her thigh, positioning it right above the deep puncture, and then threaded the end back through the buckle. Sonya whimpered as he tightened the belt. "It's going to be okay. Kerry and Ray are coming."

Her face showed confusion. "Ray?"

"Yeah," came out rather muffled as he pulled his scrub top over his head. He balled up the fabric and pressed it to her wound. "They should be here any second." He positioned himself behind her so she could lean back against his chest. He kissed her head, her skin felt cold "You're going to be okay," he said, almost more for himself to hear than her.

"I'm sorry … back at the hospital …I wanted you safe."

"I know." He gave a weak chuckle. "Just don't tell Mike. He'll never let me live it down that I got taken out by a girl."

"Mike's okay?" Her voice was weaker.

"Yeah. He's fine." He heard her mumble something like "good" then felt her go slack against him.

He gave her a slight jostle and turned her face toward his. "Sonya, I need you to stay with me."

Her eyes fluttered open briefly and a slight smile touched her lips. "You're here. I've missed you so much."

Connor could tell Sonya wasn't all that lucid but wanted to keep her talking. "I've missed you too."

She reached up and touched his cheek. "You shouldn't have tried to stop him."

"He was going to hurt you."

"But you died."

Connor's brows drew together. "I'm right here, Sonya. I'm alright."

"I know. I changed it. It should've been me instead of you. I wanted it to be me."

Connor heard shouting coming from outside. "We're in here," he yelled. He turned back to Sonya. "Help is here. You're going to be alright."

Her hand fell from his face as she lost her battle with consciousness. "I love you, …"

The rest that fell from her lips disappeared into silence. But from the bit Connor was able to catch, he was pretty sure it wasn't his name.

CHAPTER SIXTY-FOUR

Connor was slouched down in one of the padded chairs in the waiting room. He moved his hand causing the other end of the handcuff to slide slowly back and forth along the arm of the chair it was secured to. Absently he thought this was some kind of record for him. Handcuffed three different times in one evening by three different cops.

Ray told him it was necessary until he got word that all charges were dropped. Connor didn't care. He was chained to this waiting room whether or not he was in cuffs. Sonya was still in recovery after her surgery and he wasn't going anywhere until he saw her.

From the bits and pieces he gathered, the doctors had set and pinned the fracture in her lower leg, which actually ended up being the easier of the two injuries to fix. The damage to her thigh was a little more involved. The bone had a chip and there was a hairline fracture from the impact of the metal hook, but it was the damage to the muscle and blood vessels that required the most work to repair. The doctors felt the majority of the damage was done when Sonya pulled the hook out resulting in a lot of blood loss and requiring her to have a transfusion.

He glanced at the clock. It was going on two-thirty in the morning. Ray left to get some coffee about fifteen minutes ago and Connor welcomed the break. The last two plus hours spent with Sonya's partner were uncomfortable to say the least. It had been better when Kerry and Mike were here, but Mike had been treated and released over an hour ago and Kerry had left about half an hour ago after learning Sonya came through the surgery fine.

Earlier, Ray had pulled Kerry aside to talk and, with the way both of them would cast glances his way, Connor knew the discussion centered on him. It seemed after the lengthy conversation, Ray's dislike for him grew even more, if that was possible. What the hell was Kerry even telling him?

Connor didn't get Ray. He got that Sonya was Ray's partner and he should be concerned, but his acting all caveman over her rubbed him the wrong way. It was as if Ray was in… *Oh shit.* Connor closed his eyes. This really wasn't good.

A noise had him glancing up to see Ray returning, coffee in hand. He took a seat in the chair right next to Connor this time. Connor sat up a little straighter and watched as Ray took a long sip from his coffee.

"How much do you know about Sonya?" Ray asked at length.

Connor considered the question. In all their hours together he had actually learned very little about Sonya. He gave a resigned shrug. "Not much."

Ray obviously liked the answer with the smirk that appeared. "Let me tell you, kid, that is exactly how she plays things. I've seen her in action many, many times. She will learn every nook and cranny of what makes you tick. And in the end? You go home empty handed."

Connor took it as a challenge to get rid of the smirk but he didn't have much to pull from. He had a feeling Ray knew her better than anyone else, leaving him at a disadvantage. Connor replayed conversations with Sonya and came up with something Ray may not know. "I know she's always wanted to go to Disneyland."

It seemed to work as the smirk was replaced by an arched eyebrow. Connor was hoping the game would end but could tell by the way Ray slowly sipped his coffee while staring across the way he was thinking of his next move. "You know about the scars?"

Connor smiled to himself. This one was easy. "Yeah. Gunshot scars. I saw them." Ray's eyes flashed to his causing Connor to quickly swallow. He knew the last bit had Ray putting two and two together. That's what her partner really wanted to know in all of this.

Long seconds passed as Ray took another sip. "Did she tell you how she got them?"

"She said she was shot by an unhappy meth customer. He killed her parents."

"I'm impressed she told you that much of the story. It's the same one I was told."

Connor's brows furrowed. "There's more to it?"

Ray let out a short humorless chuckle. "Oh, yeah. Definitely a piece I don't think she's shared with anyone…including me."

"But you know it?"

"I have a thing for dark closets and skeletons. Occupational hazard."

"What is it?"

"Sorry, kid. Not mine to share."

Connor stayed quiet. Even though they seemed to be at a draw, he still felt like he was losing.

"She shares that with you…" Ray shrugged as he took another sip. "Well, you might actually mean something to her."

Connor went back to slouching in the chair and looking at the suddenly interesting grain pattern on the table next to him. He didn't need to tally the score. It was easily game, set, and match to Ray.

A nurse walked into the waiting area. "Detective Boone? Detective Reisler is starting to wake and has been moved into a room. You can go see her now."

Before Connor could even start to ask if he could go too, Ray was out of his seat and striding away.

CHAPTER SIXTY-FIVE

Sonya felt the light brushing of lips against her skin. "Connor?" she croaked. Her throat hurt and it was hard to open her eyes.

"Uh, no. It's me, Sonya."

Her eyes opened briefly, then she smiled. "Ray. You're here."

"Of course I'm here. I'm always here."

She felt something cold against her lips and opened her eyes to see Ray offering her a spoon of crushed ice. "It'll help your throat," he said and she opened up. As she sucked on the ice, Ray stroked some stray hair off her face.

Her forehead creased under his touch as the haze was lifting from her mind. "I'm in big trouble, aren't I?"

He grinned. "With me? Definitely."

"You know what I mean."

The grin left Ray's face. "I don't know how this is all going to go down with Peterson. If he finds out about half of the shit you pulled." As Sonya opened her mouth, he cut her off. "Don't even try denying anything. I had a long chat with your friend, Deputy Patrick." He shook his head. "What the hell were you thinking?"

She tensed and immediately regretted it. Pain was beginning to take a firmer hold with each dull throb coming from her leg. "He was innocent," she gritted out.

"So that means everything else goes out the window? Policies, procedures, laws…"

"I'm not sorry for what I did, Ray."

"Oh, you've made that very clear, but a little remorse on your part would be nice considering I also got tossed aside."

Sonya watched as the anger on his face gave way to hurt. Seeing that brought on a pain different from what was radiating from her leg. A single tear leaked out and trailed down her cheek. "That's the only thing I'm sorry for in all of this."

Ray let out a long exhale and wiped the tear away. He gave her another spoonful of ice chips before stroking her head once again. "You know it's going to be some time before you're out of the dog house with me."

"Am I going to be around long enough for that to happen?"

"You will if I have any say in the matter. You're lucky Peterson likes me. He also likes it when cases are solved and guilty people are in custody."

"Custody? Jake's alive?"

Ray nodded. "Bastard came out in better shape than you considering the fall. He's got a fractured pelvis." He paused. "We were worried about you bleeding out before we could get help. The kid did a good job keeping pressure on your wound until we could get you here."

"How's Connor? Where is he?"

Ray took on a sour look and shrugged.

"Ray," she said in the best warning tone her sore throat could muster.

He rolled his eyes and sighed. "He's worried and waiting to see you."

"Are you being nice to him?"

"Of course."

Sonya grinned. "Liar. I want to see him."

Ray smirked and pushed the call button.

Sonya was suspicious. "What are you doing?"

"Just following orders. The nurse said to ring when you woke up so they could give you something for the pain."

"I'm fine."

"No you're not."

"Whatever they give me will knock me out."

"Good. It will keep you out of trouble."

"I don't want anything until after I see Connor," she said as she attempted to sit up. Her head spun and she collapsed back onto her pillows, breathing harder.

Ray put a hand against her shoulder. "Okay. Take it easy. I'll go get him," he grumbled.

He left and a couple minutes later Sonya saw him and Connor standing at her door. Connor immediately came to the side of her bed, leaned over, and placed his lips on hers. Sonya closed her eyes as he kissed her. When she opened them she noticed Ray was gone and a nurse had entered the room.

"No," Sonya groaned. "Go away."

The nurse chuckled. "Most people waking up after surgery can't wait to see me, especially if I have this," she said while holding up a syringe.

"What's that?" Connor asked her.

"Something for the pain."

"But it'll make me sleep," Sonya said.

Connor smiled and stroked her cheek. "I think that's the point."

Sonya tried to push down the rising panic, but found it harder as her leg throbbed. "I don't want to wake up here alone."

"You won't. I'm not leaving."

"Promise?"

Connor gave her a soft brief kiss. "Promise," he whispered then gave the nurse a nod. She took hold of the IV line and injected the contents of the syringe. Within seconds Sonya was finding it difficult to keep her eyes open. "Connor?" His name came out thick and slurred.

"Yeah, Sonya?"

She let out a sleepy sigh. "Just checking," she said before the chemical induced sleep took her.

CHAPTER SIXTY-SIX

Connor listened to the music play while wishing he had foregone buttoning the top button on his dress shirt. After all the tie would have covered it so no one would've been the wiser. He probably could've gotten away with the button, but not with acting on his desire to sit in the very back of the church. Instead, he sat in the very front row staring at the caskets of his parents.

He supposed it was nice as far as funerals go. There were lots of flowers and music had been playing since he arrived. Abby Walker took the lead in planning and putting it together and he appreciated it, but he still didn't want to be here. He didn't see the point. His parents had been gone almost a month and he had done his grieving. He was told a funeral would bring him closure but he knew it wouldn't. Too much was left unsaid.

It seemed like most of the town had turned out. The church was full and Connor recognized most of the people in attendance. Sheriff Bennett even made an appearance despite the fact he was laying low. The case was still being talked about, but probably not in the way the sheriff wanted. Lucky for him it wasn't an election year.

He felt a firm squeeze of his shoulder given by Mike who was seated behind him. Connor blinked and realized everyone was standing. For what he didn't know but he obediently got to his feet as well. Soon enough they were seated again and the pastor began to speak.

Skeeter left her seat that was next to his and crawled into his lap. Once seated she began to pull on the sleeves of his shirt to move his arms. Understanding the cue, he wrapped his arms around her and she leaned back into his chest. While he kissed the top of her head, he felt Sonya give his knee a squeeze from where she sat on his other side.

He and Sonya hadn't had much time to talk even though they spent most of the days together. The last two weeks had been crazy. So many meetings and decisions had to be made. And, despite the orders to take it easy and stay off her leg, she had been there with every one and promised to remain being there through the next few weeks.

Most charges against him were dropped. The auto theft one was proving more difficult. The guy was really pissed. Luckily Thomas Dandridge was more forgiving and was helping Connor with all the legal matters. Dandridge assured him he was making progress with the man and it would be resolved before the guardianship hearing for Skeeter took place. The guardianship decision was easy even though he felt completely over his head with regards to the responsibility.

The hardest decision was with the ranch. He tried going back there but as soon as he feet crossed the threshold he knew there was no way he could stay. He needed a different place to live. As much as he wanted it to be just him and Skeeter, common sense dictated otherwise. He would need help. He was starting back to school soon and really wasn't up to speed on taking care of Skeeter full time. There were plenty of people wanting to take Skeeter in. Him? Not so much. When Lydia offered to take them both he gratefully accepted.

Despite seeing Sonya everyday and the plans they made for when everything blew over, he had been pulling away from her. Maybe it was everything that had been crammed into the last two weeks or seeing the extent to which his life was changing that made him withdraw, but more and more Connor felt it had to do with the man sitting on Sonya's other side.

The words Ray had said to him in the hospital waiting room had taken root and Connor found it difficult to supplant them especially when he hadn't really learned anything more about her. Distancing himself seemed to make it easier than investing more into whatever this thing was. He couldn't bear any more rejection or loss.

More music began to play as Connor realized the pastor had finished speaking. He hadn't listened to any of it. People were getting to their feet once more. He could tell this was the end of the service because Sonya was reaching down to retrieve her crutches that lay on the floor in front of her chair.

A group of men was gathering in front near the caskets. Ray, Kerry, and some of the other deputies were included in this group and had already found positions around his dad's casket. Josh and Brett were standing by his mother's looking around at the men as if trying to figure out if they needed to be doing something other than waiting.

Mike once again gripped Connor's shoulder signaling it was time for them to go. Connor set Skeeter down by Sonya. "You stay with Sonya while I do this. Okay?" Skeeter nodded and Connor went forward with Mike.

"You ready for this?" Mike winced suddenly. "Sorry. That was really dumb."

"Nah," Connor said. "I actually am kind of ready. Another step, you know?"

Mike nodded as they took their positions. Connor took hold of a handle on his mom's casket and took a deep breath to steady himself before starting one of the longest walks of his life.

CHAPTER SIXTY-SEVEN

Sonya watched from the distance as Connor handed Skeeter off to Lydia and remained by the graves. After the pall bearers had done their duties, they had returned to the church. Connor went through the obligatory motions of thanking everyone for coming as they trickled by him before heading back home. When nearly everyone was gone, Connor had slipped away and returned to the gravesite.

She wanted to go to him but opted to give him some time to be alone with his thoughts. What they were she could only guess. She'd had a hard time reading him lately.

Some sort of wall was going up between them. Well, another wall. Hers was always there. Connor was just building his own and she didn't know why let alone what she could do to bring it down. Maybe it was better to let it be. It would make things easier for both of them in the long run. At least easier for her.

She heard footsteps and looked to see Ray coming to stand by her. He was watching Connor as he asked, "What are your plans for the next six weeks?"

"I'm going to be sticking around here for awhile."

Ray raised an eyebrow. "For the kid?"

Sonya shifted her weight to relieve the ache in her leg. "A lot's still going to be happening. He's going to court next week to get guardianship over Madison."

"That might be a bit tough with him still being in high school. Not to mention becoming an instant parent at his age."

"Dandridge is helping him through the legal process and Lydia will provide housing and help with Madison. She's also giving him part-time employment at the bakery to make it look good for the court even though he won't need it."

"He's selling to Landmark, isn't he?"

"Yeah. We're going to start going through the place in the next couple of weeks and then he'll sign papers. Dandridge is helping with that too, in making sure Landmark doesn't screw him, setting up a trust fund for Madison, that kind of stuff."

"You think it wise giving an eighteen year old a shit load of money like that?"

Sonya shrugged. "He's got a good head and being responsible for Madison will keep him grounded."

"And you? You planning on helping with that too? Keeping him grounded?"

Sonya shifted her weight and shrugged again.

Ray exhaled slowly and asked, "So, when do I get my partner back?"

"Beginning of January."

"Your medical leave ends late November."

"I took some vacation time." She was going to end it at that but was compelled to continue at seeing Ray raise his eyebrow again. "When school lets out for winter break we're taking Madison to Disneyland."

"That's long term planning for you." Ray's focus shifted down to where his toe began working a divot in the dirt. "So after that you're coming home?"

"Yeah."

Ray paused. "What's the kid doing after he graduates?"

Sonya gave him a scowl. "Will you stop calling him that."

"That's what he is and answer the question," Ray shot back.

Sonya looked away though the scowl remained. "He's planning on moving to Lincoln to go to college."

Ray turned a full circle before responding. "You know it's never going to work — you and him."

"You're probably right," came her glib response.

"The kid is going to be so screwed up after all this. You aren't going to fix him by sleeping with him."

Sonya pivoted on her good leg and got into Ray's face. "I seem to remember a certain somebody trying to help a screwed up kid a few years back and it was far from platonic."

"You were twenty," Ray said quietly as he looked away.

"You were fifteen years older than me, my instructor, and married."

Ray threw his hands up. "What do you want me to do? Apologize? Fine. I'm sorry. I'm sorry for all of it."

Sonya let out a frustrated groan. "God, Ray, I don't want you to be sorry."

He slowly gave her a sheepish grin. "Good. Because I'm not."

Sonya rolled her eyes and couldn't help the smile that tugged at the corner of her mouth. She gave his stomach a smack and he chuckled.

He tentatively brought his hand up along the side of her face and let his thumb stroke her cheek, looking serious once again. "I wish I could have given you more. But you never really wanted more."

Sonya relaxed with his touch. She closed her eyes but it was more to block out the truth in the look Ray gave her. "You gave me what I needed at the time. Maybe that's all this will be."

"For you or for him?"

"I don't know."

Ray pulled her into a hug. "I'll always be here, you know?"

"I know."

He squeezed her tightly to him and kissed the top of her head before releasing her. "I'd better get going. It's a long drive back to Lincoln."

"Call me when you get home?"

"You bet." He gave her a wink and started walking off toward the parking area.

"Ray?"

He turned around and looked at her.

"Was I really the best candidate for the job?"

"You were. But I would have picked you even if you weren't." He turned and began walking again.

CHAPTER SIXTY-EIGHT

"Oh, hell," his dad muttered as he brought the jeep to a stop.

Connor's attention was pulled from his thoughts of starting school as a senior next week and drawn to a pitiful cry coming from a scrawny, wobbly calf just hours old. It was all alone, the herd a good half mile off, his mother probably with them.

"Let's load him up and see if we can get him to his mama," his dad said giving Connor a nod to go and fetch the newborn.

Connor hopped out and walked toward the calf. Seeing the movement, the calf's cries became louder as it stumbled its way to Connor. With a grunt, Connor scooped him up and trudged back to the jeep. His dad had spread a blanket in the back and helped him get the damp and cold calf situated. Connor crawled in next to the calf and began rubbing him with the blanket.

The jeep rumbled and bounced over the rough terrain as they made their way to the nearby grazing herd, then once again stopped. "There she is," his dad said as he got out of the jeep and came to the back to collect the calf.

Connor watched as his dad walked up to the mother and set the calf next to her. The calf was more than hungry and tried to get at her udders, but she would have none of that and quickly side-stepped him, thwarting his attempts. The baby cried and stumbled towards her. She knocked him down with a swipe of her large head and ambled off. Connor's dad collect the calf and returned to the jeep, muttered curses coming from him as he set the calf back inside.

"That damn cow has no business reproducing. Same goes for some people I know," he grumbled.

"What are we going to do with him now?" Connor asked as he let the calf suck on his fingers.

"I'm going to track down the other group and see if we can find him a home."

It took a bit of driving but they located another group of their herd. His dad stood up and scanned the cattle. "There she is," he said and climbed out of the jeep. He came to the back and got the calf. "Time for you to meet your new mom."

Connor followed as his dad strode off toward the grazing cattle. The cow he approached had a calf that was weaning age, which meant she still had milk. His dad set the calf down and pushed him up to her udders. It immediately latched on and began to nurse. The cow turned and gave the calf a sniff and continued her grazing. After the calf drank his fill the cow licked him and let him stay close to her.

His dad looked pleased as they headed back to the jeep. "I'll come back out and check on him later but I think this will work out just fine." They climbed in but his dad didn't start the jeep right away. He continued to watch the cow and her new calf. "That cow is pretty special. She'll love and protect that calf just as if it were her own." He paused. "You know that cow reminds me a lot of your mother."

Connor let out a snicker. "You'd better hope I don't tell her what you just said."

His dad looked at him blankly for a second then hung his head and chuckled. "Didn't come out the way I meant."

"Yeah, didn't think so."

His dad let out one more chuckle and grew serious as he once again watched the herd. "Shortly after your mom and I got married we found out the chances of us having kids was not so good."

"Why's that?" The question just slipped out naturally.

His dad shifted in his seat, looking uncomfortable. "Well, uh, half of your mom's plumbing doesn't really work."

Now Connor shifted in his seat. He really didn't want to hear about his mom's "plumbing" and wasn't seeing the point of this conversation.

"It hurt your mom something fierce to learn she may never be a mother. When we, uh, got you, it made us really happy...to have you as our son. Still does."

The silence stretched between them. Connor didn't know how to respond. His dad didn't do the warm and fuzzy thing.

"I know it ain't been easy between us but if I were to go back, well, I'd still want you." His dad suddenly cleared his throat. "I think you should know that."

The jeep quickly came to life indicating the conversation was over. As they were once again bouncing over the range in silence, Connor found himself wishing it wasn't.

Connor quietly stood by the caskets waiting to be lowered into the ground. He didn't know how long he'd been there but it was long enough where the cemetery workers had stopped waiting and wandered off. He thought if he stood here long enough he would feel something. All he really felt was numb.

He heard the click and soft thud of crutches approaching. Glancing over, he saw Sonya coming to a stop next to him.

"How are you doing?" she asked.

Connor shrugged and picked up a stick from the base of the large tree they were standing under. He began breaking off small pieces. "I think he tried telling me I was adopted. It was kind of cryptic and I didn't get it. We never did communicate too well."

He paused. "That was a lot of money to pay Jake every month. They had to have known he was bullshitting, you know, about wanting me."

"They didn't want to take the chance of losing you even a little," Sonya said softly.

Connor tossed what was left of the stick away and shook his head. "All that shit I pulled. They had a choice and they still wanted me and protected me."

Sonya's eyes drifted to the parking area, watching as his car pulled out. She followed it for a long time as it left. "That's love."

The silence stretched, then slowly Sonya pulled out her phone and a set of ear buds and began scrolling through the display. After a couple of taps she handed it to Connor. He looked at the screen and saw an album cover for the group, *The Calling,* and the song she cued up to play, "Could it be Any Harder." He gave her a questioning look.

"I never got the chance to say goodbye either." She gave a little shrug and looked at the screen. "I find that song helps."

Connor put the ear buds in and sat at the base of the tree. Sonya turned to leave, but he reached out and touched her hand. "Stay. Please." Sonya propped her crutches against the tree and carefully lowered herself next to Connor. He took her hand, settled his back against the tree, tapped the song to play, and closed his eyes. Soon the lead singer's voice and the words began to envelope him, working their way through his numbness. He played the song a couple more times and found it was helping.

Connor paused the music and removed one of the ear buds. "This song…when you listen to it…it's not for your parents. Is it?"

"No," Sonya said quietly.

Connor continued to look at her, waiting to see if she would tell him.

She looked down at their clasped hands as Connor's thumb began tracing slow circles on her skin. She drew in a shaky breath. "I had an older brother. His name was Max. That day…" Tears began to slip silently down her cheeks.

Connor wrapped his arm around her, the distance between them melting as he pulled her to him. Her head rested on his shoulder and he began to stroke her hair.

She began to cry, her words coming out broken between shuddering breaths. "I loved him so much. You reminded me… I didn't want Skeeter…"

"Shhh. I get it," Connor soothed her, then kissed her head. "I get it." He placed the ear bud that was dangling between them into her ear, rested his head against hers, and tapped the phone to start the song again. As the opening guitar chords started, he felt her relax against him. Their fingers laced together as they shared the music and their hurts. Connor didn't know how long this thing with Sonya would last but for now they were here and they weren't alone.

THE END